SUITCASE BOOKS

Dancing Cows

A novel by Janet McDermott

D1610568

ISBN 978-1905778-02-7

Dancing Cows

Published 2007 by Suitcase

admin@suitcasebooks.info
www.suitcasebooks.info

Suitcase Books are published by
Shorelines: info@shorelines.org.uk

Suitcase books are distributed by Turnaround Publisher Services Ltd,
Unit 3, Olympia Trading Estate, Coburg Rd, Wood Green,
London, N22 6TZ

Cover design by Ian Bobb (07799137492)
Printed by LPPS Limited, 128 Northampton Rd,
Wellingborough, NN8 3PJ, UK

British Library Cataloguing-in-Publication Data. A catalogue record for
this book is available from the British Library

jumping-off point for new journeys, and if that isn't the definition of a splendid series, it ought to be the rule for how to write one. Clearly, Robert Ludlum was not thinking of *The Janson Directive* as a one-off book but the beginning of something new. That was all the freedom I needed to accept the invitation to journey on with *The Janson Command*.

Paul Garrison
Connecticut
2012

Dancing Cows

To Edith Sterne,
for believing in my infant storytelling

To my parents, Ann and Frank,
for their unfailing support

And for Madeleine,
who makes everything possible.

1 Cows

The weirdest thing happened at work today. Even weirder than usual, that is, since everything's a bit random at our place at the moment. I arrived late, sweating and panting from cycling in the rain, to find that Eleanor had turned the heating on full against the draughts that blow in under the wonky door. I peeled off my dripping cagoule, my fleece jacket, and finally my 'Save the Rain Forest' T-shirt.

"Shelley!" Eleanor eyed with horror the spaghetti straps of my vest top, coyly entangled with black bra straps on my gleaming brown shoulders. I imagined a cartoon bubble floating above her head containing the words, Brazen Hussy!! She can be so old-fashioned sometimes. "But it's hot in here," I moaned weakly, pulling my T-shirt on again.

"Try an alarm clock," was her abbreviated response.

"Love you too," I grumbled and yanked my black and white cow apron down from its hook on the kitchen door.

I've been working in the Dancing Cows vegan cafe for about eight months now and sometimes it feels like eight years. I live, sleep and breathe nut roasts, red dragon pie, green tea and Eleanor's freckled face; which is usually white with exhaustion beneath her ginger curls as she puzzles over yet another intractable problem. She and Matt sank everything they had into setting up this place. She's always stressing about the salads, or tearing off to the wholesalers in her rusty yellow van to sort out some order they've got wrong. Matt, on the other hand, is so laid back he spends most of his time horizontal.

He thinks he can run the place telepathically from the sofa in their flat upstairs. I try his telepathy method in reverse sometimes: staring very hard at the black and white cows painted on the ceiling to see if I can will him to come down and lend a hand. Never works.

Don't get me wrong, I believe in the cafe too. I'm vegan now but I've been a vegetarian since Cheryl Fenwick and I decided to stop eating dead animals when we were twelve. Cheryl eats meat now that she's shacked up with Carl the Carnivore, but I'm still true to the cause. I remember the first time I read about animals being transported to abattoirs to be slaughtered. I saw the pictures and felt sick. I stopped eating dairy products the summer I was fifteen, when we went to the caravan in Pembrokeshire. One day we could hear this cow just lowing over and over for hours. The site manager told us they'd taken her calf away so that people like us could have her milk to drink every day for the rest of the year. I felt like each cry was coming from inside me, this huge, towering scream of grief. I just knew that never again was I going to be responsible for causing that amount of pain to another living creature. And I realised that Rehana (that's my birth mother) must have found it unbearable to give me up, whatever her reason for doing it.

Mum and Dad seemed to take it as a personal criticism when I got involved with veganism and animal rights. Or maybe they thought it was Rehana's genes surfacing despite their best efforts. I couldn't make them see it was just me, what I wanted to do. It's like working at Dancing Cows. They're so uptight about it, like if I don't rush out and get a 'proper' job right this minute I'll turn into a New Age traveller or something. Which wouldn't be such a bad thing, but I don't say that because I don't want an argument.

"What happened to all your plans, darling?" Mum complained in John Lewis's coffee shop on my graduation day. Fair enough. I had invented all sorts of schemes to keep them happy: applying to the civil service, researching a course in town planning, even attending a teacher training recruitment day. But it was all just a way of fending off their questions. Every time I nearly went to the careers office, or nearly phoned for an application form, I had this sinking feeling and my brain kind of shut down.

As I took up my post at the till this morning I couldn't resist a small glance upwards to Matilda and Winifred. I whispered,

"Don't say it, I know - late again!"

Me being late hardly mattered because the only customers all morning were my lot from the anti-vivisection campaign. They trickled in after ten to hold a meeting at the window table. I had invited them to use the cafe so I could be at the meeting too, but it didn't pan out quite how I'd imagined. I barely got a sense of what was going on as I danced back and forth between their table and the till, trying to keep one eye on the door to the kitchen and the other on the door to the street. I'd sold the meeting to Eleanor as a way of bringing in more business, but by half-past eleven Carmen, Ritchie and Dave had been sitting over the same drinks for an hour and not bought so much as a date and walnut slice. Only Angela had ordered a veggie breakfast and then changed her mind when she found out it wasn't on the house. On the house. As if! Did she think we were so made of money we could afford to feed them for nothing? Luckily no one heard: Eleanor was upstairs with Matt, 'doing the books', in other words having a row about money. And Jill was in the kitchen preparing salads for lunch.

I was just about to clear the mugs on the meeting table in an attempt to remind them that they must be thirsty, when the front door opened and this Indian woman swept in. She was wearing a cream fur coat and a dazzling emerald green sari. She stood by the till shaking rain out of a large pink umbrella, which I noticed was elegantly lined with grey satin. Her hair was oiled and twisted into a bun at the back of her head and she wore intricately carved gold hoops in her ears. Her lips were a bright poppy-red. Maybe I was staring. I hurried to the till and asked if I could help her, trying to hide my surprise that she had stepped into our cafe at all. She probably doesn't know the area, I thought, and she certainly doesn't know what we're about or she'd think twice about wearing fur in here, even if it's imitation. I could see Ritchie's shoulders twitching at the sight of it. "Tea please." She smiled warmly at me and I caught a flash of recognition in her eyes that seemed to be clocking me as Asian too, the way people do. It made me want to get her sorted into a corner as quickly and quietly as possible before she showed me up.

"Which tea? We do Assam, Darjeeling, Earl Grey, and Lapsang Suchong, with or without soya milk and herbal teas which are listed up here." I rushed through the usual patter, pointing to the blackboard. The Indian woman considered the many possibilities with an anxious frown. I was about to suggest Darjeeling when she demanded firmly:

"Camomile, please, and a honey and almond flapjack."

As I squirted hot water from the urn into a stainless steel teapot and placed it with one of our black and white mugs and her biscuit on the scratched tray, I couldn't help thinking she must be used to something better. She seemed happy enough and carried her tray carefully to a table by one of the pillars covered from ceiling to floor in flyers and ragged notices. She leaned her folded umbrella against the table leg and took off her coat, reaching awkwardly to drape it over the back of the chair and revealing as she did so a startling fold of bare caramel flesh around her midriff. Let's see Eleanor tell her to cover up, I thought with a disgruntled sniff. The end of her sari swirled dramatically across her back in stiff rustling swathes of gold embroidered silk, reflecting the ceiling light above her a thousand times in clusters of tiny sequins, making me hot with embarrassment at her gaudiness.

Jill brought me a stack of boxes through from the fridge, so I gave up on the idea of my lot buying anything before lunchtime and took her not-so-subtle hint that guarding the till does not mean giving up on all other human activity. As I was decanting salads and sandwich fillings into the bowls in front of me, I tried to steal an occasional sly glance at the new customer.

Our cafe is in a really mixed area with students, pensioners, white and black families, and newly arrived refugees, all living together in the same Victorian terraces, and barracks of boxy, 60's maisonettes. The area is sandwiched between main roads that fan out of the city up the valleys towards the barrier of dark hills looming on the western horizon. I watch Asian women passing our door every day, raincoats wrapped over long patterned kameezes, some pushing buggies holding noisy toddlers with curly black fringes and chubby hands that remind me of pictures of myself when I was little. They never come in here, and I suppose I've hardly ventured into their shops either. The clothes shops are bewildering to me. Behind the displays of shining silks, I can see groups of women chatting and laughing, but I'd never dare step in. I wouldn't know what to ask for. I can't use a sewing machine to save my life, and I'd feel ashamed not knowing things they might expect me to know.

Once I went in the Asian grocers up the road on my way home, but I hadn't realised it was a meat shop as well. A burly man in a white coat splattered with murderous stains was chopping carcasses at the back of the shop and chatting to a knot of younger men gathered around him. His friends turned and stared at me as I stood in the queue with my bunch of fresh coriander and packets of cumin and chilli powder, dying to get out and wishing my jeans weren't so tight and my T-shirt so thin and ragged. I probably wouldn't have cared if I was white, but I felt I was disgracing them, being Asian and dressed like I was. Stupid really, I wanted to tell them they had got it wrong. I may look Asian, but I wasn't part of their world, so they didn't have to look at me like that. Even if I had been brought up Asian, it still wasn't any of their business what I wore, I wasn't accountable to them. I came out flustered and reminded myself to buy my spices from the wholefood collective next time. I was thinking all this when I looked up straight into that woman's eyes and slopped hummous all down the side of the bowl and onto the shelf. I swore under my breath and looked at her again guiltily, but she was fiddling with her sari like nothing had happened. I wiped it all up and tried to concentrate on filling the bowls in the chiller cabinet.

"Shelley." A chorus from the window table interrupted me and I hurried over, conscious of the woman's gaze following me.

"You know this action at the uni labs in May," Ritchie began to explain, "There's a problem with the access. We could do with getting something in place the day before. Do you think we should - " he followed my eyes as they darted back to the woman in the sari and lowered his voice. "I think we need someone in the building overnight? Do you know anyone at the uni who could do it?"

University felt so far away already. Once I stepped out of it there seemed to be no going back. "Not really. All my mates have left now, and most of them were Arts students anyway. Look, it's nearly lunchtime and it's going to get busy soon. I'll have to stay by the till."

As I was returning to the counter, the woman in the sari interrupted me with a slightly raised finger.

"Excuse me," she began, and I thought she was going to complain about her tea. I knew she should have had Darjeeling. "Is this your cafe?"

"Pardon?" I was confused. She repeated her question, articulating very precisely and emphatically,

"Is this your cafe?"

"No," I giggled, amused at the thought, "I just work here. The owners are upstairs." I glanced behind me to see if anyone else had heard this bizarre suggestion, but Jill had the volume on the stereo turned right up in the back, blasting out Manic Street Preachers.

"Are they Indian as well?"

"As well as what?" I eyed her suspiciously.

"As you." Her gaze was unflinching.

First I was supposed to own the business; now I was assumed to be from a country I had no connection with. "No they're not," I muttered, trying to stay calm. "Is there anything I can help you with?"

"I'm sorry. Excuse me asking so many questions, but I'm intrigued by your cafe, it's so unusual. It's vegetarian isn't it?"

"It's vegan actually." Here I felt on slightly safer ground. I perched on the edge of a neighbouring table to continue. "That means we don't use meat or dairy products in our food, and we only use organic produce. We try to show how you can eat well and stay healthy without exploiting animals or destroying the environment." Out of the corner of my eye I noticed Carmen standing up and realised I had missed the end of the meeting. I curled my fingers around the edge of the table, itching to launch myself across the room to catch the others before they disappeared. Thing is, I felt anchored to her curious eyes fixed on mine.

"How interesting. It sounds very spiritual, a very Indian way of thinking."

Her languid words stung me into action. "It's not meant to be and I'm afraid I'm not religious. Excuse me." I hopped off the table and steered my way across the room to the disintegrating meeting.

"Shelley, are you okay for the same time in two weeks?" Carmen looked up from her diary as she saw me approaching.

"Actually, can we do it after the cafe closes? I can't really concentrate if I'm working here," I explained. "You can come any day after six, I'll sort it out with Eleanor." There was a shuffling of pages and a bid for the pub as an alternative venue on Dave's part, but Ritchie was worried about being overheard. Finally we agreed another date in the cafe.

The room went fairly quiet after they'd gone. I gathered up their dirty mugs and spoons and wiped the table in the silence, uncomfortably aware of the woman sitting behind me. I felt bad for ignoring her, but I didn't know what else to do. I couldn't say to her, it's no good you going on about India to me because I don't know anything about it, and anyway it's Bangladesh, actually.

"I'm not religious either, you know." Her rich musical voice suddenly floated out into the empty room. "I used to be quite political like you when I was younger."

"Really?" I grunted ungraciously, without looking round.

"I don't often come across people brave enough to take direct action in this country. Of course, we were brought up on direct actions in India, you know, hunger strikes, sit-ins, lie-ins, even self-immolations… "

I flashed an awkward smile at her as I manoeuvred around the table. I had no idea what she was talking about. Now she was starting to seriously irritate me. She must have overheard Ritchie talking and seemed to think she knew all about us. I glanced desperately at the kitchen door for a way out of the conversation, but reggae beats thudded out from Jill's inner sanctum and Eleanor had still not descended to organise us for the lunchtime rush. Business must be bad, I noted fleetingly. Normally she would be down by now, and some days so would Matt to drawl witty pleasantries at the customers and mess up the till, moaning, "Shelley darlin', come and fix this bloody thing fer' us."

The front door suddenly swung open, crashing loudly

against the table behind it, and a dishevelled boy with darting angry eyes beneath his combat-style cap burst into the room propelled by a shove from two more following close behind. He shouted something unintelligible that sounded like 'Al Qaeda' at the woman in the sari and the others growled echoes of the same taunt. Their white faces were blotched and pimpled and they mumbled in gruff teenage voices, clenching their fists and kicking at the tables. The woman never moved a muscle, not the faintest flinch.

Oh my God, I'd better do something, I thought, suddenly remembering my responsibilities. But the first boy seemed to have run out of steam, pinned to the spot by the woman's calm stare.

"This is a vegetarian cafe. If you're interested in halal you'll have to try somewhere else," she smiled with perfect charm.

The first boy looked desperately at the others, swept his arms across a couple of tables sending sugar bowls and salt cellars flying and ran out, followed by the others, shouting a straggled chorus of, "Kill the Paki bastards!" In the stillness that followed it took me a while to realise the pounding I was feeling was not Jill's music still pumping away in the back, but my own heart thudding in my chest, even louder than the roar of traffic blown in through the open doorway. The woman and I looked at each other.

"Wow," I breathed. "You were pretty cool."

"I'm used to it," she shrugged. "It's not their fault, actually. It's the parents, you know. They're like all young men, trying to prove themselves, they just need a bit of guidance."

I closed the door and began picking up the pieces of a

smashed sugar bowl. The woman drew a chair out from under her table and patted the seat, saying, "We can tidy that up in a minute. Why don't you come and sit here? I'm Veena, by the way."

Tentatively, I sat down on the chair beside her and told her my name.

"Shelley," she frowned, puzzled. "Is that Bengali?"

"It can be English or Bengali, but mine's the English version."

"Hello, Shelley." She stretched out a plump hand with long elegant fingers, which I shook self-consciously. She smelt of sandalwood, like the incense I used to burn in my room in halls of residence, only more fragrant and mingled with coconut oil. I noticed the creased divide between her pink palm and the silken brown skin on the back of her hand and was struck by the contrast. For a moment I was in the playground again: 'Why aren't your hands brown on the inside, Shelley? C'mon, tell us. Why? Why?' Children pushing, hot breath all over me, rough hands pulling my hands open, turning them back and forth so they could all stare. Then I wanted to cut my hands off I was so ashamed.

"I'm going to an interview in the Asian Women's Centre down the road, Awaaz, you must know it?" Veena withdrew her hand carefully and I realised that I had held it too long. I nodded, a vague picture of purple and pink paintwork and windows full of posters flashing through my mind. "I'm far too early, it's not till one o'clock. Anyway, they'll probably give it to a younger person."

"You look the perfect part for an Asian Women's Centre to me." I was feeling bad now about having been so grumpy earlier. "You'd have my vote. But what do I know?"

"Enough," she patted my hand with something that felt like affection. "You're an Asian woman and you've voted for me, so the job's mine." Her laughing eyes were full of kindness, but I couldn't carry on talking to her. She wouldn't say those things if she knew. Any minute now she was going to start asking questions again and I would have to close down the conversation or hand my life over to be prodded and picked at like a prize marrow. I couldn't do it.

Eleanor's sharp voice suddenly startled me out of my seat.

"Shelley, what are you doing?" I realised that somehow three people had materialised at the counter.

"A sugar bowl smashed. I'm just clearing it up," I dumped the fragments of china onto Veena's tray and hurried off to get a dustpan to sweep up the sugar scattered across the floor, while Eleanor attended to the queue of customers.

When I returned Veena was putting on her coat. Even at close quarters I couldn't tell if the fur was real or imitation. I decided I didn't want to know.

"Good luck with your interview," I volunteered instead.

"I hope I haven't got you into trouble," she whispered.

"By the way, I love your cows." She picked up the amazing silver-lined umbrella, unhooked her bag from the back of the chair and flashed a parting smile to me as she made her way to the door. As the cascading folds of her sari rustled past me, I inhaled a last heady breath of sandalwood and coconut and wanted to follow her, like a rat after the Pied Piper.

"Friend of yours?" Eleanor quizzed when I joined her

up front again.

"Not really."

"Veena? What are you doing in there?" Ramesh's impatient tones call to me from the dining room.

"Just coming." I reply, compliantly. But this task will not be hurried.

I cut open a mango and the juice runs down my fingers. Carefully, reverently, I carve the pulpy flesh from the stone and arrange long slivers of golden fruit on a large plate. Licking my fingers, I can taste again the dusty streets of Patna, red clouds rising under my bare feet as I play by the river after school while glistening black water buffalo wallow in the shallows. I see clothes flapping on balconies, and smell the air thick with cooking spices and the smoke of kerosene oil. I remember craning over the wooden gate to watch for my father returning from the lawyers' chambers at Mahendra Ghat. As the light fades from the lilac-washed sky and the day's stifling heat relaxes its grip, men gather around the paan sellers and chai stalls in the street. Inside I hear my mother chatting with the chokrah about the family next door and the outrageous hikes in ghee and sugar prices, their conversation washed over by the clanging of temple bells rising from the banks of the holy River Ganga. It's forty years ago now, but still I miss that shimmering expanse of water, the blue silken currents sliding by the old stone steps in the dry season, and the foaming brown floods beating angrily against crumbling banks in the monsoon. I long to rest my eyes on the river's delicate, dangerous curve. Here everything is so concrete and sordid and cluttered, the Earth itself is sealed beneath choking layers of brick and tarmac and cannot breathe, and there is so much work to do to maintain the complicated machinery of our lives, such lonely barren work.

When I carry the plate ceremoniously into the dining room, Anil and Pooja are staring with glazed expressions at the flickering percussive television perched on the sideboard. Ramesh is sitting up expectantly and has moved his dinner plate away from him with the knife and fork placed carefully together at an angle to indicate that he has finished his main course. He learnt this and many other tips from 'Good Manners: How To Move in the Best English Society' by Dr P. T. de Souza, B.A., PhD, R.S.A., bought secondhand at a bookstall in New Market before we left Calcutta twenty-five years ago. I notice the dark grey jacket of his suit on the back of his chair and realise that he hasn't changed out of his work clothes. That means he is expecting to go out again later. I feel a faint stir of pleasure at the thought of an evening without him, maybe indulging in a few soap operas with Pooja, or initiating casual chatter with Anil over coffee, trying to tease out little confidences from him on this rare occasion when he has chosen to grace us with his presence.

"Here we are, folks," Ramesh announces proudly. "Mangoes from India - well, the subcontinent. When we were young you could only get them for a few weeks of the year, you know. When the season came, we couldn't eat enough of them, we'd make ourselves sick, ask your mother."

I smile dutifully as I divide the fruit onto smaller plates. "Oh, Mum, I forgot to say, someone called Farah rang for you, she said she'd try again later," Pooja informs me without shifting her gaze from the screen. The plate in my hand lurches wildly.

"Did she leave a number?" I try not to look too distracted.

"No, she said she'd ring back, she didn't want to leave a message. Who is she, anyway?"

"Just someone from the surgery," I keep my eyes on the plate as I tell this lie.

"When you've quite finished your message service, Pooja, maybe you'd like to taste some of this mango I bought specially for you both," Ramesh barks with annoyance, and I feel a twinge of triumph watching his little surprise fall flat.

When he breezed in from work and with a flourish presented me with a small wooden crate of neatly packed fruit, I didn't know what to say. Seeing the orange-flushed mangoes gleaming in their beds of purple tissue paper, I felt confused and overwhelmed. He so rarely does anything on impulse and this was a gift so intimate, so touching, whispering of forgotten, special times. Mangoes, the colour of sunshine, the colour of saffron robes flashing in a crowded street, flickering flames in clay divas around a shrine, strings of fresh marigold flowers threaded into my hair in the morning on my way to class. And in the warm evening, in the shadows of the peepal tree behind the college wall, Ramesh, spreading heavy fingers on my back beneath my thick plait, pulling me close, wilted marigold petals scattered on the ground.

"So, what do you think?" he pressed me impatiently, "I found them in that mini-market on London Road, when I went to get the car washed. They've come direct from Pakistan, for Ramzaan the bloke told me. I thought we ought to do more to keep the children in touch with their heritage, you know."

I turned away from him to clatter pans on the draining board and hide my disappointment. Wanting to impress his father, of course, how stupid of me.

"You should have warned me," I snapped. "I would have done lamb or chicken, it doesn't seem right having mangoes after pasta, but it's too late now."

Why do I allow myself to hope? And why do I care so much about something so small?

He smacks his lips ostentatiously, looking around the table for a response. Pooja is transfixed by some drama on the television.

"Tell us about Dadaji's garden, Daddy," Anil prompts, trying to compensate for Pooja's inattention.

"Your grandfather had so many mango trees in his compound. The house in Defence Colony came with the job, of course. It was a huge place with a team of servants just to look after the grounds," Ramesh obliges, his good humour restored. "Your uncles and I were very naughty, we used to climb on the walls and try and shake the mangoes down before they were ripe."

"Did you have mango trees, Mummy?" Pooja turns to me.

"No, we didn't have a compound like your father's. We lived in the middle of the city by the river. Our mangoes came from the bazaar or from the amwallah who used to bring them round the streets on a wooden handcart. Let's eat, shall we?" I avoid Ramesh's eyes, disturbed by a tide of anger that is rising in me.

As I bite into the soft fruit and taste again its wild pungent sweetness, I see my mother eating mangoes at the end of her life, masticating slowly with her crooked, gaping teeth, savouring the luscious tang of the juicy flesh and sharing a conspiratorial smile with Pooja, her last grandchild, as they polished off the best mangoes in the bowl before the men came home from work. How can Pooja not remember that visit? How can the smell of mangoes not bring these memories flooding back for her?

"Mangoes were Ammi's favourite fruit," I murmur almost to myself.

"We'll have to take you to India again soon." Ramesh beams at his children approvingly. "You can see your grandfather in Delhi and eat mango fool and mango lassi and all those delicious things." I wince at his tone and see the scepticism in their eyes as they smile weakly at him. I feel sorry for him and hope he doesn't see it is too late for all that.

The phone rings loudly, jangling through the house like an alarm, and I rush into the hall to pick it up first.

"Hello, is Veena Kumar there, please?" a woman's voice says cautiously.

"Speaking."

"Oh Veena, it's Farah here from Awaaz ringing about the job."

"Oh yes, hello," I murmur, my heart pounding. Her voice is mellow and bobs with that faint evocative lilt of the subcontinent that I love to hear.

"I'm happy to say we'd like to offer you the job."

"I don't know what to say." I breathe, reeling. I was so sure I hadn't got it.

"Would you like some time to think about it?" She sounds hesitant. "I can ring you back in the morning."

"Oh, no," I recover myself quickly. "There's no need for that, I'd love to do it. I accept. Absolutely."

"Well, that's great. You had me worried there," Farah laughs, "We need to follow up your references, which might take a week or two. When I've done that I'll ring you again about a start date. Is that okay?"

"Fine," I nod. I suddenly find myself imagining Sanjeev Patel ranting at Ramesh, 'Why didn't you tell me Veena was looking for other jobs, man? She's really landed me in it now. Where am I going to do get another bloody receptionist that speaks Hindi, Urdu and Bengali? Can't you tell her? She's your wife, for God's sake!"

"I'll be in touch," Farah finishes, briskly. "Bye for now."

"Bye," I murmur and replace the receiver thoughtfully. I wanted this. I wanted more than a few shifts on reception in a doctor's surgery for our old friend Sanjeeev. I wanted to go out every morning like Ramesh and matter somewhere else. Now it's happened I am in shock, I don't know who to tell.

I have a sudden impulse to tell Shelley, the girl in the cafe this morning. I see her round face in front of me, her small flared nose and that tell-tale look of the eastern Himalaya in her dark almond-shaped eyes, Assamese maybe, or Sylheti, I never got a chance to ask. If I had she probably wouldn't have told me, she made that clear enough. Even after those boys burst in so clearly targeting both of us, she wouldn't admit any connection between us. From her voice, and the slogans scrawled on her T-shirt, and her short black hair rising in a thicket of fuzzy spikes above the black and white hairband that matched her apron, I guessed that she had grown up here. But I could tell nothing about her family. And I could see she understood nothing about me. It hurt me a little that she didn't seem to hear that I was on her side. I warmed to their little huddle around the table plotting the downfall of some oppressive force, their earnestness so different from the jaded boredom and materialism I see in Pooja and Anil. I wanted to tell her I too had marched with jute pickers and lain across the Esplanade tramlines in the midday heat, dust and oil in my hair and sweat drenching through my choli in unseemly patches. When Ramesh and I were students there seemed to be something to demonstrate about every other week, marches, sit-ins, hunger strikes, it was all so desperately important. I remember the sinking weight of bamboo poles in blistered hands supporting cotton banners painted with red, angry slogans, the press of bodies in the shouting crowd marching down Chowringhee. "Congress traitors! BJP wasters! Communists! Zindabad!" Laughing, jibing children running alongside us, the chanting deepening to a thunderous echo as we turned into Park Street, hemmed in between high, peeling, colonial buildings, harsh horn blasts from stranded taxis a random descant to our chorus. I have never been able to describe adequately the thrill and passion of that time to my children.

I felt those memories nudging me gently, awoken today in the cafe, rising from the trays of pulses and vegetables and the catchy little exhortations on the wall, 'A pure diet is a pure heart', 'Eats Without Meats'. Surely no Anglo-Saxon penned those? I could imagine them engraved in curling calligraphy behind plastic frames on the paan-stained walls of an Indian coffee house. Like the signs painted lovingly and reproachfully along the Grand Trunk Road from Patna to the Nepalese border: 'Better Late Than Never'; 'Safety: Safe Tea'; 'Cut the Gossip: Let Him Drive'; and five miles later, in complete contradiction, 'Make Short the Miles With Talks and

Smiles'. Those cows on the cafe walls, waiting silently to catch the eye of the unwary customer with their sudden presence, they were not the patient ruminating cows of English picture books, they were the cows of my childhood, swaying arrogant bony hips through bustling lanes and bazaars, confident, serene, yielding to no one. I find myself smiling, now, at the eccentric wit of the artist who created such a bizarre shrine and I wonder if he, she, has ever encountered Nandi, the white bull. The cafe today seemed from that other world of roadside tea stalls and dingy coffee houses teeming with college students planning revolutions beneath creaking ceiling fans. I felt suddenly surrounded by friends again.

"Mummy, is everything all right?" Pooja asks softly from the dining room doorway.

"Yes darling. Come on, let's finish our dinner." I usher her back into the dining room and push everything else, the job, the cafe, Shelley, to the back of my mind.

Later, burying myself in loading the dishwasher, I can almost believe the whole day has never happened. It would be easier to believe that. I feel I have been stupid ever to think I could break through the layers of habit laid inexorably like sediment on the bed of a river, year after year, and hardened into permanence. How will everything get done? Who will do it, with me out all day? How will I fit it all in? I can't change this household now, even though it is changing without me. Anil is drifting away. Despite living here, he is absent in mind and body and we hardly see him. Next year Pooja will be gone too, across the Pennines to Manchester if she gets the grades she needs. Then there will just be the two of us, or rather just me and my loneliness and the interminable edgy silence of waiting for Ramesh to come home and ignore me.

I have never become used to the silent interiors in this country. I used to dread coming home in the morning after taking the children to school; that chill feeling like steel shutters crashing down behind me each time I closed the front door. The emptiness of the house seemed to drain me of all energy and churn my brain into a thick soupy porridge through which I could reach no decision or meaningful act. Sometimes I used to stare out at the neat cardboard-cut-out avenue and imagine that the city had been mysteriously emptied of its inhabitants and I was the only person left alive. I would wait for minutes at a time, maybe half an hour, by the living room window, until a car drove past or a woman clipped by on smart high heels and I was reassured of the existence of other human beings. Then I would be thrown into a panic that there was no time to finish all my housework before I had to pick the children up and I would rush around the place starting six things at once, then leave them all half done when three o' clock suddenly came round. Standing in the kitchen remembering this, I know I have to take the job on, whatever the consequences. I feel as if I am standing on the edge of a precipice, and I know I have to jump.

3 Sky

I never told Eleanor about the boys bursting in that morning, I don't know why. I was going to when I'd swept up the sugar, but after the Indian woman, Veena, had gone, we suddenly got really busy and there was no time for anything until about three o'clock that afternoon. By then, I didn't feel like talking about it any more. Seems silly really, but it felt private, something that had only happened to Veena and me and wasn't to do with anyone else. I think they must have seen Veena come in, or maybe they were watching us through the window and saw there was no one else around. Not that I'm bothered. I mean it gave me a scare at the time, but Veena was right, they were just little boys showing off to each other and Veena made them look pathetic. She was wicked. That surprised me, she looked so posh in her silk sari: I'd have expected her to scream and panic; but it was me that froze. Now I wish I had asked her about all that direct action stuff she was boasting about, we could do with someone like her when we do this releasing rabbits thing at the university.

By the time Eleanor and I finally sat down at one of the tables in the middle of the afternoon to finish some left over salads and lasagne, I had put the incident away somewhere inside my head and Eleanor was preoccupied with the state of the business, as usual.

"Bit of a slow morning," she reflected gloomily, picking at her plate of salad. I watched her thin arched fingers clenching her fork as she stabbed random lettuce leaves, the taut angle of each joint elegantly poised. Her hands were the thing I noticed first about her when we met, the way she moves them when she talks. When they interviewed me for the job I was quite in awe of them both. Matt was relaxed and offhand, he seemed to be trying to put me at my ease, but his flippant asides just made me more nervous because I didn't know when to take him seriously. Eleanor was politely distant behind her round metal-rimmed glasses. Come to think of it, she's hardly worn them since. She talked sternly about ground rules and terms and conditions, yet her hands fluttered as she talked and seemed to be having an entirely different conversation.

"We'd love you to join us," she said enthusiastically on the phone the next day. "Don't be put off by the interview, we're really very easy to work with. I just think it's better to know where you stand with people from the start, don't you?" Eleanor is an unpredictable mix of steely precision and sudden enthusiasms which bubble up from time to time despite her caution. I've been here a few months now and as time has passed, I've slowly warmed to her.

"It's always slow when the weather's bad, " I tried to reassure her.

"I don't know," she sighed, abandoning her fork on the plate and leaning back. "Matt thinks we should start later in the morning and stay open till nine in the evening. But I think then we'd have to have a different menu. People expect something special for dinner, don't they?"

I shrugged, thinking, what does Matt know about it, he's hardly ever here? But I never know whether to say what I think to Eleanor about Matt. He doesn't seem very clued up about what's happening. He creeps around the low-ceiling kitchen with his stooping shoulders and enigmatic smile like some Victorian overseer; either too grand, or too scared, to get his hands dirty. Is he an incidental add-on or is he the essential other half of an inseparable Eleanor-and-Matt whole? Sometimes she treats him like a business partner, makes arrangements around him, allocates time to him, like the wholefood co-op, like another recipe project. She doesn't talk about him much to me. But when they're together they communicate through their eyes, and they speak a sort of clipped private language and finish off each other's sentences like they've been married for years. I can't work it out.

"Have you seen the stuff about the racist attacks on the flats?" Eleanor suddenly started on a new tack, taking me by surprise. "A Bengali family have had their windows broken and there are some Somali families who are virtually living under siege."

My heart did that little jump that happens whenever I hear anything connected to Bangladesh. Stupid really. As if what's happening to a Bengali family on the Washington Road flats has anything to do with Rehana giving birth to me twenty-two years ago. But I always feel it, that little thud inside, like when you're falling asleep and suddenly you seem to step off a cliff. Luckily, no one ever seems to notice.

"Yeah, we got something about it this morning." I pulled myself back into the room, recalling the flyer I had skimmed through and stuffed into my pocket as I took the post up to Matt that morning. I had been more concerned to see a red bill in the pile, which Matt waved a dismissive hand at when I pointed it out to him, drawling, "Dinna worry yoursel' Shelley, babe, I'll sort it."

"There's a new campaign starting up. They're hoping to organise some kind of community patrol on the flats," Eleanor continued, earnestly. "Matt and I are thinking of going to the next meeting as it's practically in our backyard."

"Me too." I pulled the crumpled leaflet from my pocket and smoothed it out on the table. She looked at me searchingly.

"I wouldn't want to muscle in on your patch, but from where I stand, it's just as much about us as it is about you," Eleanor said. I felt cornered by the concern in her green eyes, and too transparent. I suddenly remembered about the boys in the morning. It seemed obvious to say something now, but it also felt too late.

"Of course it is," I replied. "Actually, I'm glad you're going, I hate going to meetings on my own." Once spoken, I believed it.

Eleanor sat back in her seat sipping her mug of black coffee and watching me quietly, her legs folded under her at one end of the old church pew she and Matt rescued from a house clearance. She has a soothing, cat-like presence. She belongs to this cluttered anarchic space she has created and I almost don't need to look up to see her slight form curled on her favourite seat in the corner. It dawned on me the cafe is actually Eleanor's home and she welcomes all of us in - staff and customers - as part of her family. I felt a rush of affection for her generosity in giving us this space that nourishes others and has saved me from being in thrall to some monolithic institution that would have squashed my spirit.

When I left the cafe that evening I wheeled my bike, Sky, down the road to the Asian Women's Centre at the bottom of the hill. I had always known it was there, but had never really stopped to look at it. Now I was curious, and I wanted to know what it was that Veena thought she was too old for. By the time I reached the building the grey blinds were shut tight in neat overlapping vertical strips. There was a sign on the glass door in different languages, and posters in the windows advertising advice sessions and classes in Basic English, Computer Skills, Sewing, things that seemed to have nothing to do with me. There was a light on upstairs and I wondered if the interview panel were still up there dissecting the candidates' answers, or whether the light had been left on by mistake in the rush to get home after a long tiring day.

With a shrug I resolved to forget about it and move on, but at that moment the light went out. I heard voices at the side of the building and the loud two-tone siren of an alarm being set. A group of women came round the corner talking urgently and rapidly.

"If you do the phone calls, Shahnaz, I can write for the references and start on the contracts."

"Don't be silly, look at you, you're not well. Leave it all with me - we don't know if she'll accept yet, so no point chasing references. And don't come to work tomorrow, eh?"

"Hello, can I help you?" I jumped as a slight woman with short wavy black hair and a long sharp-featured face approached me.

"Is this Aah - Aw - the Asian Women's Centre?" I stumbled over the name, not sure I had remembered it correctly.

"Awaaz? Yes, that's us. It means 'voice' in case you're wondering. We'll be open at nine-thirty in the morning if you want any advice." Her eyes shone with a zeal for service.

"I was wondering about the interviews?" I ventured.

"Yes?"

"I know someone who applied, I just wondered who got it." Even as I started speaking I realised how stupid this was, I only knew her first name and, anyway, why should they tell me?

"We haven't notified the candidates yet. Why don't you ring your friend later on tonight? We should have spoken to everyone by then."

"Okay, thanks," I flushed awkwardly and retreated from the scene, leaving them to a loud and effusive round of goodbyes. I realised I was unlikely ever to see Veena again, and felt very silly trying to follow the trail of one of the hundreds of people who come in and out of the cafe every year never to be seen again.

I lifted Sky into the gutter, clicked the strap of my helmet under my chin, and settled myself onto the firm, padded saddle, then leaned my weight forward over the handlebars as I pushed off from the kerb. The tarmac had a rough grain that grumbled slightly beneath the hard tyres as I sailed along, my legs pushed against the gently rising gradient. Most of Sheffield is gradient, one way or the other, which was a bit of a shock after the level expanses of the Thames Valley, but I've got used to it now. People at uni thought I must be mad, or very skint, to cycle everywhere, but I couldn't imagine how other students survived without a bike. Any other mode of transport is so expensive and so fraught with hassles, waiting at bus stops, waiting in traffic jams and hunting for parking spaces. Walking, my second best option, just takes too long.

Sky is a pink-and-silver-painted ten-speed women's tourer with drop handlebars and derailleur gears. I've had her since my fifteenth birthday, which is around when I seemed to stop growing, leaving me several inches shorter than most of my svelte English friends. I can only just rest my toes on the ground with the saddle on the lowest setting, I should think it's rusted fast in that position by now as I've never needed to raise it. I call her Sky because that's what I feel like when I'm on her, I feel like I'm flying and I can go anywhere, do anything. It's kind of a private little world of your own being on a bike. On a bus or a train there's loads of other people to stare at you, or bug you with their chattering, and even in a car there's the radio or you have to talk to people you're with. On my bike there's just me, and the wind, and sometimes I really feel like I'm up there on my own in those high white clouds, and there's nobody to understand, or not understand, it's enough there being just me and Sky and the wind.

From the Asian Women's Centre I followed the River Sheaf to the Broadfield pub and then climbed up through Nether Edge and over the hill, dropping down towards the River Porter at Hunters Bar. When we all finished our degrees and Megan and Dee left Sheffield, I tried to get someone else to share our student house in Crookes in the west of the city, but everyone I knew was leaving or had other plans, and the agent wanted it sorted like yesterday, so in the end I let it go and took this one bedroom flat over a workshop near Hunters Bar roundabout. It's only meant to be temporary because I didn't really want to live by myself, but I'm getting quite attached to it and since Tiger attached himself to me, I don't mind there being no people to talk to when I get home any more.

Tiger is a large mean-tempered tabby cat with a look of the wild in his piercing hazel eyes and tapered fangs. I reckon he's got at least three homes he visits in a fairly random rotation, so I always feel honoured when he chooses to stay with me. I'm trying to teach him to be a vegan. I've known people with vegetarian dogs that they've trained from puppies, but never a vegetarian cat. I guess they're probably just too close to being wild animals and that's fine, but I've told Tiger there's no way I'm ever going to buy him canned whale blubber or farmed fish. He takes it in his stride and still drops in regularly for his veggie sausages and water.

That day he wound himself around my ankles as soon as I swept into the backyard and propped Sky up against the wall under the concrete staircase - which gives some protection from the rain, but not much. As I chained Sky to the plastic drainpipe, Tiger arched his striped back against my calves and lamented loudly my callousness in shutting him out in the rain all day.

"What happened to all your mates then, Tiger?" I teased him, "No one home to let you in?" I was harried up the steps to my first floor entrance by Tiger's hungry wails. I don't know why climbing them is such a drag, but no matter how fit I feel, or how easy I find the hills on my bike, I always find those last fourteen steps just kill me. As soon as I turned the key in the lock and pushed the door hard, Tiger was through the opening and into the flat with a triumphant flick of his back legs. On the bristled coir doormat lay a couple of advertising circulars, one of Mum's pink floral envelopes, which I had been expecting, and an airmail letter from the States, which was a surprise and gave me a warm glow at the sight of it. Hugh and I split up amicably and without fuss a long time before he went to Philadelphia University last year, but I still miss him sometimes and I love his quirky, self-mocking letters, the sloping longhand in old-fashioned black fountain pen ink, the pretentious references that pass me by, as he knows they do, but he shares them anyway because he refuses to modify himself for anyone, and the occasional attentive question just when I am beginning to wonder if I exist in this correspondence.

First I attended to Tiger in my cramped galley-style kitchen, separated from the main part of the living area by a formica-topped breakfast bar, filling his dish of water and putting down a plate of yesterday's soya mince from the fridge. Then I put an old camping kettle full of water on the gas flame for myself. Having eaten so late in the afternoon at work, I would just have some toast and a mug of Barleycup tonight. Working in a cafe all day is a real turn-off as far as cooking goes, and so is living on your own. While the kettle was purring busily, I drew the frayed velvet curtains in the sitting room and turned on the 'coal effect' gas fire and watched the fake lumps of coal turn slowly red when the gas flames flickered over them. When I first moved in I thought the fire was really naff, after the open fire we had in our Victorian terrace in Crookes, but I grew to love its instant, effortless heat and the friendly purr of the cleverly concealed gas jets. Tiger became immovable from the faded rag rug in front of it whenever I switched it on.

The kettle's screaming whistle pulled me back into the kitchen and I put together a tray of steaming Barleycup, toasted rye bread with hummous and olives, and a thick slice of carob cake. I slipped my letters onto a corner of the tray and carried it through to the sitting room, where I placed it carefully on the wooden crate I used as a coffee table, draped in a red and white tasselled Palestinian scarf. Tiger followed me, licking his lips from the scraps I had given him, and curled himself into a perfect grey and brown streaked circle on the hearth, letting out a long sigh as he shut his eyes. Sitting back on the lumpy sagging settee, I nibbled half-heartedly at my toast and turned to my letters. I opened Hugh's first and found that he had given his first lecture as a postgraduate research student and felt he had finally 'arrived'. I felt a twinge as I heard in that the unspoken message that he wouldn't be coming back. All his earlier misgivings about cultural gaps, misunderstandings, his alienation in American academic society, seemed to have vanished in the clouds of euphoria surrounding his new success. What I love about it here is their naive enthusiasm, he enthused, They're not afraid to care, to be emotional about thinking, there's none of that British embarrassment at being earnest - that's it! - they're so unashamedly earnest, it's so sweet and so liberating.

God, Hugh, listen to yourself I suddenly wanted to say. What happened to the evil of American imperialism? I could almost hear the strains of 'God Bless America' wafting out of his letter and wanted to rip it up. The warm glow had gone and I wished the letter lay back on the mat unopened.

I turned to the pink envelope. A faint perfume of Nivea hand cream rose from the floral printed pages inside and I could see Mum turning and folding and massaging her hands, the skin slack and creased with age, as she sat in front of the television in the evening watching soap operas and hospital dramas. She always finds so much to say in her letters, and never fails her self-imposed fortnightly deadline. I can't keep up, but I usually manage once a month with the odd phone call in-between. In this one she told me that our elderly neighbour was going into a nursing home and the house was up for sale already, her children appeared to be wasting no time in realising the family assets.

Your father says they need the money for the nursing home costs, but she's told me herself many a time how selfish her eldest is and how little he bothers about her feelings. Still, your dad says keep out of it, so I say nothing, poor old dear. I read on. That woman rang yesterday from London, the post-adoption woman. Something about a support group for adults who were adopted as babies, but I told her you were living up north and you wouldn't be interested. I was surprised they had our details still, but I suppose they keep everything on computer these days. As if that explains why they still have our details. As if the computer has a mind of its own and stubbornly clings to the information it has accumulated. I could tell she was upset. What she really meant was: I thought you told them you weren't interested, so why are they still contacting you now? My shoulders tensed and a knot of unease sat in my gut. Mum and Dad didn't like me going to look at my adoption files when I was eighteen, they were worried I'd get upset and they were hurt that I wanted to know about Rehana. Afterwards I told them there was nothing in the files and I had no further interest in her, which was how I felt at the time. And I was very hurt by that flat empty brown folder, lifted out of a drawer that was packed with bulging files waiting for other adopted children. I was hurt to see all the school photos and updates Mum and Dad had sent about me lying untouched. I felt so rebuffed, so disregarded. The whole thing had been a bit of an anti-climax. I didn't know what to say to the social worker who showed me the file and offered to counsel me on its contents, and I went back to university relieved that it was over. But since then it has never quite been over, something has continued to worry away inside me, like picking at a scab and finding that the wound underneath has still not healed.

Why had Mum answered for me? I couldn't travel to London, it was true, and I wasn't sure I'd go to a group about being adopted because I didn't see why I would have anything in common with other adopted people, unless they were also Asian vegan animal rights activists who liked cycling and cats. But I wanted to be able to say that myself, and I just might have wanted to hear what else the woman had to say. I read mechanically to the end of the letter, but I couldn't take in anything else. I let it fall onto the cushion beside me next to Hugh's discarded letter and picked up my mug. I sipped the burning malted drink and watched the quiet blue flames of the fire slip into channels and gullies between the glowing coals and flare up in sudden bursts of orange in random corners. Trying to retrace the day in my mind, I wondered where the boys this morning had come from and whether they had anything to do with the stuff in the anti-racist campaign leaflet. I wondered about Veena's fate in her interview, and the intriguing goings-on behind the grey blinds of the Asian Women's Centre. Maybe I could go to one of their women-only swimming sessions one afternoon, or learn a bit of Bengali, that would really freak Mum and Dad out. Maybe I could even learn to sew, and then I could pop in and out of those mysterious clothes shops confidently buying swathes of material and little paper bags of buttons and fastenings. Implausible, but not impossible.

I finished my toast, but put the cake back in the tin, I wasn't really hungry. I decided to go to bed early and left the kitchen window slightly open so that Tiger could jump out onto the offshoot roof below, if he got the urge to wander off into the night.

Ranks of double radiators barely take the edge off the penetrating cold in this large echoing hall and I am grateful for prickly thermal underwear beneath the satin folds of my sari. The rows of grey plastic chairs have been filled in a haphazard fashion from the back leaving a line of empty chairs at the front. I sit in the middle and wonder if I should move forward to show a bit of solidarity with the thin, bearded man facing us, who is looking anxiously from the door to his watch and back again. It is nearly quarter past seven and I wish he would start. If only they had an agenda of some sort I could at least predict how long this will last. After all, it takes only a few minutes typing and the press of a photocopier button to produce that much organisation. We did better in our back room in Lenin Sarani, (more commonly known as Lower Circular Road, but we liked to support the Communist government's renaming of colonial landmarks), with Mitra's second-hand Phillips typewriter and the Xerox machine in the Standard Trunk Dialling booth round the corner. I close my eyes to ward off rising irritation. I breathe deeply and attend to the slow lift and fall of my diaphragm. I roll my creaking shoulder blades gently and straighten my back against the cold unyielding plastic, wishing I had worn a thicker cardigan.

I am attending this evening's meeting on behalf of Awaaz and I feel worn out already from working all day, providing dinner at home, which I had no time to eat, and dashing out again to make it here for seven. Even though I have finished at the surgery now, after lengthy recriminations from the doctors - and Ramesh - I still find it difficult juggling everything. On a day like today everyone wants me at the same time. The look on Ramesh's face when I laid out the dishes on the table and then put my coat on over my sari was his most sour and thunderous. Sitting here now I feel sick at the thought of it, and it is almost not worth staying in this seat a moment longer to endure such a weight of displeasure. Even Pooja is angry that she will have to clear up alone, that I am not there to make her cups of tea and cocoa all evening while she ploughs through her 'A' level texts, which she is suddenly serious about. But if I go home now I have to face Farah in our supervision next week and hers is a different displeasure, more veiled and damning. She will seem to understand, but I am not the gullible little housewife she thinks I am and I see the contempt in her velvet curtain of sympathy for my 'busy family life'. I can feel the muscles in my neck twisting into hard knots as I think of her thin tapered eyebrows slightly raised in my direction and her clipped comments dropping icily onto the table between us. I will always be too soft, too fluffy, too much of a mother hen, for her. I spend too much time with the women, I am too familiar with Riffat, who is only an admin worker, I am not focused enough, I am not quick enough, my ideas are too modest or too woolly. I am not the woman she wanted the management committee to appoint. I'm not supposed to know this, but Riffat heard them talking the day after the interviews.

The man at the front clears his throat loudly.

"Ah...Excuse me, everybody, if we could make a start... I'm Ralph Heaton and I'm Chair of this Anti-

Racist Campaign, which was set up last month by residents and workers in Moorfield to counter racist attacks in our area. The first item on our agenda today is to finalise the name of the campaign so we can print the publicity - Come in, there are plenty of seats at the front here - no, just here..." He motions three latecomers down to the empty chairs beside him as they try to creep in unobtrusively at the back. With a little jolt of surprise I recognise the young woman from the vegan cafe I went into on the day of my interview, Shila was it? - no, Shelley. She is following a ginger-haired woman in a blue denim jacket to the front of the hall. The man who entered with them slides into a spare seat at the back. I try to catch Shelley's eye as they sit down two rows in front of me, but she is too busy whispering to her companion as they settle themselves under Ralph's stern gaze.

Ralph begins his introductions again and outlines the current systematic harassment of a number of asylum seeking families that have recently been housed on the council estate behind the London Road shops. I want to suggest the problem is wider than this: various women in different situations have come into Awaaz in the past fortnight worried about racist attacks; but I feel wary of speaking in such an unfamiliar forum and Shelley's presence is oddly inhibiting.

The man who came in late with Shelley interrupts Ralph's preamble to make a point. His voice is quietly authoritative with a surprising uplift at the end of each sentence, which I recognise as possibly Scottish or Irish, but I find it impossible to place regional accents in this country. I hope Shelley will turn round when he speaks, but she and her friend merely exchange a look of recognition and I realise they know what he will say and maybe have heard it many times before. "Matt Ferguson, Dancing Cows Cafe," he begins. "It's a real step forward for local people to begin organising in this way against the power of the state and the forces of international capital - "

"Give it a rest, mate!" someone calls from behind me and I struggle to turn and watch them both.

"I'll keep it brief," Matt continues, unflustered. His thin mouth has a slight ironic twist as if he is suppressing a smile. "I suggest we call this campaign Sheffield Against Fascism in Europe, or SAFE for short, it's easy to remember and places us in a bigger picture, connecting us with people across the continent mobilising to resist fascist states and the corporate power of multinationals... " He is very assured and seems to have thought a lot about the meeting before he arrived, I am impressed and intrigued.

"I thought something with a more local feel, something people can really own," Ralph counters. "Something like the Moorfield Anti-Racist Alliance, maybe?" He looks round the room for support and a number of murmured comments compete for the space. By the end of the meeting Matt's inspired acronym seems to have captured the field. I notice Matt exchanging a glance with the red-haired woman, he nods very slightly and she raises her hand to speak.

"Eleanor Charles, Dancing Cows Cafe. I think we need to be clear that our role is not to defend individual victims of racist attacks, but to raise awareness in the wider community of the realities of racism and fascism and to confront the government about their role in creating and perpetuating racism."

"That's not exactly what we agreed in the last meeting." Ralph looks uneasy. "We have already proposed and agreed a rota of volunteers who will sit with families who are being targeted by the racists and carefully document anything that happens to them. The police will only take it seriously if they've got evidence, which means dates, times and accurate descriptions. It's important to record everything. We can provide cameras, notebooks, tape recorders, and mobile phones to call for help if things get sticky." My hand shoots up before I quite know what I am doing and as Ralph's gaze slips across to me, I feel my heart beginning to pound and a hot flush creep over my face.

"The woman over there - maybe you would like to share your experiences?" he invites with an encouraging smile and I realise he thinks I have come to the meeting because I have experienced an attack myself.

"Veena Kumar, Development Worker at Awaaz Asian Women's Centre." My voice sounds strange to me, very high and strained, and a pulse is beating violently in my throat. Ralph's smile fades behind his clouded and uneasy eyes. I continue, "I was wondering what people do when there isn't someone to sit with them. I mean, an attack could happen at any time of the day or night - couldn't it? You can't cover everybody all the time."

"We're doing our best. What does Awaaz suggest?" He barks his response so quickly I almost jump. I sense him reacting to something other than my words and realise I have no sense of how Awaaz is perceived in the wider world or where we are located in the web of other networks and interests this area seems to be crawling with.

"I understood this was an exploratory meeting so I'm

just trying to understand how this is going to work." I try to steady my voice and out of the corner of my eye, I am dimly aware of a black-fringed oval face turned towards me as I plough on. "What about having some kind of a telephone rota so people could be available to come out when there's an incident - when someone needs help?" Shelley flashes a cautious smile of recognition at me and mimes a clapping action to applaud my intervention.

"I thought that was the job of the police," a voice behind me interrupts.

"I really think we should have more discussion about our aims in offering this support before we plunge into it," a woman's voice sounds anxiously behind me. There is a ripple of dissenting asides around the hall and Ralph looks slightly desperate as he calls the meeting to order. I put my hand up again, the fierce beating of my heart has subsided now and I can dare to look around the hall. "Maybe I could offer a real example," I feel a thrill of something long forgotten, a delicious harmony between the original thought as it forms in my mind and the shape it takes in my voice and speech as it bursts into the world. I stand up to continue. "A young woman came into Awaaz earlier this week. She was rehoused in Moorfield quite recently from a women's refuge, so she has no support networks in Sheffield and lives on her own with her three-year-old child. On Sunday night someone smashed the bolt on her back gate and painted racist graffiti on her front and back doors. Now she's really scared because she knows she's a target, but she's no idea when or how the next attack will happen. Is the primary purpose of this organisation to physically protect her in her home? Or will it put pressure on the police and the housing department to protect her? Or is it going to campaign more generally in wider forums to raise awareness about these attacks?"

As I sit down again I find myself wishing, childishly, that Farah could see me. I have asked a question that has relevance and meaning and can focus the debate, I have been precise and pertinent, not soft and woolly. I can do this, I realise, and I am back in that old exhilaration, raising my shrill angry voice above the deadening whirr of ceiling fans to rally the student body and meeting Ramesh's silent shining eyes across the heads of the crowd. I feel a stir of desire at the memory of that intoxicating time. The passion we shared to change the world, and that heady sense of potency and danger. We were at the front line, we faced the khaki-uniformed police with their batons and rifles, our sweating hands clasped beneath my dupatta, Ramesh's hot hoarse breath in my ear in the instant before the charge, 'Whatever you do, don't let go.' Why do I not wish that he could see me now?

I know, with startling certainty, that he would not approve, worse still, that he would be embarrassed to see his sedate respectable wife making a show of herself in public. He would condemn me for the very things he admired and adored in me thirty years ago. Words fly back and forth across the room and I barely hear the ensuing debate as memories of Calcutta swim before my eyes and I try to grasp the depths of our transformation, the infinitely tiny steps by which Ramesh and I have travelled from that moment to this. At what moment did we let go of each other, at what moment did we let go of our dream? I try to imagine asking him and know he will say he hasn't let go of anything, he still serves the disadvantaged and oppressed, in his legal aid work and his duty work at night with people whose lives are in shreds. But I know he doesn't do it any more for a cause, or a dream, he does it for the mortgage and to have white leather settees and pay Anil's university fees, and to send photographs to his parents of an avenue with cherry trees and front lawns. And my part is to smile in the photos and keep the settees clean. I have no business going out and finding a new cause of my own.

My attention is plucked back into the room by a mellow young voice that I recognise.

"Shelley Wright, Dancing Cows Vegan Cafe, Moorfield. I was thinking, maybe the campaign should find out first what kinds of support the people being harassed are asking for and then we can think about what we can realistically deliver?" Shelley turns her head to glance shyly at me as she speaks. She seems a kind of benevolent spirit springing up unexpectedly at moments of fluid possibility. The day I met her, the flow of my life changed, blessed by the guardian cows in her extraordinary cafe. In the midst of this English city I thought I knew so well, I discovered a ramshackle cafe that embodied the highest Hindu principles of non-harm to living things in its stained menu. And here she is again at a moment of revelation. I see that my life is not as set in stone as I thought it was, a little flurry of silt has been stirred up from my river bed and I feel the sand shifting beneath me. I see that I have changed and am changing still.

The meeting resolves to set up a rota of volunteers living in Moorfield willing to take short walks around the neighbourhood in the evenings to observe any activity, and another rota of volunteers available to be phoned to go out immediately to support someone who has been attacked. I refrain from putting my name down knowing it is not my position to be putting myself on any volunteer rota, I am here as a worker. And if I were not working at Awaaz I would have been oblivious to all this in the leafy private estates of Hallam three miles away. But thirty years ago I was out every night of the week making a stand alongside the poor, the homeless, the oppressed. I hardly recognise the person I have become now.

At the end of the meeting everyone files into the car park and stands around in shivering clusters checking diaries, stamping feet, breathing vaporous clouds into the frosty air. I stand outside the clusters and am about to go when someone catches my arm lightly.

"Hi, Veena. It's so great to see you. Congratulations on getting the job." "Shelley." I grip her hand warmly, but when her friends appear beside us, she pulls back self-consciously and I am reminded that our contact was for the briefest of moments.

"Veena, meet Eleanor, my boss - "

"Fellow worker," Eleanor murmurs.

" - fellow worker," Shelley laughs, a wry intimate glance passing between her and Eleanor, " - and her partner, Matt." Matt grunts an inaudible greeting and Eleanor stares at me curiously in the soupy gloom.

"You certainly gave them something to think about in there," Eleanor says in a slow gravelly drawl, and I'm not sure whether she is approving or sarcastic. "It's good to see Awaaz getting involved in this sort of campaign."

"We do a lot of campaigning work, actually." I realise I sound a little cool. This woman is unsettling me and my hackles are raised, but I don't want to snub Shelley's friend. A small man in a woolly hat interrupts us to talk to Eleanor and Matt, and I take the opportunity to turn to Shelley. "It's so good to see you, Shelley. You must come down to Awaaz and I'll show you round. What about tomorrow when you've finished work?"

"Aren't we meant to be going to see that German film at The Showroom tomorrow?" Eleanor cuts in, leaning across from her other conversation.

"That's not till eight," Shelley looks surprised at the speed of her interruption. "But maybe another time would be better, I'll pop in one day next week. We're off to the pub now. Why don't you come along?"

I am tempted. I have hardly seen the inside of an English pub in the twenty-five years I have been here, and I know that in the intimate processing that follows the formal meeting lies the heart of political business, the forging of alliances, the search for soulmates, the discovery of love. I see Ramesh's dark gaze meeting mine across the table in the gloom of the Indian Coffee House as he endorses my argument too vehemently, and Santosh nudges Nitin in the ribs and guffaws triumphantly,

"Oho, look Nitin. Ramesh has found his guruji."

Then I remember how incongruous my sari will look among the denim jackets and beer glasses, and I think of Pooja waiting for her cocoa.

"Thank you for inviting me, but I need to get my bus," I decline, aware of how prim and formal I sound. I can see that Eleanor is relieved. We depart in opposite directions, calling back our goodbyes, and as I head for the dank, draughty bus shelter. I catch wind blown fragments of their raised voices debating which pub to visit first.

Wednesday is meant to be my half-day at work. It doesn't always happen, especially in term times when students with no lectures drift into the cafe in the afternoon filling up the tables for hours on end with their bags and files. By four o'clock the faint acrid scent of weed begins to coil around the pillars and I know there will be no shifting them till six and very little money spent. Sometimes Eleanor persuades me to stay on with promises of an afternoon off later in the week, but the Wednesday after the S.A.F.E. meeting I decided to visit Veena in her new job at the Asian Women's Centre and I was determined to leave dead on two. I left Sky in the yard where I knew she'd be safe, and tucked some Dancing Cows menus and Vegan Society leaflets into my bag as I went out of the main door to give me an excuse for turning up at Awaaz.

When I arrived at the centre I nearly walked on. Through the half-open blinds, the rooms looked warm and yellow in the misty afternoon. I could see a figure sitting at a desk downstairs and others moving around upstairs. They seemed solid and absorbed in their own world and I felt as insubstantial as the mist outside. I didn't exist for them, yet. I could just walk on and no one would ever know I had been there. A voice in my head began to caution me. What if Veena isn't there today? You should have rung first. And beneath that, more quietly whispered, what if they don't think I'm Asian? And beneath that, almost inaudibly, what if I'm not the right sort of Asian? Excruciating memories pressed in on me. 'You look Chinese.' 'You're very

English.' 'Are you South American? - you remind me of a Peruvian friend I had.' 'Your face is so unusual.' 'You don't look Asian.' I doubted this was going to be worth the effort, going through all that exposure and confusion again, putting myself on the line, starting again with a whole new lot of people with their old questions and assumptions. This is why I didn't want to leave Sheffield, I thought. I shuddered and tried to get a grip. Come on, I told myself firmly, you're just delivering some leaflets for the cafe for goodness' sake. I pushed open the front door and stepped into the end of a long bright room decorated with posters and lined with untidy racks of leaflets and magazines. The room was carpeted in ribbed grey cord and divided by an elegant curve of pine veneer desks separating the waiting area from the office space. In the far corner a half-circle of low easy chairs surrounded an area strewn with toys and coloured bricks. A woman in flowing pink clothes with long immaculately combed black hair was seated at a computer by the window. She swung round in her swivel chair and flashed me a cheerful smile framed by magenta lipstick.

"Is Veena here?" I ventured awkwardly.

"She's in a meeting, luv." Her gruff Sheffield accent was a surprise emerging from the delicately sculpted lips and her ease began to soothe my prickles of anxiety. "Can I 'elp? I'm Riffat. Administrator."

"Shelley - from the Dancing Cows Vegan Cafe down the road. I've got some menus and information about veganism I'd like to leave here somewhere..." I looked around uncertainly.

"You can give 'em to me, if you like. I'll put 'em in the rack." She stretched out a thin arm encased in gold bangles and took my wad of papers. "Mmmm... interesting. Don't know if you'll get much business from us, though. We're that busy in 'ere I'm lucky if I get to t' sandwich shop for me dinner most days. You can wait for Veena, if you like. Her meeting started at half-twelve so they should be done soon. Do you want a cup-a-tea while you're waiting?" There was only acceptance and welcome in her eyes. I began to relax.

"No thanks," I said and retreated to the soft chairs. Riffat resumed her tapping on the computer. Looking up at the leaflets in the rack on the wall, I could see lots of standard leaflets in different languages about things like welfare benefits and diet in pregnancy, a bit like a doctor's waiting room. Then there were posters advertising English classes, computer classes, a diploma course in interpreting and translating. I noticed an Indian dance class for beginners starting after Easter and thought that might be fun, maybe I could persuade Eleanor to come with me. But then I realised the class was probably only for Asian women and she wouldn't count. It struck me that I didn't actually know any other Asian women. As I began to feel more relaxed I wandered over to the magazine rack and picked out a magazine. The cover design was a black outline of women in saris working in a rice field. I flicked through its sepia-coloured pages. It had a faded price sticker on the back, "Rs. 20/-", and I realised it must have come from India. I skimmed the contents page. It was in English, but some of the titles just didn't make sense to me, "Eve-teasers flushed out". What did that mean?

Suddenly the front door opened and a slight young woman in shalwar kameez and a frayed denim jacket ushered a small child into the room, the woman muttering to her under her breath as she pushed her in. The little girl's eyes were brimming with tears and she complained in an insistent monotone.

"Ammee, doodh, doodh, ammee…"

Looking around, the woman caught my eye. Pulling a crumpled letter out of her handbag, she began speaking to me in a language I didn't understand. I fished helplessly in the catacombs of my mind for a response, but could only find textbook French from schooldays.

Riffat swung round and intervened, replying to the woman in her language in gentle rounded tones that I would never have guessed were there from her flat Yorkshire vowels earlier. She gestured to me and the woman laughed at her mistake.

"Sorry I talk to you in our language," she called across the room. "You don't speak?"

"No, sorry," I smiled. "I don't speak." I loved the idea that I didn't speak, it was such a turning of tables. I was also hugely, disproportionately, flattered that she had mistaken me for an Awaaz worker. I was beginning to feel like I could belong here.

The little girl, spying the toys, waddled over to the corner with an excited squeal, her previous distress forgotten.

"Huma! Ethay aa!" the woman called sharply.

"It's all right," I reassured, suddenly seeing how I could be useful. "I'll look after her. What's her name?"

"Huma. She is naughty. She understand only Punjabi," her mother looked doubtful.

"We'll be fine," I said confidently, thinking that Huma looked very amenable to me.

"Fikar na karo," Riffat reassured the woman.

Huma sat down in front of the toy box and began

pulling with frustration at the quilted jacket bulging in front of her.

"Shall I do it?" I suggested, and I reached over and began to unzip it for her. I half expected her to panic as I fumbled the zip, but she accepted my help as though it were the most natural thing in the world. Maybe she was used to big people she didn't know taking charge of her. Maybe that's what it's like being a small child, I couldn't remember. If small children inhabit my universe at all, it's usually on the outer perimeters, as unpredictable and messy appendages to cafe customers. I felt honoured when she allowed me to help her take the jacket off. We built brick towers and played jangling tunes on a miniature wooden xylophone for a while.

When Veena came clattering down the stairs with a smartly-dressed woman I recognised from the day of the interview, she found Huma and me on the floor creating swirling patterns on old computer paper with satisfyingly thick creamy wax crayons. Veena looked very different in a tailored black suit and cream silk shirt. Her midriff folds, that showed so openly below the taut line of her sari blouse that day in the cafe, were now swathed by a broad black waistband that, despite its stout stitching, was beginning to take on the unruly creases of her body. Her soft plump face and tightly pinned coil of luxurious black hair reassured me that, beyond the stiffly padded shoulders, she was still the same person.

"Hello!" I chirped brightly.

"My goodness. Hello, Shelley." Her face broke into joyful recognition after a moment of confusion. "How nice to see you. Farah, Riffat, this is Shelley who works in that cafe I was telling you about."

"We've met," Riffat laughed, "And she's made herself at home."

"Nice to meet you," Farah smiled politely. Her eyes drifted over me with a faint shred of recognition and passed on. "Can we book in our next supervision, Veena?"

"Of course," Veena hurried over to where Farah had opened a large blue hardback book on the table. I guessed that Farah was in charge, and I noticed that no one had introduced Huma's mother, who was waiting patiently to continue her discussion with Riffat. When the next meeting had been booked in the diary and Farah had spoken briefly with Riffat about the minutes she was typing, she left with a parting glance of curiosity towards me. I noticed Veena's shoulders sink with relief and a look of mutual sympathy and understanding pass between her and Riffat as the door closed behind Farah. Veena came to sit by me, and Huma immediately thrust her drawing onto her lap.

"What's this, beti? Achcha. Very pretty. Yeh kiya hai?"

Huma explained her picture in a breathless confiding rush, pointing out significant marks and watching Veena's face intently. I wasn't sure if she was speaking another language or her own baby talk. Veena expressed great admiration and then turned to me. "So, you've come to see what Awaaz is all about?"

"I came to see you." I explained simply.

"Oh, how sweet of you." She squeezed my hand with emotion. "And as you see, here I am." She flung her arms wide to demonstrate her undeniable presence and I laughed at her enthusiasm.

"And how is it?" I realised this was not the place to ask such a question as I noticed Veena's eyes flicker in the direction of Riffat's bowed head. Riffat seemed absorbed in filling in the form Huma's mother had brought.

"Oh, it's all very interesting. There's a lot to learn and it's very different from my other job. Now I'm working so near to your place, we must make a time to meet up properly." This was clearly not a 'proper' meeting. I felt myself in uncharted territory. I didn't know how Veena made friends, what kinds of things she was into, I didn't really know if we had anything to talk about. The smart black jacket had thrown me, and I felt I was losing a memory of sandalwood scent rising from creased brown skin and quiet remarks that irritated with their certainty and fascinated with their cadences.

"So, what did you think of the meeting last week?" I prompted, grasping around for a common point of interest. "I thought what you said was really cool."

"Thank you. I thought it was interesting," Veena's tone was cautious and I could see she was being diplomatic. "We'll have to see how it works out in practice. I haven't seen it make any difference yet to women I know who've been attacked." As she said this, her gaze drifted across the room to Huma's mother and I drew in a sudden breath of comprehension.

"That woman you talked about in the meeting with the three-year-old child...?" I said, lowering my voice. She looked at me sharply and I felt embarrassed and crass. I shouldn't have mentioned it, but it was she... never mind. I didn't want this to be so difficult.

"Did you put your name down on one of the rotas?" she asked as if my last sentence hadn't been uttered.

"On both rotas." I was going to say more, but I noticed her looking anxiously at the clock on the wall. "Have you got something else to do? I don't want to get in the way of your work."

"I'd love you to stay longer, Shelley, but I do have this report to type up and I really need Riffat's help now she's finished with Tasleem. She's only here till three o'clock."

I wondered where the woman had gone who charmed me into neglecting a mounting queue at the Dancing Cows counter, but I didn't argue.

"No problem. I only came in to drop off some leaflets," I smiled brightly. I began gathering up the paper and crayons and helping Huma back into her outdoor jacket.

"Do come back again," Veena urged wistfully, and then, more decisively, "In fact, come to my house for lunch on Sunday."

"Actually," I said "I've been helping Eleanor sort out the backyard on Sunday mornings," I hesitated, not sure if our casual acquaintance was up to something so heavy and formal.

"Dinner then," she insisted. "We usually eat at seven, so come any time after five. Here, I'll give you my address."

I could see no way out of this so I allowed her to write her address on a crisp compliment slip from the front desk. Slipping the paper into my bag, I said a quick goodbye to Riffat and followed Tasleem and Huma, who were also making for the door.

As we stood on the wet, windy corner outside the centre, Tasleem pressed me to go to her house for a cup of tea. Sidestepping sprays of dank oily water thrown up from the roadside drains by lorries thundering past, I mumbled something about shopping and having to cook dinner.

"I can give you dinner," Tasleem insisted. "Please, you

have been so kind to Huma. She likes you." Huma was complaining loudly once more and stretching her arms out to be carried.

"Just a cup of tea then." I gave in to the cheerful impulse that leapfrogged over old inherited warnings in my head not to get involved. "Coming Huma?" I held my hand out and she grabbed it with an excited skip as we set off. Her small plump fingers clutched around mine felt warm and strange. I hadn't held someone else's hand in mine since Hugh left Sheffield and Huma's hand was so tiny and light in comparison, so achingly trusting as she led me up the hill away from Awaaz, leaving behind the dense, cluttered valley floor I spent so much time studying for my dissertation. The river which formed the valley now lies hidden behind derelict factories and echoing steel-roofed warehouses, a muddy green trickle most of the year flowing bravely between high brick walls, at points disappearing under whole buildings, the forgotten artery that once fed the grinding shops and the forges, that kept the valley alive and humming with its soft Pennine waters. And, following the river's course faithfully, the railway, running swiftly behind factories and backyards of old terraced houses, sailing over and under blackened gritstone bridges, hidden now, like the ancient river, behind plastic-trimmed fitness complexes and prefabricated retail units stacked along their barren access roads.

"Geography is History," Doctor Carter used to tell us, "In any landscape we look at, urban or rural, we can see the story of what has gone before. It is our task as geographers to read that story." My passion was ignited instantly and Sheffield became my playground, a city with contours, its history writ large and unambiguously, like Rome's, across its seven hills and its dark industrial flood plains and I am still tuned in to those resonances in the stone and soil around me.

Tasleem led us down a dark ginnel in the centre of a terrace of Victorian workers' houses. To reach her back door we had to pass through her neighbour's yard and as I glanced up at the window I saw a woman in an apron with dyed blonde hair watching us from her kitchen. I smiled and she returned an embarrassed twitch of her lips and moved away from the window. When we were safely inside I asked Tasleem about her neighbour.

"She was nice in the start, she give Huma sweets and chocolate biscuits when we are outside. But now she doesn't talk to me. She has one son. He goes to the big school out of the town where the buses go - Totley -," she giggles suddenly at another thought. "When I first get this bus I keep thinking, how is this bus going to 'Toilet'? What is this place, Toilet? I am not reading it properly!" Her laughter was infectious and soon even Huma was laughing, although she had no idea what it was about.

"So, this boy?" I reminded Tasleem.

"Oh yes. He ask me if I am asylum seeker. I say no, but he says I am and he calls me very bad language. When I tell his mother she just says, you know what boys are like, but she doesn't stop him to do anything. And then last week my gate is smashed and they put paint on my doors. I don't know it is this boy or some other boys."

"I'm so sorry, poor you." My sympathy seemed so inadequate. "Why did they call you an asylum seeker?"

"Oh-ho! English boys round here, they think asylum

seeker is very bad. One Somali lady across the road from me, she has six children with her and she is alone like me looking after them. They say she is asylum seeker and they throw stones at her. She can't run fast, you know, she's big lady," she pushed her elbows out to indicate the woman's size, "and something wrong with her leg, I feel so sorry for her."

"So this boy next door, is he still giving you trouble?"

"Not much. I don't let Huma play outside when he's at home." She frowned and shook herself into action. "You want cup of tea?"

I nodded politely, "No milk, thankyou," I smiled.

She went out to the kitchen and I produced a pencil from my patchwork bag and a little rainbow-coloured notebook on which I drew a succession of barely recognisable animals for Huma. She bounced on the settee with delight at each drawing and copied my naming of the animals in a lisping burble, looking sceptically at each drawing as if she found it hard to believe too. Then she suddenly realised her mother wasn't in the room and ran out panic-stricken on solid stamping legs calling, "Ammi! Ammi!"

From the kitchen I could hear Tasleem reassuring her in Punjabi. Her intonation leapt wildly and warmly as she coaxed Huma and her voice sounded more vigorous and brash and brightly humorous than in her laboured English. I felt a bit excluded from that intimate experiencing of the world in a language I had no access to. I thought about Rehana speaking Bengali somewhere on the planet and realised I could have grown up thinking and feeling, even dreaming, in totally other words and rhythms. I felt a kind of deja vu, a shifting within, that suddenly placed me in Huma's shoes, being comforted in the language of another continent, a language of sweating crowded bazaars and sleepy villages wilting in relentless sunshine. Bengali is a gentle musical language full of sibilants and soft shushing sounds like whispered endearments, I couldn't imagine myself speaking such a language, yet, sitting in Tasleem's front room, I felt sparse and light without it. I stared through the window at the watery fading sky and the lamps flushing from strawberry red to orange in the darkening street, and thought of that other life, that strange parallel life that accompanies me everywhere, like a shadow, teasing me with glimpses of the person I might have been.

Tasleem and Huma came back into the room with tea and chocolate biscuits and I pulled myself back into the present.

We talked about the classes Tasleem did at Awaaz and she told me she had only been in Sheffield for a few months. I told her about my work in the cafe, which fascinated her.

"I want to have job," she announced firmly. "When Huma goes in school I will get job. I don't want staying alone all day in the house. Too boring. I like to do something interesting." She looked at me hopefully and I wasn't sure if she thought I might be able to produce an interesting job for her. I realised I had no way of gauging if we were on the same wavelength or not. I couldn't even quite tell what meaning her sentences really carried because maybe the words she translated in her head had a different significance from their English renditions. Was, "I like to do something interesting", a statement, a wish, a request, or something uniquely Punjabi that was a little bit of all of these without an exact translation? Maybe, if I knew her better, I would learn the meanings her words carried and understand more accurately her intentions. I felt as if her few words were invested with far more richness and subtlety than my rambling sentences.

"Will you come again?" Tasleem asked me as I began to gather up my things to go.

"Of course," I replied, enthusiastically. "If I come earlier in the day next time we could take Huma to the park. Have you been to any big parks here?"

"There is a park at Mount Pleasant with a swing that Huma likes."

"Oh no, I mean a big park with lots of play areas and a pond and a cafe," I explained. "We could go to Graves Park and see the animals in the Rare Breeds Centre and have lunch in the café. Huma would love it." I felt quite excited myself. The prospect of Huma discovering it all made the outing seem much more special.

"Will you come every time?" Tasleem asked anxiously. I turned the phrase over in my mind, puzzled by it.

"I don't understand what you mean," I had to say. She thought hard about how to say it differently.

"Will you come lots of times or only one time?"

"Oh, lots of times!" I exclaimed, realising I had given her no idea of my intentions. I felt bad that I had so much power in our newborn friendship and she had none. I tried to estimate what would be realistic for me. "I could try to come once a week. How about that?"

"Okay," she smiled, satisfied. "You give me your telephone number?"

"So when I don't come you can phone me and tell me off," I laughed, retrieving my notebook from Huma.

I walked away from her house that day cradling a warm

glow that was a combination of Huma's hand in mine as we walked and the musical modulations of Tasleem's Punjabi playing over and over indistinctly in my mind.

I stand at the smooth, grey, marbled worktop chopping tomatoes and cucumber on an old wooden chopping board. We have expensive ceramic surfaces installed in the kitchen, but, to Ramesh's annoyance, I persist in using the same old boards I bought on the market when we first came to Sheffield. My face is flushed from the heat of the gas flames under various pans on the cooker and my hair hangs down my back in a thick heavy plait, bouncing gently against my spine when I move like an old familiar friend reminding me of schooldays. I have pulled the pallu of my turquoise cotton sari round my back and under my arm and tucked it safely in at my waist away from the flames and hot oil. It's so easy to have an accident with open flames and flapping saris, and so easy to fake one as well, 'cooking accident', they would say in tiny insignificant print in the newspaper, and my mother would tut and shake her head.

"Cooking accident - pah! Another dowry death, but they won't investigate," she would sigh. "Too many business connections in that family." But in refusing the dowry system for her own daughter she lost me entirely to another continent and a cold, distant way of life that was a kind of death for both of us.

The doorbell chimes its corny 'Big Ben' anthem and I feel embarrassed knowing Shelley will find it distinctly un-'cool'. I hear Anil welcoming her in his slightly gruff casual way. I can picture him stooping over her uncomfortably in the narrow hall, his loose limbs retreating awkwardly into the cloak cupboard, a shy smile tweaking the corners of his lips.

"Hi. Shelley? Come on in. Mum's just in the kitchen. Do you wanna park your coat in here?"

I turn as Shelley follows Anil through the kitchen doorway. A forest of stiffened black spikes stand up all over her head and her purple and green top dazzles with its sequins and tiny silver mirrors. I know the torn hems of her jeans and the plunging round neck of her top are fashionable at present, but I dread Ramesh's judgement of her as a bad influence on Pooja. Still, I am happy to see her and that's what matters.

"There you are, Shelley." I put my knife down and wipe my hands quickly on a tea towel hanging on the side of the cupboard. "I've been looking forward to this so much. I do hope you're hungry."

"I'll say. It all smells delicious," she replies and breathes deeply the aromas that fill the house.

"Let's go and sit down for a bit," I suggest. "Anil will finish the salad and make us some tea, won't you Anu beta?" Anil nods agreeably and establishes Shelley's tea requirements with the ease of someone used to having guests in the house. I can see that Shelley is impressed and I am grateful to him for rising to the occasion after he was in such a bad mood about her coming this morning.

He didn't get up till nearly midday and came down to find Pooja and me discussing vegetable dishes and fruit chaat in the kitchen.

"What's going on?" he snapped suspiciously, and when I told him I'd invited a friend for dinner he just exploded. "You can't. Why didn't you tell me?"

"I'm telling you now, beta. What's the matter? You don't have to stay in if you've got something else to do," I reassured him, perplexed at his reaction. Then he just

68

walked out of the room throwing his arms up in despair and went back upstairs and didn't mention it for the rest of the day. His behaviour at the moment is very worrying.

I take Shelley into the front room, which we keep mainly for guests or more formal occasions. I follow her eyes to the white leather suite and draw my breath in as I realise we are looking at the hides of dead cows. She doesn't blink and calmly selects a deep armchair beside the red velvet curtains that descend to the floor. We were so proud of their long elegant sweeps when we chose them, but now they seem overdone and ostentatious to me.

"We're waiting for my daughter, Pooja, and my husband," I explain, to distract her from the glass cabinet she is eying curiously. I am not sure what she will think of our china ornaments and crystal vases and the ranks of gilt-framed family photos. "He's up at the golf club - you might have passed it on the bus?" She nods. "And Pooja's at her friend's doing exam revision, but she promised me she'd be back for dinner. So, how are you?"

"I'm fine. We've been clearing the backyard at the cafe all day, so I feel very healthy," she informs me, stretching her arms expansively to indicate hearty physical exercise.

"Do you live at the cafe, then?"

"No, that really would be sad," she laughed. "I rent a little flat on my own in Hunters Bar. I just went in today to help Eleanor clear the yard so we can use it in the summer for customers to sit outside."

"That sounds nice. Sitting outside seems to be very popular these days." I pause, digesting her comment about the flat. "You live on your own, then?"

"Yes." Her lips push outwards into a stubborn pout. "It's great, actually. When you deal with other people all day long it's nice to have a bit of peace and quiet, and I have got a cat. Sort of."

"I know that's what young people do in this country," I comment, hearing the regret in my voice, "But I don't see the point of Anil and Pooja paying all that money to unscrupulous landlords when we've got space for them here. And they'd just keep coming back to get their clothes washed and their meals cooked."

"Living at home's not the same as having your own place, though, and doing your own thing," she asserts. She says what she thinks. I like that. When they were little Anil and Pooja used to protest about everything. Now they humour me to my face and do something else behind my back. I preferred the arguments.

"I suppose you're right," I agree. "But it doesn't stop me wanting to hang on to my babies." Shelley looks quite taken aback and I laugh defensively. "I know they're practically grown up, but they'll always be my babies to me even when they've got children of their own."

"I just can't imagine my mother calling me her baby," Shelley admits, and adds, thoughtfully, "I suppose she's always treated me in quite an adult way... maybe it's because there were only the three of us."

"I think it's also to do with a different attitude in this country," I suggest, intrigued but wary of probing as I remember how touchy she was in the cafe. "In India there isn't this thing of leaving home and being separate from your family like you have here. You never really leave your parents' home unless you move to your in-laws, and then you just take on another set of parents. You're always someone's child until there's no one left in the generation going before you. Even when you're a parent yourself, you're still someone's child as long as your parents and your in-laws are alive."

"But that's like you're not allowed to live, that's so claustrophobic," Shelley says, sounding appalled.

"It's a different way of living," I try to explain. "The Western way can be so lonely." A shudder runs through me as I remember the gales of loneliness that howled around me when I first came to this country.

Shelley looks unsure and doesn't respond. Instead she asks how my work is going.

"Oh, I really don't know," I screw up my face in pain. "It's all turning out quite difficult. I'm not sure I've done the right thing at all." I hear Anil approaching with a rattling tray and add hastily, "Don't say anything, though."

He sets down before us two cups of tea, one without milk, and a plate of biscuits, and then checks a few details with me about the salad and warming up the curries.

"I'll leave you to it then," he steps back decisively. "Have a good gossip about me, won't you," and he flashes a dazzling smile at Shelley as he turns to the door.

"What makes you think we'll be talking about you?" she calls after him indignantly.

"I'm sorry, he's too cheeky that boy," I apologise. His flirtatious manner annoys me and I want to say, hands off, she's my guest.

"He's a student," Shelley comments benevolently, as if her own student days are now far behind her. She notices my frown and adds, "But you worry about him?"

"I worry about him not talking to me," I murmur, half to myself. "I know there's something going on."

"Have you asked him?" she suggests, somewhat obviously, I feel.

"You probably think I ask too many questions," I laugh, wagging my finger at her. "But I've learnt my lesson with my own children. Ask too many questions and you just get lies. I suppose he'll tell me when he's ready, or when he needs my help. As long as he hasn't gone and got some poor girl pregnant, I worry about him tying himself down too young." I see a shadow pass across her eyes and feel a lurch of horror as comprehension dawns in me. "Oh, I'm really sorry, Shelley, did I…?"

"No, no." She hesitates and takes a deep breath. "Okay, what the hell. It was my mother, actually. She was still at school when she had me." I feel a kind of thud in my chest and think of how young Pooja would be to be a mother.

"And what about the boy? Or the man?" The words are out of my mouth before I have time to consider whether I should be asking such questions.

"She wouldn't say who he was. They said probably another boy at the school. Nobody knows." Shelley shrugs in a gesture of helplessness. The possibilities run through my mind, a classmate, a neighbour, a member of the family even, uncle, brother, father. These things happen, and of course the girl cannot say. Poor Shelley. I shake my head sadly. "I wouldn't let Anil ruin a young girl's life like that. Even if he wouldn't stand by her, I'd support her myself. Your poor mother, she must have been very lonely and frightened… "

"Birth mother," Shelley corrects roughly, "I don't know what she felt, I never knew her. She was fifteen. I don't think she'd even been in the country that long because she was in special English classes at school. It was all a bit of a disaster. I suppose she had to get on with her own life somehow, so she gave me up for adoption. I was with a foster carer for a few months and then Mum and Dad adopted me. They're English, but my dad's been to India a lot. Anyway, they're my real parents, they loved me and looked after me, not her, so they're the people who matter to me, " Shelley says, examining her fingernails intently.

"Of course." I try to assimilate all this information. I leave what I hope is a respectful pause. Then I can't stop myself probing further. "Have you ever met her? Your birth mother?"

"Nope," she responds abruptly. "And there isn't any more to find out, before you ask. The family went back to Bangladesh after she had me and no one ever heard from her again." She sighs, looking down at the toe of her shoe, which is digging a little depression in the woollen tussocks of the Berber carpet. Then she looks up at me defiantly. "People always want to hear some tear-jerking, long-lost, reunion story and think I'm in denial if I don't want the same. There wasn't much to go on in the first place, and then they lost track of her and that's that. It doesn't really bother me, I'm happy getting on with my life in the present, thank you."

"The present and the past are connected, though, aren't they? I believe they are all one in the end." As I offer this I see her spring to retaliate and then she seems to let it go.

"Fair enough," she shrugs. "But I don't."

I sip my tea and study her for a moment. She is so self-contained and confident. I smile. Here I am, twice her age, so solid and settled in my big house with my husband and children, and I don't feel any different to how I felt all those years ago when I arrived here, lonely and miserable and too terrified I might fall apart to admit it even to Ramesh.

"So we ended up talking about Anil after all," I joke, trying to lighten our mood and her eyes meet mine in a kind of truce.

"You were saying about the job," she reminds me. "You seemed very busy when I came into Awaaz the other day."

"I know, I'm sorry about that." I hesitate.

"Riffat seemed nice."

"Yes, she's lovely, she's been really helpful and looked after me when I've done things wrong or when I don't know where to find something. There's so much to remember, all these policies and procedures."

"It's hard work when you're new," Shelley commiserates. "I was hopeless when I started at the cafe, I just forgot things all the time and half my food couldn't even be served, we had to eat it ourselves or bin it."

"I know I'm learning," I sigh, "but I feel really stupid having to be shown what to do all the time. I thought it was all about working with women in the community and all I've done so far is go to meetings and read hundreds of policies and guidelines and minutes."

"That Farah wasn't very friendly," Shelley observes, bluntly. "Is she your boss?"

"She's the chair of the management committee." I am relieved at her directness. "She's very businesslike and frightening. She fires things at me that I don't understand, but I don't say, I just sort it out with Riffat later."

We both jump at the sound of a door slamming loudly at the back of the house. "Mum! I'm back!" Pooja appears in the doorway, brandishing a rucksack full of books. I have no idea if she has actually opened the bag while she has been at Kate's, or even if she has been to Kate's, but I do know she doesn't tell me half of what she's really up to.

"There's no need to shout, Pooja, we're just in here," I remonstrate quietly. "Shelley, meet my daughter, Pooja."

"Sorry, Mum," Pooja says to me in passing and looks curiously at Shelley, running her eyes over the frayed hems of her jeans and the glittering top. She is clearly flummoxed and I realise I didn't brief her sufficiently this morning. Shelley is nothing like the middle-aged lawyers' and doctors' wives in saris and gold jewellery it is usually my duty to entertain. I find a mischievous pleasure in unsettling her preconceptions.

"Hi. You run a cafe or something, don't you? That must be hard work." Pooja volunteers.

"It's okay. I don't mind the work." Shelley meets Pooja's appraising gaze head on and I feel unexpectedly proud of her.

"And you're a strict vegetarian? We had fun thinking of what to cook tonight, didn't we, Mum?"

"I'm vegan. I hope you didn't go to any trouble?" Shelley looks guilty.

"Of course not," I assure her, glaring at Pooja, "Indian food is full of vegan dishes, as I'm sure you know. Pooja, why don't you go and help Anu lay the table. I'll come through in a minute."

By the time everything has been organised for dinner Ramesh has returned home. As he enters the front room he also raises his eyebrows in momentary surprise before clicking effortlessly into gear as the jovial host.

"So, Shelley - or is it Ms… ? - "

" - Wright, but Shelley's fine," Shelley smiles awkwardly. "Would you like a drink before dinner?" He swings opens the cabinet in a corner of the room with a grand flourish to reveal an array of sparkling glasses and dark bottles with gold lettering on their labels. His heavy eyebrows twitch as he speaks and light bounces off his shiny mottled brown forehead. I can see that Shelley is not sure how to respond to him and I wonder what she expected. "Sherry? Port? Dubonnet?"

"A sherry, please, medium," she suggests uncertainly.

"So you work with my wife," he states rather than enquires, as he pours the drinks.

"Sort of," she murmurs, sipping the sherry and looking anxiously at me. I can see she doesn't want to contradict anything I have said. I want to tell her it's okay, he has just got it wrong, as usual, because he wasn't listening to me when I told him about her.

"She works in a cafe near Awaaz," I interrupt. But he is intent on his own line of inquiry now.

"I suppose you feminists don't approve of us men very much," he challenges with an amused smile.

"Ramesh..." I protest, needing to check on things in the kitchen, but not wanting to abandon Shelley if Ramesh is going to start playing his lawyer's games with her.

"I don't really approve, or disapprove, of men in general, and I can't speak for anyone else," she responds evenly.

"You must think we're against you, or why set up a place we're not allowed in?" The edge of annoyance in his voice is for me, not Shelley.

"It's not about shutting people out, it's just about having a separate safe space for women," I intervene. "You supported women organising separately in India, so

76

don't pretend it's something new or revolutionary here. Anyway, dinner's ready. Let's go through to the dining room."

I usher the two of them unceremoniously into the dining room and place Shelley beside Pooja and opposite Anil. Ramesh and I sit at opposite ends of the rectangular dining table. There is a flurry of activity as we help ourselves, and each other, to the array of steaming dishes, salads and pickles spread out before us. As we begin eating a small reverent hush falls on the room. Ramesh and I still eat with our right hands, mixing the rice with dahl or dahi and moulding it into sticky balls which we balance on our fingertips and nudge into our mouths with our thumbnails. The younger ones use forks to chase their rice grains around the plate, which I have tried but find an impoverished and frustrating experience, separating me from the delicious blending of texture on the fingertips with taste on the tongue that makes the meal whole.

"This really is lovely, Veena." Shelley breaks the silence.

"Yeah, Mum. It's great. Who needs meat?" Pooja endorses with enthusiasm.

"Everyone needs meat for a balanced diet," Ramesh pronounces, chewing heavily.

"That's not true actually," Shelley counters in a quiet firm voice, "We can eat and digest a wide range of foods, we don't need meat to live."

"I admire you, living according to your principles," Anil addresses Shelley, looking seriously into her eyes across the table, and I notice Ramesh's eyebrows begin to narrow into a frown.

"You wouldn't know a principle if it hit you in the face," Pooja laughs at her brother.

"And you would I suppose?" he flares peevishly.

"Have you got any brothers?" Pooja turns to Shelley, who shakes her head. "Very sensible. Don't ever get any, they're a complete pain."

"So what does your father do, Shelley?" Ramesh interrupts, looking sternly at Pooja.

"He's a head teacher in a primary school, and my mum works in personnel in Reading City Council."

"You're a long way from home, then?"

"I came to Sheffield to go to university and just sort of stayed on."

"Like so many. Sheffield is full of students who've stayed on, we're famous for it," Ramesh comments, sounding like a disgruntled elder of the borough. I do wish he wouldn't put on such pompous airs sometimes. "Dad thinks students do nothing all day - based on his own youth, of course," Anil confides across the table. Ramesh makes an explosive noise, but his mouth is too full to protest. "He doesn't understand how tough college is these days."

"What did you study, Shelley?" I interrupt, realising I don't know.

"Geography."

"What can you do with that?" Ramesh looks dubious. "Apart from draw maps, perhaps?"

"Actually, it's not all maps, it's useful in lots of things like planning and land management... " Shelley's voice trails off under his sceptical gaze.

"Or you could teach it," Pooja adds helpfully

"So what are you doing with your geography right now?" Ramesh persists. I am beginning to feel he is bullying her and I don't like to see it, I feel ashamed of him.

"Well, I'm not really using it at the moment. I'm working in a vegan cafe, but I may go into environmental work in the future," Shelley sounds unusually cornered and I realise she can be young and uncertain too. I want to cradle her from Ramesh's slamming certainties.

"Mmmm..... a CV as a waitress isn't going to get you far, is it?"

"You're always advocating starting on the shop floor, Dad," Anil interrupts, winking at Shelley.

"Yes, where there's something else to aspire to. I don't quite see the progression here, but I wish you every success. You're certainly an enterprising young woman," Ramesh concedes with a forced smile.

"What are you doing, Anil?" Shelley asks, swinging the focus away from herself.

"Accountancy here in Sheffield. I wouldn't recommend it," he replies dismally, "Hell of a slog - "

"But brilliant career prospects," she finishes, with a conspiratorial flash of her eyes.

"Absolutely, dear thing," he replies, and they burst out laughing.

"You may mock, but you'll see the value of it when you've got a family to feed," Ramesh warns, rising abruptly from his seat to slip into the kitchen and rinse his hands. There is a very slight shuffling of relief as he leaves the room.

"Actually, I need to have a chat with you about uni," Shelley addresses Anil, casually. "I've got a friend at your place who needs a bit of help. You couldn't call into the cafe some time, could you, so I could fill you in?" She holds his gaze for a moment.

"Sure." He nods and helps himself to more rice. I'm glad she had the sense to wait until Ramesh had left the room, but I am starting to wonder if inviting Shelley to dinner was such a good idea.

When Ramesh returns to his seat, Pooja and I begin to clear the plates away and Anil carries the serving dishes into the kitchen.

"We have fruit chaat or kheer for dessert, Shelley, but I'm afraid the kheer is made with milk," I explain.

"Chaat will be lovely," Shelley smiles and turns to Ramesh. "You've been in Sheffield a long time, then?"

"Nearly twenty-five years," he confirms with pride, "And we've been in this house most of that time as well. Properties round here were much cheaper then of course and I set up in my own partnership relatively early in my career."

"Did you find it hard getting into? I mean, law's meant to be very elitist, isn't it?"

"I specialised in criminal cases and legal aid work, and I did a lot of immigration cases. Still do, in fact. I have a bit of a monopoly on that client group, as you can appreciate."

"You mean the Asian community?"

"Precisely. People want someone they can feel safe with, speak their mind to, you see, and speak in their own language, of course."

"Like the women who come to the Asian Women's Centre," Shelley points out slyly.

"I suppose so," he concedes, laughing. I am pleased to see him give her credit and I start to relax a little. I suppose he doesn't mean to bully, he's just so used to that environment he can't help bringing it home with him sometimes.

"And there's all that duty solicitor work you do for the police. That gets you known in the community," I point out, dishing out the desserts Pooja has brought in from the kitchen. I notice Anil has not returned. "He's called out at all hours of the day and night, you know, when other solicitors' offices are closed. The interviews can go on for hours. They need him sometimes for his Hindi and his Urdu, you see, they haven't got anyone else who can do that side of it."

"Yes, yes, it's just part of the job, Veena," he looks irritated and my tension returns. What have I said now? I get tired of trying to read his moods. The door in the hall slams and Ramesh looks at me accusingly. "Has Anil gone out without saying goodbye?" Pooja jumps in quickly.

"He said he doesn't want any dessert. He's gone out for a walk."

"I apologise for my son's rudeness, Shelley." Ramesh kneads his brow with the thumb and forefinger of one hand. "I don't know what to do with that boy sometimes."

You don't do anything, I find myself thinking vehemently, it all falls on me. But I keep quiet.

"Oh, there's no need to apologise," Shelley responds hastily, "I wasn't really his guest."

After our meal we have tea with cardamoms and I offer to show Shelley the garden. Carrying our mugs, we walk out onto the lawn bordered by rose beds and dark green rhododendrons, their heavy purple and red buds just starting to show. The low sun filters through a line of silver poplars at the bottom of the garden and a cool breeze chills me through the wool cardigan I have buttoned over my sari, sending a shiver up my back. I am amazed at how Shelley can stand there without a cardigan or jacket on, but she has grown up in this country and has plump young arms. She seems to have none of the obsession with being slim I see in Pooja and her friends.

The lawn is spongy underfoot and its miraculously dense green blades shine with the intensity of a rice paddy where the slanting evening sun catches them. As saffron is the colour of India for me, so the green of wet grass shining after rain is the colour of England, and I celebrate it wherever I find it, on swathes of rolling hillside or hemmed into a tiny pocket of turf between concrete and tarmac. Particularly hemmed in by concrete and tarmac, actually, where it is the colour of hope, bursting forth irrepressibly through the cold dead weight of human construction. I think Shelley would understand that.

We wander over to a set of white plastic patio chairs tucked away in a corner.

"Beautiful rhododendrons," she compliments. "Did you plant them?"

"No, they've been here for years. We're forever cutting them back. Actually they're one of the reasons we chose the house." I remember holding my breath waiting for Ramesh's reaction, knowing it would be his decision in the end, based on his checklist of garage, central heating, two reception rooms downstairs, one for formal guests and another for ourselves, and all the legalities of surveys and buyer chains. I only knew I had to have the dark emerald-leafed bushes dripping with ruby-red and cerise-pink flowers, so loud and brilliant and tropical.

"They are magnificent," Shelley agrees. "But they can be a terrible weed if they get into the countryside. They take over whole hillsides."

"They remind me of bougainvillea at home, and the red hibiscus flowers we used to wear in our hair." I explain and decide to risk another question. "Have you ever been to Bangladesh, Shelley?"

"No." She looks cautious. "My father went to India a lot when he was younger, but we've never all been as a family."

"Why not?" I am amazed, but not surprised, given her guarded responses whenever I mention India.

"Couldn't afford it, I suppose, or too busy. We've never been much of a family for holidays. Some years we didn't even go on holiday in this country. Mum just took me to my granny's in Blackburn for the summer while she was working."

"You really should go to Calcutta - or Bangladesh - but Calcutta's easier and it's all Bengal. It was all one before Partition." I try not to sound too prescriptive, but I cannot hide the urgency in my voice. "We haven't been recently, but we used to take Anu and Pooja every two or three years."

"And did they like it?"

"They loved it when they were little. But it was more of a struggle as they got older, they didn't like leaving their friends for so long and we stopped going altogether when they got into their exam subjects. They've both been doing exams every year at school and college for the last five years."

"And now?"

"Now it's a bit awkward. They're very desirable marriage partners. We don't want to offend anyone by refusing marriage offers, so it's better not to go. I just keep telling people they're still studying, which is true, of course. Actually, I want them to be free to make their own choices. There doesn't seem to be any alternative when they've been brought up here, does there?"

"I don't think so, but I would say that wouldn't I - I'm not in your position," she reminds me.

"No, you're not," I murmur, looking at her quirky, impish haircut and the dark brown irises of her Himalayan eyes. "But I think you would say the same thing wherever you were placed. You're that sort of person, independent and single-minded."

"Is that good or bad?"

"Very good." I slap my hands on my knees. "Believe it or not, that's how I used to be once."

"I do believe it." She smiles shyly. I feel we are becoming friends.

Another weird couple of days at the cafe and I'm in this kind of surreal situation that I can't get my head round because maybe it didn't even happen. On Sunday morning I woke up to blue skies flooded with sunshine, and sped down the empty main road to the cafe, pedalling madly from sheer joy at not being late for once, full of inspiration for our evolving continental patio idea. Eleanor wasn't even dressed when I got there. I found her in the cafe kitchen in her blue silk kimono, brewing fresh coffee and making toast in the veggie breakfast grill to carry back upstairs to their warm, rumpled nest in the upstairs flat. While she was waiting for the coffee to percolate she chatted animatedly to me about what she called our 'horticultural venture', and I leafed through her Sunday paper, which I had picked up off the mat on my way in. I couldn't quite relax, something about the gaping of her casually tied kimono and the faint tracery of bluish veins on her chest above the shadowed parting of her breasts, too much information on this lazy, decadent Sunday morning. I felt sympathy for Ermyntrude and Matilda's blushes, and embarrassed thinking about her and Matt having sex in the flat above my workplace.

She had been on at me for ages to help her clear out the backyard. We both had a fantasy that on sunny days we could put tables and chairs out there and our customers would eat al fresco. Matt was scathing about our 'poncy middle class' aspirations and refused to get involved, but we were convinced it would boost trade dramatically, and had already begun calling it 'The Garden' to get ourselves in the mood. Now the moment to tackle the yard had arrived we approached it like a campaign and drew up detailed plans after work, complete with hanging baskets, tubs of flowers, a brushwood screen to hide the bins, a bay tree and even a small fountain in the bottom of an old barrel, bubbling up over a stack of large rounded pebbles where, we imagined, people, or their children, would be unable to resist the temptation to throw in coins and make wishes.

Once Eleanor had stirred herself into action, she supplied me with thick gardening gloves and I set to work collecting the old bricks and plaster left behind by the builders when the kitchen was extended and flinging them into a wheelbarrow. She then wheeled it up a neat little ramp she had constructed out of the old back door into a dinky yellow skip that had been delivered to the back gates on Saturday morning. Then there was all the disgusting congealed litter and black slime on the blocked drains to clear, and after that, thickets of weeds bursting through the old flagstones and swarming up the high back wall, which bulged alarmingly around a massive sycamore trunk on the other side.

"We'll have to get him next door to cut that tree down," Eleanor frowned, eyeing the vast branches waving above her, erupting with bursting new leaf buds. "It cuts out too much light in the summer, people want sun when they're sitting outside. They can always have umbrellas when it's really hot."

"You can't cut down a tree!" I protested. "That's murder."

"Oh, don't you start. I've got enough problems with Matt."

"But it's a living thing. That one could be a hundred-years-old."

"Hardly." Eleanor was sceptical, and ruthless when she had made up her mind. "We'll plant something else, don't worry. Two if you like. Then we'll be increasing the total number of trees on the planet. But it's got to go. Anyway, you're quite happy to pull up weeds, and sycamores are weeds, believe me." I had no answer for that, except to feel an incipient twinge of guilt about the ranks of rosebay willow herb massed in the corner oblivious to my approaching spade and fork.

The sky above the uneven horizon of the back wall was so vast and blue and airy I could almost imagine the sea lay the other side. A cold April wind tugged at my shirt and brushed my exposed neck. There was a time when long thick hair covered my ears and warmed my neck and Mum was always on at me to tie it back or the knots would be a devil to comb out. I liked the heaviness of the loose mane bouncing on my back and only regretted it when I had to sit at breakfast wincing and squeaking as the relentless brush ploughed through my tangles and Mum snapped, "It'll hurt more if you pull away. Just sit still."

"Why don't you let me cut it off?" Dad would butt in unhelpfully, "Then you'll have little bouncy curls like when you were a baby."

"No," I would grimace stoutly, raising protective arms over my precious hair.

"Leave her alone, Pete," Mum's quiet voice spoke volumes and I could feel her looking at him across the top of my head in that way she had of closing down a dangerous subject, "It's not her fault her hair's so knotty."

And I knew whose fault it was, the one who was

responsible for all the little imperfections in our life, my dense matted hair, my tempers and my secretiveness; my dark skin, which Mum spent so much time trying to be positive about, when it obviously worried her. Once I heard her once tell Aunty Jill how much lighter-skinned I was as a baby. "Apparently they all start off light but we didn't know that. Not that I mind, Jill, but I worry about how she's going to get through life, I just want things to be easy for her, you know."

As I leant over the pile of debris and felt the strain in my back and my calves, I was reminded of countless childhood Sundays spent on the vegetable patch at the end of the garden turning soil, planting, weeding, potting out. The sun was always shining and we always had a flask of tea for Mum, a flask of hot cocoa for me, and lots of chocolate digestive biscuits, 'for energy'. That morning I felt we could do with some advice from Mum, but she doesn't approve of the Dancing Cows. It was such a long time since I had consulted her on anything I wasn't sure I knew how to ask any more.

"I hope we're going about this the right way, we're not exactly experts," I confided to Eleanor. She pushed back her ginger curls and stood up, a wide smile lighting her round face, a pink flush on her cheeks.

"It feels all right to me," she gasped. "And it's bloody good exercise. I feel like something out of Thomas Hardy."

"So where's that manservant, Matthew, with our cider and sandwiches, that's what I want to know?" I joined in.

"In bed and not likely to emerge before dinner." Her face darkened with resentment and my laughter fell flat. "In fact, I shall go and put the kettle on myself." Eleanor planted the legs of the barrow firmly on the ground and marched indoors.

I finished the corner I was working on and squatted on the step by the back door, enjoying the warmth of the spring sunshine. Eleanor brought out two mugs of Barleycup and sat on the step beside me.

"I do love the sun," she sighed, her hands enclosing the steaming heat of her mug. "It puts me in such a good mood."

"Roll on summer, then," I teased.

"Oh dear, am I such a grumpy Griselda?" Well actually yes, I thought. But there was something quite small and vulnerable in her worried eyes, and the realisation hit me that she really wanted me to like her. It was a bit of punch in the guts when I seemed to spend my life trying to meet her impossible standards. Everything felt upside down for a minute.

"Only when the coffee machine packs up," I managed to respond, clinging to the safe ground of her obsession with real coffee.

"You're never grumpy, Shelley." She looked at me curiously. "How do you manage to sail through life so easily?"

"I don't know," I replied, shrugging. I wasn't quite sure what she meant. "Maybe I'm not a very deep person."

"Of course you are," She sounded quite cross. "Look at how passionate you are about your animal rights stuff, and how you throw yourself into things."

"Things?"

"You know what I mean, like the anti-vivisection group, and S.A.F.E. You don't agonise about it. You just do it. You're amazing." She looked at me fondly and I felt embarrassed by her attention and strangely shy. "You've been through much more than me, but you just don't seem to be ridden with angst like the rest of us."

"What do you mean?" I felt baffled and uneasy.

"Well, you know, being adopted…? And growing up in a white family?" Eleanor faltered, looking more uncertain of her ground.

"Being adopted isn't a problem, you know, it's just a fact. Anyway, I don't dwell on it." I finished abruptly.

"It's not as easy as that. Sometimes things dwell on you whether you want them to or not," Eleanor countered, looking at me sceptically. "Maybe it's just me, some white middle-class thing. I just wish I was more like you."

"You don't mean that," I stated bluntly. I decided I preferred it when she told me off. I couldn't get my head around the idea that she had noticed me at all, never mind to such a detailed and considered extent. Feeling exposed in the chill wind, now that I had been sitting still for a while, I reached across to my jumper, discarded on the steps when we first started digging, and pulled it on over my T-shirt. When my head popped out of the neck of the jumper I met Eleanor's eyes still studying me intently.

"Stop looking at me," I laughed. "You're making me nervous."

"Sorry," she apologised and stood up, shielding her eyes against the glare of the sun as she appraised the piles of earth and rubble now littering her yard. "Come on, let's get back to work before that sun disappears."

I looked up and saw a gaggle of fluffy white clouds advancing slowly across the previously pristine blue sky and I knew they heralded the end of the sunny morning. I felt triumphant that for once we had beaten the clouds and squeezed the best hours out of the day.

"We should do this more often," I said as we left our mugs on the steps and returned to the damply turned clods.

"What? You'd give up your only lie-in of the week?"

"To enjoy the sunshine I would," I said out loud. To myself I thought, lie-ins are overrated when you've got no one to lie in with.

As if on cue, Matt appeared at the back door and, shading his eyes against the sun with his forearm, called up to us.

"Hi, you two. How's it going?"

"Brilliant!" Eleanor called back, "You've missed a lovely morning."

"What about lunch? Will a fry-up do?"

"You bet," I nodded, enthusiastically. Eleanor just raised an eyebrow at him.

"Come in at one o'clock, then," he instructed and disappeared indoors again.

"What's brought that on?" I looked at her, amazed. She shrugged her shoulders and pursed her lips in a worried frown.

"You don't want to know," she muttered.

Well, she was right about that.

This morning I arrived at work to discover the kitchen had become a battleground. Eleanor was hissing murderous comments under her breath and Matt was stomping around, moving piles of crockery and pans to no effect. The surfaces were scattered with boxes of food in various painfully early stages of defrosting and there was no sign of Jill.

"Morning. Where's Jill?" I ventured, braving the stormy atmosphere.

"She's quit because the microwave's bust and Matt shouted at her," Eleanor spat frostily.

"Don't be stupid, that's got nothing to do with it. She's got another job." Matt slammed a cupboard door.

"But she would have worked her notice if you hadn't pissed her off with your snide remarks."

"Where's her new job?" I interrupted, as the temperature rose.

"Town Hall canteen, would you believe?" Eleanor laughed bitterly, "Cooking bacon and egg breakfasts and meat pies and God-knows-what."

"But why?"

"Better pay, a pension scheme, paid holidays, minor stuff like that," Eleanor's sigh had an uncharacteristic note of defeat.

"Completely cynical, she's got no politics," Matt pronounced.

"That's easy for you to say, she's got a family to feed. No wonder she was upset when you spoke to her like that," Eleanor glared at him with venom.

"Of course I didn't say that to her face. What do you take me for, woman?"

"Don't 'woman' me, Matt. You're doing no good here. Why don't you take that microwave and get it fixed or get another so we can get back to defrosting things in five minutes instead of five days? Shelley and I can manage, can't we?"

No choice. I shrugged indifferently. Typical Matt that, making himself so unpleasant you end up begging him not to do any work.

After he had gone Eleanor and I salvaged what we could, made some fresh dressings, hummous and salads and cooked some risotto and vegetable bakes to tide us over until the freezer stuff defrosted. We worked in desperate silence for a while but once we had opened up and dealt with the first trickle of customers Eleanor brewed some herbal tea and seemed to relax a little.

"I'm sorry this is putting an extra strain on you, Shelley," she apologised as we sipped our mugs of steaming lemon and ginger.

"Oh, it's all right. I'm sure we'll get someone else in soon."

"I didn't mean Jill leaving, actually. I meant all this arguing between Matt and me," Eleanor sighed wearily.

"I wasn't going to say anything, but as you mention it, are you two okay?" I wasn't used to Eleanor volunteering anything about her personal life.

"Not really," she admitted, a tremble in her voice, "We argue about everything, and the cafe's losing money, you know, we're in a really bad way."

"How bad?"

"Terminal," she muttered and put her hand over her mouth as tears welled up in her eyes.

"Oh Eleanor, I'm sorry."

"I'm all right really," she sobbed. "I just don't know what we're going to do. You'd better watch the till." I peeped through into the cafe and saw a small queue forming again.

"I'll just serve this lot. You stay here," I ordered firmly and left her blowing her nose on a piece of kitchen roll. When I had dealt with the queue she emerged with bleary eyes and a red nose looking like a small child. I always thought of her as so 'stiff upper lip', tough and reserved, now she just seemed to have wilted unnervingly.

"I think you should go upstairs and have a rest before

lunch," I suggested, "You look worn out."

"Thanks, Shelley, but I'd rather be doing something," she replied heavily.

The rest of the day passed in a mood of slightly hysterical bravado as we tried to cheer each other along. Underneath the banter I kept expecting Eleanor to break down again and the whole thing was a bit of a nightmare. Matt returned in the afternoon without the microwave. He reported tersely that another one would be delivered the next day and went straight upstairs. I tried to get Eleanor to go up as well, but the cafe was too busy with students and women with children on their way home from shopping or the park, and we both ploughed on until closing time without a break.

As we unloaded the last dishes from the dishwasher I tried to offer some more support to Eleanor. "Is there anything else I can do to help with the cafe? I can work some extra hours if you need me, I don't mind about being paid," I volunteered.

"No, it's all right. I can manage down here on my own on the odd afternoon and you're here most of the time anyway." She stacked the plates mechanically and loaded them onto the shelves with slow exhausted movements. I didn't know how to get her to stop.

"Let's just sit down a minute and talk about it. Please," I urged her and I led her back into the empty cafe and sat her down at a table. I made some peppermint tea and insisted she take a cup. When we were both seated she started to explain.

"The real problem is Matt. He wants to sell up, you see. He thinks if we close down now we can still get something for the building, but if we carry on much longer we'll be in so much debt we'll end up with nothing."

"Close it down? But you've put so much into it," I gasped, horrified, "What would you do?"

"He's got relatives in Australia, he thinks there's a better life over there for him and he wants to do some travelling in the Far East, go to China. Basically, he's bored. I've no idea what I'm going to do."

"Are you splitting up then?" I studied her strained, sad face. She nodded wordlessly and looked hard at the huge cows gazing back in mute understanding.

"I'm sorry." I followed her gaze around the jumble of tables and posters and prancing two-tone Friesians that had become my world too in the last year

"There must be something we can do," I urged her, energetically, "We can keep the cafe going ourselves. We do all the work anyway. We don't need him to make it work."

"We haven't got the money, Shelley. We'd have to buy him out and we haven't got any capital. No bank's going to give us a loan when they see the state of the books. You should get out while you can, you know. You could get a really good job with your degree and all." She looked at me sadly, tears standing in her eyes.

"Well, I don't intend to leave yet." I leaned across the table and gripped her arms. I was surprised at how frail and bony they felt in my grasp. "I need this place. I don't know what I would have done with my life if I hadn't got a job here."

"And I don't want to lose you, Shelly." Her voice broke loudly and shakily into the silence around us, as the tears rolled down her face.

"Oh, Eleanor, you wouldn't." I leant across the table and

flung my arms around her shoulders. We hugged awkwardly and I manoeuvred myself around the square corners until we were standing together our arms around each other laughing and squeezing tightly. She was shivering in her thin shirt and plastic apron.

"I'm sorry. I'm just in such a mess," she muttered, burying her head in my shoulder. I tried to move back to tell her it didn't matter, but she clung to me and her face was very still against my neck. Neither of us moved, and our stillness extended into the hushed silence. I could feel the wetness of her tears on my neck and her breathing against my hair. Her mouth was pressing lightly against the skin at the base of my neck, where the collar of my T-shirt had been pulled back in our embrace. I began to feel hot with embarrassment. The warm insistence of her lips ran through me like a shock as I suddenly realised she was kissing me. I shifted my position slightly and she let go, pulling a tissue out of her apron pocket to blow her nose with.

"There may be something we can do," she said briskly, picking up our mugs and walking through to the kitchen without meeting my eyes. "Let me talk to Matt. I'll have to see how long he's prepared to wait for us to come up with a plan. Whatever happens we'll have to replace Jill, we need at least one other person to cover all the shifts." I followed her into the back and found her staring gloomily out of the window at the ornate metal wall brackets waiting for baskets of brightly trailing lobelias and petunias, and the clean swept flagstones waiting for patio tables and chairs. Sycamore branches dotted with tiny green leaf buds were waving jauntily against a soaring cobalt sky, triumphant against Eleanor's murderous plans.

I continued to move things around the kitchen aimlessly, but I was shaking. I could still feel the pressure of Eleanor's arms across my back, the warm solidity of her body against mine, the fierce intimate stillness, and the touch of her lips on my shoulder. My face was flushed with confusion as I clattered saucepans and pretended not to see her doing the same.

"Can anyone get any service in here?" a male voice interrupted suddenly from the cafe area. Shit. I had forgotten to lock the front door.

"We're closed!" Eleanor called back, and under her breath to me she muttered, "Wanker, can't he read?" I laughed and hurried through to find Veena's son, Anil, grinning at me over the counter.

"Oh my God, Anil," I exclaimed, disorientated.

"Charming," he mocked. "What happened to 'Come down to the cafe any time Anil'?"

"No, it's great to see you." I recovered myself. "We're closed now, but I do need to talk to you. Maybe we could go for a drink or something?"

"I take it you're not here for the food, young man, coming in at this time?" Eleanor interrupted sternly, peering round the door from the kitchen. She seemed to have recovered her usual tough exterior.

"It's okay, Eleanor, I'm dealing with it," I said, flushing slightly. Eleanor peered closely at Anil.

"Why don't you get off Shelley, I'll clear up," she suggested.

"But don't we need to talk about the business?" I reminded her uneasily. I felt we had left everything unresolved.

"It can keep till tomorrow," she assured me and I was grateful to be released from the awkwardness between us. Seizing the opportunity, I quickly untied my apron and grabbed my coat and bag from behind the door. I followed Anil out into the street.

We meandered into the city centre meeting the rush hour crowds dashing and scurrying for the bus or the softly purring tram, everyone focused on home, their automatic pilots steering them faultlessly through the melee. Here and there another free floating soul like us wound an indecisive path amongst the clicking locks and slamming shutters and the piles of litter fluttering in deserted doorways. Anil slowed his long strides to keep pace with my short determined steps. I felt a huge relief to be out of the cafe and there was a desperate edge to my own flight from work. As we walked we deliberated over where to go for a drink and why it wasn't practical to open the Dancing Cows in the evening.

"You could make a packet opening at night, there isn't a decent vegetarian restaurant in the city," Anil pronounced.

"And you'd know, as a lifetime vegetarian yourself," I sniped scornfully.

"I do know other vegetarians apart from you," he retorted, "And I know it's bloody difficult trying to find somewhere a diehard vegan like you can eat unless it's Indian - and then we might as well go home - the cooking's much better and you don't get dirty-minded waiters eyeing you as if you're a naughty boy for being out with - " he faltered and I looked at him quickly.

"Yes?" I prompted crisply.

"A girl you're not married to," he finished lamely. "The point is where are we going to go for a drink?"

"The Showroom?" I suggested. "There's plenty of

space and I want to pick up a film programme for this month." Anil was fine with this and we strode decisively down hill, the dark galleried stone arches of the old Midland Station below us and the swelling green hills of Norfolk Park rising beyond the platforms on the far side of the valley. As the evening sunlight caught the concrete battlements of Skye Edge flats and turned them gold, I was seized by a sudden desire to put my arm through Anil's. I felt as if I was back with Hugh again, wandering the autumn pavements and parks behind our halls, kicking deep piles of wet leaves, our fingers entwined, asserting our coupledom. I hadn't thought of Hugh for ages, not since that last letter, which I hadn't been able to reply to yet because it upset me so much. When we first split up I thought of him every day, a mixture of pain and frustration and sheer pique that he had made the decision alone that we were not right for each other. I was angry that he hadn't discussed his thoughts with me, and hurt because I didn't agree with him, I missed his lanky figure and large bony hands, his long pianist's fingers stretching out to me in a gesture of mingled pleading and surrender. Like holding out an open hand to a shy animal, urging: trust me, it's only a hand, I won't bite. But take that hand and it's not so easy to disentangle your fingers. It took me months to lessen the pain at the mere thought of those tender papery fingers across my skin and his thoughtful eyes staring into the fire over a bedtime mug of Earl Grey tea. Now I'm not sure it was Hugh I missed or just the affirming togetherness of it all, the shared jokes, the secret allusions, the intimacy of his lean flat white body, so unlike my own, the tenderness of his gaze across a sea of bowed heads in the vast catacombs of the library, that hallowed special state of having 'somebody'.

Pushing my hands firmly down into my jacket pockets, I preserved a discreet distance between Anil and myself. We sat down with our drinks in a corner of the Showroom Bar. I told him about the Dancing Cows and our imminent demise and he commiserated and poured scepticism over my idea that somehow Eleanor and I could find the capital to keep the place going on our own.

"Can't see it myself, but what you need first is a decent accountant," he advised solemnly.

"You offering?"

"Yeah, I could take a look at your books if you like," he responded.

"Seriously?"

He nodded and I eyed him thoughtfully. "That's great, but I had actually been wanting to ask you another favour."

"Oh yes?" His eyebrows lifted. "Sounds ominous."

"Well, it is. Very." I took a deep breath. "It involves breaking rules. I was wondering if you could get me, or someone else, into the Biology labs at your uni over the May Day Bank Holiday." He looked at me blankly. "I'm in an anti-vivisection group and we want to highlight some research on animals they're doing by displaying a big banner from the top floor of the building and taking photographs of what they're doing to the animals to send to the press, stuff like that. And we might rescue some of the animals if we can manage it."

"And what would I have to do?" he asked, warily.

"Just get me a student pass - I'd ask to borrow yours, but we haven't got anyone in the group who looks like you, so it would have to be someone else's, preferably either a white male student with a kind of ordinary nondescript sort of face, or an Asian girl with short black hair like me - what do you think?" I screwed up my face in exaggerated anticipation of a refusal.

"You're mad," he laughed. "But I'll see what I can do. Can I see what the other people look like apart from you?" I nearly hugged him. I couldn't believe he was okay about it.

"They're a bit paranoid about being identified, but I suppose you need to know what we all look like to get a pass that really matches one of us."

"If you want to do it properly you, or whoever, needs to start going in and out of the building a few days before so the porters get used to your face." He was beginning to get hooked into the logistics of it all, and then another thought stopped him in his tracks. "But why haven't you got anyone else in there doing all this for you?"

"We did have," I admitted slowly. "He got arrested on the last campaign, got kicked off his course and the police know his face now."

"Oh." He looked at his shoes thoughtfully as this information sank in.

"I do understand if you don't want to take the risk. I'd hate to get you into trouble with your tutors."

"Stuff them. My course is boring me rigid anyway, it wouldn't kill me to get thrown out," he muttered gloomily.

"That's terrible," I said. "You can't go through three years feeling like that, it's such a waste."

"Do you think so?" There was a strange distant expression on his face.

"Of course - I mean, if you can see yourself as an

accountant in three of four years' time, then great. But if you hate it so much now, what makes you think you're going to be any happier later?"

"Life's not all about being happy, there's responsibility and earning a living and stuff."

"You sound like your father," I teased.

"God, no, a fate worse than death." His dark eyes widened in mock horror and the coppery brown skin of his cheeks creased into a wide smile. He had very long eyelashes for a man, I noticed, and I wondered if Asian men generally had long eyelashes or if it was just him.

" - Or maybe you've got responsibilities I don't know about?" I suggested mischievously. The smile vanished from his eyes.

"Meaning?" He stared back at me defiantly.

"Meaning, is there something you're not telling your mum?"

He looked down at his drink and there was a long silence as he swilled the remains of his lager around the glass. I felt bad for pressing him and uncomfortable as I remembered that I hardly knew him. He raised the glass to his mouth and gulped the dregs down quickly.

"I'm sorry. I've no right to ask," I apologised.

"It's not what you think, you know, you or Mum."

"I don't know why you don't talk to Veena, she's probably more radical than you or Pooja, if you only knew." I laughed at the look of scepticism on his face. "You should try talking to her about her job. They do really interesting stuff at Awaaz. I bet you've no idea what she's into."

"She just thinks I've got someone pregnant, Pooja told me," he responded sulkily and I could see how Veena still thought of him as her little boy. I was no longer sure

I wanted to know his guilty secret, whatever it was.

"Look, you're right. I really don't need to know anything and it's probably better if I don't because it would be awkward with Veena. Anyway, I need to go home and feed the cat." I sat up purposefully.

"Oh no, come back to ours for dinner. We could surprise Mum, she loved having you over, and there's always food in our house. We could firm up some more details of our Secret Mission. Go on." His eyes lit up excitedly at the idea and I allowed myself to be persuaded by the thought of Veena's warm smile and another divine meal.

The crowded bus is overheated for this time of year and steamy with dripping raincoats from a sudden spring shower that caught me at the bus stop down the road from Awaaz. In my seat I am jammed up against the streaming window by a broad-shouldered young man in a heavy leather jacket, who sits with his knees splayed open so that I have to turn my own into the wall to avoid contact along our thighs. I resent this and eventually I start to relax my leg beneath the protective covering of my damp raincoat so that my thigh presses increasingly against his in the hope that he will move his leg away. He seems oblivious to my body and the warm bulk of his leg remains stubbornly in place as he flicks his thumb over the keypad of his mobile phone, texting industriously. I shuffle further towards the window and stare out grimly at the grey streets sliding past. Now I really do feel exhausted. A dull pain sits in the centre of my forehead, pressing on my skull. I know why it's there. As soon as I stepped out of the management committee meeting at Awaaz I noticed it creeping in, as I relaxed the iron concentration I had maintained through two hours of heated debate and galloping business items. I am constantly racing to catch up and always losing. It seems I am not cut out for this. But I am in it now.

I love the homely familiarity of arriving at Awaaz in the morning, making a first cup of tea with Riffat. She reports on the half day's work she has already completed: feeding her husband on his return from a night on the taxis, coaxing sleepy three-year-olds out of bed, putting a wash on, taking a call from the Punjab where her parents, resting after lunch, persist in not understanding the precision timing of Riffat's early morning departures, negotiating twin tantrums about wearing coats when the sun is shining, and, at a point in the car when all seems lost, discovering a miraculous new sideroad that cuts out a whole junction on the way to nursery. I soak up the details, nostalgic for that vivid, hour-by-hour rollercoaster ride I had with Anil and Pooja: the small arms round my neck, round my knees, the flow of questions and chatter and complaints teasing me out into the bright sunshine of their presence, the volatile impatient playful person I was in those moments, dancing in that sunshine, while other quieter parts of me shivered alone and forgotten in unlit corners of the house. With Riffat I share the remnants of that life, the struggles I still have with Pooja to eat properly, tidy her room, tell me her movements so that I know she is safe, and the campaign I wage to stay in Anil's life. Riffat and I speak less often about our husbands - I don't know why. I have missed for so long this intimacy with other women. Riffat is all the sisters I never had, the sisters-in-law in India I had scarcely met before Ramesh's scholarship came through from England. She is naughty and mischievous and delightful, we are girls together at the back of the schoolroom.

And I do still feel like such a new girl. I have my own desk with its smooth grey wood-effect finish and locking drawers, and a terrifying high-backed swivel chair like some oil company executive. I don't know what I'm going to put in all the drawers. I feel rather embarrassed at their emptiness, but I trust they will fill up in time, giving me the air of being established and productive. Riffat is my fount of wisdom and I feel bad that she is not paid more when I depend on her so completely. I told her I had suggested a pay rise for her to Farah to recognise the extra responsibilities she takes on and she laughed affectionately,

"You're a right softie, Veena. There's no chance with Farah in charge, and, anyway, I wouldn't want the aggro. This way at least I can go and pick me kids up at half-three every day and forget about Awaaz till the next morning."

I could see her point. I have worried endlessly since I started. I sit at my desk in the upstairs office comparing my pathetic scraps of paper and scribbled notes with the authoritative towers of documents left by my predecessor and I feel quite overwhelmed. But then there is the real work of meeting other women, listening to their stories, bringing them together in an English class or a confidence building group and weaving their difficult, suspicious, idiosyncratic strands into a single piece of brilliantly coloured cloth. I have fought so hard not to surrender to the many expectations there are of me. Shafia draws me to one side to share gossip about the aunty who runs Rani's Fashions and her wholesaler from Leicester, who used to deliver new suits to the shop once a month and now appears twice a week; Rukhsana Bibi wants me to find a job for her daughter so the Home Office will let the daughter's new husband come from Pakistan; Zaibun is seeing a boy at college from an inferior caste and can't get contraception from the family doctor who knows her parents, and Tasleem, bringing up a child alone, rehoused from the refuge, just misses her mother and needs someone she can turn to. I worry constantly about being perceived as having favourites, and yet I already know there are some women who have no one else, who will be coming to see me here for a very long time. Farah says don't get personally involved. But there are so many resonances for me in each encounter. I am constantly pulled back into the cardamom-scented, silk-veiled secret places of the extended family, where I move slowly and clumsily, like a visitor in my own home. I find myself navigating according to my mother's voice, harvesting her wordless knowledge of life's unfolding. I feel myself becoming her.

The bus slows down past the familiar configuration of orange, red and white lights above the late opening supermarket, and I excuse myself roughly past the unhelpful young man and struggle to the front of the bus. As I step off into another flurry of hostile, steely rain, I feel an explosion of frustration with Ramesh for assuming total control of the car, and with myself for going through all the trauma of acquiring a driving licence sixteen years ago and never practising my skills. Now I cannot handle the massive gleaming Audi of which he is so proud. Of course Shelley would applaud my dependence on public transport. She would have everyone on bicycles and buses. I can't find much consolation in her dewy idealism as I begin the weary trudge up the last hill to our house. Not only is Sheffield devoid of a decent watercourse, but it is plagued with calf-straining hills at every turn. The damp dripping air smells sweetly of wet gardens and freshly turned earth and seems to dissolve my headache by degrees as I plod up the hill in the fading light. As I approach the house I am greeted by a display of warm yellow lights blazing from every window.

"How many times do I have to tell you to close the curtains if you put the lights on?" I chide irritably as I dump my bags on a corner of the dining room table, which is buried in Pooja's files and papers.

"Sorry, Mum." Pooja is unconcerned. "By the way, Shelley's here."

"Shelley? I don't understand." A stab of panic pierces me as I wonder if I have forgotten some arrangement I am supposed to have made.

"Anil met her in town or something, and they came back together - " I hear laughter pealing from the front room.

Why shouldn't they, I suppose. Stay cool, I tell myself in Pooja's language. But I feel flustered and very uncool as I check my hair in the hall mirror. My headache has returned with the bright indoor lights and close, dry, centrally-heated air. After a long day at work I am hardly ready to be sociable again so soon, and there is something muddy and disturbing in this unscheduled overlapping of our lives. It is not something I have come to expect in the neatly boxed and delineated routines of English suburban life. But I enjoy Shelley being here. I gather up what reserves of goodwill I have left after two hours of committee meeting and burst energetically into the front room.

"Hello, Shelley. How lovely to see you."

Shelley is in a deep chair by the fire and Anil is perched on the arm of the settee with one foot resting casually on the coffee table leaning forward towards her and rocking with laughter.

"Hi, Mum," he swings round.

"Hello Veena," Shelley smiles, "Sorry to surprise you like this - "

"I invited Shelley for dinner, Mum. Thought she looked like she needed feeding up - "

"Watch it." I notice Shelley's easy familiarity with a slight tensing of my shoulders.

"We met in the cafe and went for a drink, and then Shelley wasn't doing anything tonight so - here we are." He throws up his hands in a helpless little-boy gesture I know so well.

"Well, that's wonderful." I try to sound pleased, "But I haven't anything vegan cooked, will dahl be all right for you?"

"Oh fine, please don't worry about me. Anyway, it's Anil's call, he can worry about what I'm going to eat."

"Of course," Anil jumps up at this cue, "Shall I get you some tea, Mummy?"

"Yes please, darling, and get Pooja to help you put the dinner on, I don't know what she's doing working in the dining room when she's got her own room to study in."

"Her room's a tip, you should see it," Anil confides to Shelley, leaning over her as he passes her to get to the door. She doesn't move her legs aside to let him pass, but lets his knees brush hers in the narrow gap between the coffee table and the chair. I am reminded of the young man on the bus. Is it just a general lack of manners or propriety in all young people? Or different thresholds of intimacy and bodily contact? Am I so old-fashioned?

I settle into the armchair opposite Shelley with a long sigh and silence trickles back into the room like sand settling after a wave's retreat.

"You're getting on well with my son," I remark as casually as I can manage.

"He's good fun." Shelley avoids my eyes and changes

the subject. "Have you had a good day?"

"Yes, until the management committee meeting."

"Whoops." The humorous twinkle in her eye is irresistible.

"Exactly." A smile creeps across my own face and I let out a long sigh of exasperation. "The only person I really trust there is Riffat. It shouldn't be like that in a women's organisation."

Shelley shrugs her shoulders. "I've never worked in a women's organisation, so I wouldn't know, but I guess you can find yourself working with complete shits anywhere."

I resist the maternal impulse to check her swearing, but I feel a distance opening up between us in that word. The waters are muddied again and my head hurts. I plough on.

"But working in a place where you're supposed to share the same vision, you expect to pull together."

Shelley's smile fades.

"Actually we're in a bit of a mess ourselves right now. Matt has really stabbed us in the back and the cafe might have to close."

"Shelley, I'm so sorry." And I am, but in my head a surprising new voice cuts in harshly, telling me I have had enough of other people's troubles for one day, I cannot listen to another sob story tonight, and especially not from an attractive young woman who has designs on my son. I try to silence this uncharitable incarnation and Shelley sails on, unaware of my struggle to hear her. "Eleanor's trying to sort it all out with Matt, so it might be okay. But we've lost Jill in the process and we're really under pressure to cover all the shifts. It feels like the vision's gone right out of the window and we're just fighting to survive."

"I know what you mean." I shake my head, as much to rally myself as in sympathy with her. "All the Awaaz committee seem to worry about is our funding. I thought we were there to fight women's oppression and now I sit in meetings arguing about whether we can afford to provide tea and biscuits in the drop-in area. It makes me wonder sometimes if I'm in the right place." There goes that voice again, impatient to get my story in first, wanting to be heard above the rest. Childish. What's the matter with me today?

"You were really political when you were younger, weren't you?" Shelley focuses intently on me as if she has noticed my need.

"I was." My reply is cautious, but her eyes are bright with curiosity.

"Well? What did you do?" she invites. I look down at my hands folded in my lap and try to remember what it was all about.

"I got involved in the Communist Party when I went to university in Calcutta. There were lots of us in my women's hostel who joined the Women's Wing of the students' union and I was elected a shop steward. West Bengal had just become a Communist state in the elections of '75 so it was all really exciting. It wasn't long after the war in '71, and Calcutta was bursting with refugees who had come across the border from the East." I see the incomprehension in her eyes. "You know? When East Pakistan became Bangladesh?"

"Of course." She gives a short dismissive laugh and lowers her eyes from my gaze and I realise that she doesn't know. Bangladesh is such a young country, but she is younger still and why should she know about things that happened before she was born in a country she's never seen? I feel overwhelmed with sadness that she doesn't know.

"Shelley?"

She looks up and smiles a desperate, forced smile. Her voice is harsh and strained when she speaks.

"Carry on. So, then what?"

"There were lots of shortages." I want to smooth the moment over for her. "Lots of workers' strikes and demonstrations about the plight of the refugees. As students we had to show our solidarity with the workers. We thought there was going to be a revolution. It was our cause, the destiny of all those who work by hand or brain." The long forgotten words resonate in my mind, kindling the faint embers of an old fire within me. Where did all that passion go? When did I lose sight of that bigger picture? I struggle to explain what it was all about. "It must sound so outdated to you now. But it used to make sense, it had a name. Socialism. Communism. It was about fighting the oppression and exploitation of the poor and putting ownership of industry in the hands of the people. We fought tooth and nail for it, both of us did."

"So why did you stop?" Shelley breathes, she seems captivated now.

"Ramesh got a scholarship to do a PhD in England."

"But why did you stop?" Her question confuses me and I wonder what more explanation she needs.

"I came with him, we were married," I begin to say, and then I remember that we weren't married when he was offered the scholarship. We got married so that I could get a visa to come with him as his wife. I remember that my mother pleaded with me not to go, advised me that a love marriage would not be enough to sustain me alone in a strange land without the rest of my family. But I didn't feel I had a choice at the time, I couldn't bear to lose him. "I suppose I came because I was in love with Ramesh," I explain more precisely. "We tried to get involved in student politics here for a while, but I wasn't a student any more and Ramesh was working so hard on his PhD, and then we had the children and life got so busy there wasn't time for anything else. When you have a family the years just slip away." Shelley nods, but I can see she doesn't really understand. How could she?

I also know that isn't really it. There was something else. When we came to Sheffield we found our way of doing politics didn't fit somehow. We went to meetings in those first few months full of hopeful enthusiasm and everyone smiled politely when we said things and then carried on the meeting as if we had never spoken. Our language seemed to jar and people looked embarrassed when we offered to help and suggested we wait till someone had time to 'show us the ropes'. They never did and we slowly stopped going. We never talked about it, it was too painful somehow. When I think about it now I feel hot with shame, although it wasn't our fault if we were naive or inappropriate and I still don't understand what we did wrong. We have never talked about any of those things that happened when we first came to England. I feel a shiver down my back as I realise how set in stone that not talking has become and I try to shake off the thought by turning to Shelley.

"So when you go off on your actions and demonstrations for animal rights, don't forget I really do understand what it's all about. You can tell me anything,

I won't be shocked."

"I know. I think I realised that when you put those boys in their place that day in the café," she laughs. I'm pleased she noticed that and remembers it, and I feel the knots of tension slowly uncoiling in my shoulders as I let her tell me more about the current crisis in the cafe's finances.

Anil returns with mugs of tea and announces that he and Pooja will do dinner as I must be tired.

"I think this is for your benefit," I whisper to Shelley suspiciously, after Anil has returned to the kitchen. "They don't usually worry about me being tired."

I try to tease out what I feel about her and Anil from the blur of exhaustion and fuzzy emotions churning in my gut. I didn't bring her here to flirt with my son, is a thought that keeps surfacing, or is he flirting with her? Or neither? Young people today are so much more at ease in the company of the opposite sex, they seem to be able to be genuine friends, 'mates', without any flirting being implied, or so Pooja is always telling me. But I find it hard to imagine why a woman and a man should want to be friends without a sexual attraction lurking somewhere. What could they have to share otherwise, when men and women inhabit such completely different worlds? I have never had a friendship with a man, not the sort of friendship I had with other girls at school and college, and I can't imagine what such a friendship would consist of. Maybe it's just a lack of experience of male friends in my youth. Young women in this country grow up with boys at school and at home and have a completely different outlook from the one we had. They all merge together somehow, into an amorphous population of cropped

114

heads and torn jeans, more neutral and less defined by their gender than we were. Maybe it's possible for them to scarcely notice gender at all and just be people. I doubt it somehow.

Gradually the evening meal is assembled by my bickering but good-humoured children. Ramesh is out working late, so it is a light-hearted, informal affair washed down with mango juice and more tea, and accompanied by much banter between the young people. I am pleased to see that Shelley is more than a match for Anil's stumbling wit.

"That was wonderful, Veena. I've got to be getting back now," Shelley says as the plates are being cleared by Anil and Pooja.

"Why don't you wait for Ramesh, he can give you a lift," I urge, wishing for the second time that day that I could drive.

"No, honestly, I'll be fine, it's not late," she insists.

"I'll walk you to the bus stop," Anil volunteers.

"Oh, isn't he sweet?" Pooja teases. "That's so gallant."

"Shut up, Pooja," Anil mutters furiously, and a flush spreads across Shelley's face.

"You don't have to." She looks at him directly and I see a hesitation in his eyes. There is more going on between these two than anyone is admitting, maybe even to themselves, I conclude.

"The bus might be ages," Anil explains, pushing back his chair and standing up decisively. "If you've missed this one, I could show you where to get the other one at the top of the hill. Come on." He fetches Shelley's coat from the hall and she follows him out, exchanging promises with me to have lunch together soon and to visit more often.

After she has gone I am left wondering again about her Bengali roots. She has such a Bengali face. Even before I knew she had that connection, I had placed her in the green wooded hills of Assam, or the waterlogged Sylheti plains. She seems indifferent to the coincidence of my years living in Calcutta, across the Sunderbans delta from her family in East Bengal. Strangely for a geographer, she seems to have no sense of the geography of our two lives.

9   Tasleem

My flat seemed particularly cold and uninviting when I finally got home from Veena's late in the evening. It might have been the contrast with the carpeted and upholstered luxuries of Veena's house, but despite the fun we had had at dinner, I wished I hadn't gone. Anil made it sound so easy, a bit of a laugh, surprise Veena, eat lots of nice food and have a good time. But when I got there I felt as if I might have overstepped some invisible line with Veena, it was like I'd spoilt the closeness we had the first time I went there. And I should have been fascinated hearing about her past, but I was unsettled and out of sorts in a niggly unspecific way. When she was talking about Bangladesh, I just couldn't handle it. I felt like my head was going to explode or something. I was also still trying to digest what had happened in the cafe with Eleanor before Anil turned up.

And I really didn't know what was going on with Anil. As predicted, when we got to the bus stop I had just missed a bus - which made me think: did he already know I'd miss it, before we even left the house? - so we walked up the hill to the high windswept road that runs along the top of the escarpment beside the golf course. In the fading light we could see over the golf club wall across the valley to the scattered cottages and farms at Stannington and beyond to the darkening Penistone moors on the northern horizon. In the west the reservoirs at Rivelin Dams glinted silver, reflecting the last light from a thin band of pale turquoise sky trapped between towering cloudbanks above and the black silhouetted plateau of Moscar Moor below.

"Amazing views you have up here." I said, looking out across the hills, and Anil murmured agreement.

We stood by the bus shelter, listening to the rustle of wind in the leaves and the amorphous, voiceless hum of city traffic drifting up from the valley, the unending backdrop to our lives. There's always noise in a city, I thought, and I longed to get out onto the moors, the distant undulating green and purple swells that appear at unexpected moments sailing beyond the blocked, chequered, squarely piled skylines of the city.

"Look Shelley," Anil began, after a pause. "I'm trying to work some stuff out at the moment that my folks don't know about, I'm sorry to be secretive, but with you knowing mum and everything... "

"It's okay, honestly. There's plenty you don't know about me." I asserted, coolly.

"Oka -ay," he pretended to back off with raised hands. "Sorry."

"I just meant it's fine," I qualified, smiling at his theatrics. "I don't need to know. And thanks for helping us out with the action. Look, here comes my bus."

The bus pulled up, I paid and found a seat by a window. Anil was waving at me from the pavement. I carried the view of his laughing smile, and black hair bobbing as he danced on his toes to catch sight of me, all the way home.

As I entered the cold, empty flat, I could smell the decaying rubbish in the kitchen bin, which no longer shuts properly because a plastic hinge has broken on the swing lid. Refusing to face it, I went all round the flat switching lights on and drawing curtains. Only after I had I lit the gas fire to make it feel more homely, filled the kettle and set it to boil, did I lift the black plastic bin liner out of the bin and begin to knot its corners tightly to trap the putrid smells. The jaunty ring tone of my mobile phone going off in my jacket pocket stopped me in the middle of this process and as I leapt across the room to the jacket hanging on the back of the door, I heard the sigh of the abandoned bin bag collapsing and spilling rubbish onto the floor.

"Shit!" I fumbled desperately in various pockets to silence the tinny jingle.

When I finally located it, I clamped the thin metal case to my ear and barked, "Hello?" as I swivelled round to survey the ruins of my bin bag.

"Shelley?" Tasleem's voice echoed tentatively in my ear. "Chupko, Huma!" she hissed at Huma, who was crying in the background. "Shelley, I need you help me. Those boys break my window. Can you come?" I paused for a moment, trying to get my brain into gear. I saw Huma's beaming face and her precious plump little fingers catching mine. This was the sort of crisis I was supposed to know about as a S.A.F.E. volunteer, but my mind was blank.

"I phone the police. They coming in ten minutes," Tasleem added helpfully. God, she's more sussed than me any day.

"Okay, Tasleem," I tried to sound competent. "Just hang on, I'm coming."

"Thank you, Shelley, thank you. I go now, Huma crying. Goodbye." The phone clicked off. I stood by the door staring at the smeared crumpled packets and slops of food strewn across the floor and tried to think. If I cycled really fast I could be there in ten minutes.

Ignoring the bin bag crisis, I turned off the gas fire and the gas flame under the kettle and checked my jacket pocket for keys, money, diary with useful phone numbers. Then I remembered I had left Sky at the cafe when I went out for a drink with Anil earlier and we never returned to collect it. How dense of me not to remember. It would take me thirty or forty minutes to walk to Tasleem's, and possibly just as long waiting for a bus at this time. But I never used buses and had no idea of the timetable.

I suddenly thought of Eleanor and before I knew it I was dialling the number of their flat at the cafe. I could hear the shock in her voice when she answered and I knew she thought I was ringing about earlier in the cafe. "Listen, Eleanor, it's about S.A.F.E.," I cut in quickly. "I know you're not on the rota tonight, but I've just had a call from a woman in Highfield called Tasleem who's had her kitchen window smashed. She's called the police and I need to get over there now, but I left my bike at work. You couldn't give me a lift, could you?" There was a silence as she thought and I began to feel this was a very bad idea. "I know it's really late… "

"No," she said slowly. "No, it's fine. But you shouldn't be going on your own. Remember the training? Always go in pairs. I'll come in with you when we get to the house. Just give me five minutes."

As I tucked my phone away into my pocket I was relieved. She sounded quite her old self really. Maybe it would be all right after all and we could forget that odd moment before.

But when I slipped into the passenger seat of her car, waiting beneath my window with the engine running, she seemed tense and distant.

"Shelley, I'm really not sure about this," she sighed, switching the engine off and turning to me. In the darkness her eyes were pools of light. "We're talking about a racist attack here, we can't just go diving in. Shouldn't we ring the people on the rota and let them deal with it?"

"But she's rung me," I insisted, desperately. "I have to go and I can't get there quickly without a car."

"But how did she get your number?"

"I gave it to her - we met at Awaaz and I've been to her house a couple of times." I tried to stay calm and resist the urge to shake her into action.

"You don't seem to have very clear boundaries between your personal involvement and your work as a S.A.F.E. volunteer." I heard the disapproval in her stern tone, but I found it difficult to take her seriously.

"I know. I'm sorry. I just gave her my number so we could meet up and stuff. But, Eleanor, can we please go? Now?" She looked at me, surprised, and turned the engine on without another word. We drove in silence through the dark streets. I thought she must be offended until she suddenly asked me, in a light conversational tone as if nothing had happened,

"So did you have a good evening with your friend? What's his name?"

"Anil. Yes thanks. He's Veena's son actually - you know Veena from Awaaz?" She nodded, keeping her eyes on the road. "He came to see me about the action at the uni. He's a student there and he's agreed to help us out."

"That's brave of him, he must like you a lot to get involved with your madcap schemes." Eleanor glanced sideways for a moment and caught my smile at the memory of his easy enthusiasm for our plot. "You like him, don't you?"

"Oh, he's all right," I waved my hand dismissively. I knew what she was getting at. "I like him, but not like that. I mean he's a bit young." Eleanor laughed out loud. "All right," I protested indignantly. "I know I'm young too, but he's even younger, he's still living at home."

"Sorry." She became suddenly serious. "Honestly Shelley, I don't think of you as young. I didn't mean to laugh." It's not like Eleanor to apologise. I couldn't think how to respond so I just looked out of the window.

When we reached Tasleem's street it seemed deserted. But as we got out of the car the back of my neck prickled uncomfortably and I found myself looking round in all directions as we approached her solid blue door.

"Who is it?" a voice called from within when I knocked. "Shelley." I answered loudly, and the door was unlocked and opened cautiously.

"Shelley! Come in, come in." Tasleem looked exhausted and red-eyed and, as our eyes met, hers begin to fill with tears. She led us into the living room where Huma was tearing up magazine pages and arranging them very precisely on the black laminate coffee table. She ran to her mother when she saw a stranger enter and clutched a handful of material from Tasleem's kameez firmly in her grasp, twisting her head sideways into the hollow at the back of Tasleem's knee.

"Hello, Huma, do you remember me?" I called to her gently.

"She's feeling shy, lots of people in the house." Tasleem began to explain.

I jumped with fright as the doorway behind her

suddenly filled with the large stooping frame of a police officer.

"Sergeant Hoyland. Pleased to meet you. Friends of Mrs. Bibi's are you?" He seemed relieved at our appearance. "We're just on our way out. Not much we can do, I'm afraid. She says she saw someone, but she admits it was very dark and there are no other witnesses. We've called our Crime Scene Investigator and he'll be round within the hour. There may be some fingerprints on the back gate and there's a shoe print in the flower bed outside the back door, so please don't go out there till he's been."

"But you do know who's done this, don't you?" Eleanor challenged him. "We've been telling you about the youths that have been harassing black families around here for ages. We even know where some of them live and we've reported them before."

"And you are?" He looked distastefully at Eleanor.

"A volunteer for S.A.F.E. Anti-Racist Campaign. Aren't you going to take a statement from her?"

"It's very difficult in cases like this, she can point the finger at whoever she likes, but who's going to back her up around here?" The sergeant eyed Eleanor suspiciously as he retreated down the narrow hallway before us.

"Look what they did to my kitchen!" Tasleem clutched my arm in agitation. A second policeman was standing in the kitchen amongst the shards of glass and china talking on his radio. My eyes fell on a large red brick lying on the floor by the cooker with a chalk circle drawn around it. I shuddered violently, realising it could have hit Tasleem or Huma if they had been in the room. A cold wind blew in through the window. Jagged glass fragments were still embedded in the wood frame. The yard beyond was plunged in threatening shadows accentuated by eerie yellow light from the street lamps. The yard gate was swinging open into the ginnel that ran between the houses.

"What a mess," I breathed in horror. "Shall I sweep it up for you?"

"I'm afraid it's best not to touch anything till the SOCO gets here. We'll get someone to board up the window after that," the second officer intervened, putting away his radio. "Best go back in the other room, love."

"Have you interviewed the neighbours?" Eleanor persisted quietly, still addressing Sergeant Hoyland, and I felt a rush of admiration for her determination.

"If the lady wants it taken further, that's her business don't you think?" his reply was loud and flustered. "You've to be careful things don't escalate. Like as not, it's kids who are too young to be prosecuted anyway, so you're onto a loser. Take my advice, love, I've seen it before. You're not doing her any favours stirring things up. What she needs to do is apply to the housing for a transfer, move somewhere else. They should never have put her down here on her own with a little kiddie."

"Why should I move? I don't like moving house again. It's not fair," Tasleem interrupted, looking angrily at the policeman. "This is too much for me to bear, this moving again. I want to stay here. You take these naughty boys away." She wiped her eye with a corner of her dupatta and I reached out and squeezed her other hand. Gripping my hand tightly, she continued, "Tell me what I must do."

"All right," Sergeant Hoyland sighed, shaking his head. He looked at Eleanor when he spoke as if she was in charge. "When they've been to board up the window she can come in and make a full statement. But she'll need an interpreter to go through her rights properly."

"Couldn't the duty solicitor do that?" I asked, thinking of Ramesh.

"Duty solicitors are for people who are being accused of something and ask for a solicitor for their own protection, not for reporting a crime. Anyway, they're not interpreters."

"Yes, but there is someone who can speak her language, I know him," I argued.

"Who's that then?" the other policeman interrupted.

"Ramesh Kumar. He works for Eaton and Dashwood on Queen Street."

"We know Eaton and Dashwood all right, but they've never given us a duty solicitor and certainly not one that can speak Asian, like," Sergeant Hoyland stated with an air of authority.

"But he's on the list." I was perplexed at this response. "You must know him, he's always being called out. Unless he's on a list at another station?"

"Oh no, we'd know him. We always know if there's someone can speak Asian. We're desperate on this patch to get hold of anybody that can do interpretation. No point interviewing them otherwise, see, it's not admissible in court, and they're very fond of saying later they didn't understand the question."

"They?" Eleanor repeated, half to herself. I was more concerned about the fact that neither policeman seemed to have heard of Ramesh. I couldn't understand it.

"Could you find out if he's on the duty solicitor list, please?" I asked, as sweetly and politely as I could manage.

"I told you we've never heard of the bloke," Sergeant Hoyland insisted irritably, "He probably meant he was on duty somewhere else. But I'll check now when I call through." He took out his radio and moved over to the window.

Tasleem loaded a tray with cups of tea, plates of biscuits and bowls of roasted dahl and peanuts and I carried it into the other room for her while the policemen talked on their radios. The tea was made with boiled milk and was sweet and strong and frothy.

"I'm so sorry you've had all this trouble, it must have been awful," Eleanor said to Tasleem.

"Yes, very bad people here," Tasleem agreed fiercely "Some bad boys living on this street."

Tasleem told us she had been expecting another attack after the last incident. She slept with the lights on every night and kept her mobile phone under her pillow. She had also noticed more taunts when she went out in the day, "Why they hate me so much?" she asked and Eleanor looked helpless.

"It's not you, they don't even know you," I tried to explain. "I think it's because they're fed up with school or they can't get jobs or they're angry about something else and they just want someone to blame - it's easy to blame someone who looks different from them."

"Maybe the police will get them this time," Eleanor coaxed optimistically. "If they take fingerprints, and they've already got the addresses you gave them before... "

"But it won't be finished now and I have to live here every night by myself," Tasleem sighed, looking intently at my face. She leaned across to me suddenly, pressing my hand, "Why don't you stay here with me, Shelley?"

"I don't know," I faltered, completely taken aback and a little embarrassed. "I'm quite settled where I am actually."

"You can sleep in the big bedroom. Huma, she sleeps with me, she is scared to stay by herself since we leave Birmingham. Those boys won't do trouble if there is someone else living here with me."

"But she can't. She's not looking for anywhere to move to - " Eleanor looked at me in alarm when I said nothing. I knew there must be reasons why I had to say no to Tasleem, but I couldn't seem to name them at that moment. And a small seed of interest began to take root in my mind. I held it gently, cradling it, exploring it, making its acquaintance.

"I'll have to think about it," I said slowly. Eleanor stared at me in horror.

"Yes, yes," Tasleem beamed. "You think and tell me."

The sergeant came into the room and addressed me triumphantly.

"No such person. At least, not on the duty rota. Some of the lads think they've heard of an Asian solicitor at Eaton and Dashwood and he might have done the duty list a long time ago, but never while I've been here and that's nearly five years."

"Oh. Well, thanks for finding out, I must have made a mistake." I tried to sound grateful.

"The SOCO's here now, round the back," he continued. "So we'll be off. If you want to make a statement come down to the station in the morning."

"Yes, I will." Tasleem said with determination. "Thank you."

We stayed until the window had been boarded up and all the policemen had gone. By the time we left, Huma had fallen asleep again, unnoticed, on the settee. She looked very peaceful, her long black lashes resting on honey-smooth cheeks, one hand still clutching the end of Tasleem's dupatta. Tasleem tugged it free, unconcerned, as she stood up and my hand twitched, wanting to stop her in case she woke Huma, but she clearly knew how deeply her daughter slept. She knows everything about her, I thought, watching them. That must be so amazing. I supposed Mum and I must have been like that once, but I couldn't remember ever feeling that kind of intimacy, I couldn't remember us being inseparable like Tasleem and Huma.

Driving home, I could sense Eleanor's intense disapproval. Her knuckles were stretched taut and white around the steering wheel and her tired eyes were chained to the road.

"You think I shouldn't move in with her, don't you?" I ventured at last.

"It's your life, Shelley," she clipped briefly, reproach dripping from every syllable. I turned my eyes aside to the solitary pavements sliding past in a murky orange light and felt the weight of our disagreement sitting tightly on my chest.

"I didn't say it just to make her feel better, you know. I am serious about it."

"It's not that," Eleanor cut me short, swinging us wildly round the roundabout and up the last hill to my road. "You don't seem to have thought it through at all. How can you raise her hopes like that when you don't know what you're doing? There's a child involved. You can't just move in and then move out again after a few weeks if it doesn't work out. It's a big commitment. And you won't be able to come and go like you do living on your own. Tasleem doesn't go out in the evenings. She'll worry if you're not home by seven every night. And what about your anti-vivisection stuff? What's she going to do if you get arrested? She's not even a vegetarian, never mind a vegan, she won't understand. And what if you got involved with somebody? You couldn't take them back to her place and you couldn't stay over somewhere else because the whole point of you being there is for Tasleem to feel safe at night."

"But I'm not involved with anyone," I protested weakly and fell silent as I remembered our hug.

"But you could be any time - hang on a minute," she twisted herself round to reverse into the space we had left two hours earlier.

"Shall I just jump out?" I suggested, trying to be helpful.

"Nope. I've got it," she insisted, and swore quietly and viciously as she misjudged the distance. I sat very still in order not to add to her stress.

When she had finished edging the car back and forth in minute shifts, she switched off the engine and sat staring blankly out of the window.

"Look, about what happened earlier... " She breathed deeply. "I'm sorry, I was a bit upset."

"It's all right," I lied, not knowing what else to say. I wanted to make it all right for her.

"I do care about you," I blurted out. "And it's fine your caring about me. I just don't think I care in the same way." I stole a sideways glance at her and could see her eyes harden in the light from the streetlamp.

"It's all right, you don't have to be nice." She spat the word with contempt. "It just makes me feel more of a fool than ever. Let's just say I was a bit tired and emotional and try and forget it."

"Okay," I agreed quickly, relieved that we had dispensed with 'it' so easily.

"You'd better get indoors out of this cold," she said briskly. I opened my door and stepped out of the car, searching for words to ease things.

"'Bye," I managed feebly. She started the engine up again without looking at me and I watched her drive off. Once in the flat, I shut the door firmly behind me, and slumped down on the settee without putting the light on.

"Shit. Shit. Shit." I swore quietly in the gloom. I felt washed out and miserable. Everything was such a mess. And then there was that weird business about Ramesh. Why had he been telling Veena he was going out to work in the evenings when he wasn't? It looked well dodgy. Should I tell Veena? I drew the curtains against the cold void beyond, starless and faintly orange above the zigzagging black line of the rooftops across the street. Ignoring the rubbish still lying on the kitchen floor, I headed straight for bed. I undressed quickly and crawled into the excessively spacious double bed, hugging the cold quilt around me until I had warmed a cocoon for myself. I wished Tiger had not disappeared tonight, I could do with his uncomplicated warmth and solidarity. Right now, he was quite possibly the only living thing on the planet I'd feel totally safe and comfortable with, I was in a quagmire with everyone else. It took me ages to get to sleep.

I have discovered a small park just up the road from Awaaz with a quiet corner I have claimed as my own. A wooden bench with splintered remnants of peeling green paint is tucked under a privet hedge opposite an old beech tree. I go there when the weather permits and I manage to squeeze a lunch break in between meeting women and running groups, which is not that often. I have slipped away to my secret corner today to meet Anil, at his request, and I am in luck as there's no one on my bench. The spring sunshine is surprisingly hot and gleams on the beaten metallic surfaces of the slide and climbing frames in the children's play area. The spreading grey branches of the tree above me are studded with buds just starting to unfurl into light green heart-shaped leaves, luminous in the sunlight. My jacket lies abandoned over the back of the seat, and for a while I remain completely motionless, absorbing the healing warmth of the sun through the skin on my arms and face. I listen to the birdsong in the dark hedges behind me. I dig out my cheese salad sandwich and a can of fizzy orange from the flimsy plastic bag they gave me in the sandwich shop. Although it's after two, I haven't eaten yet. It was hard enough just getting out of the office so close to the Annual General Meeting next Monday.

"I have an appointment," I told Shahnaz economically and I blush remembering my evasiveness. Meeting my son sounds frivolous to me, like washing my hair, or going shopping, whereas 'an appointment' sounded firm and immutable and precluded further enquiry.

"I'll be passing by your place around lunchtime, today, Mum," Anil dropped in nonchalantly at breakfast this morning, his dark sleek head bent over his cereal, brown elbows resting untidily on the table. "Would you like to meet up?"

"If you can make it at half past two, that would be lovely," I agreed, hiding my surprise. I suspected the reason he was suggesting this was to tell me the something he had found too difficult to say at home all this time. "Let's meet in that small park near Mount Pleasant, by the children's playground."

I watched his jaws working energetically on a full mouth and his lips smacking with satisfaction. He is such a little boy still when I feed him. The sweet daily pleasures of nourishing a child came so effortlessly with Anil, part of the simple affection that rolled between us in slow leisurely tides, lapping the quiet shores of our separate lives. With Pooja there was conflict all the way, especially over food, sulky silences hanging like clouds over the table, lovingly prepared morsels rejected on the plate, and the endless worry over her frail limbs and stubborn refusal to grow. The tension between us would spark in the air as soon as I entered the kitchen to cook and would still be there at bedtime in her desperate clinging hugs and quirky grunts and snuffles into my shoulder.

I pull the ring on the can. It cracks and fizzes, a confident young sound, and I feel a thrill of illicit pleasure as I sip the frothy drink, as though I have sneaked out of school. Not that I ever did such a thing at Calcutta Girls High, stranded at boarding school in a strange city hundreds of miles from Patna. How desolate that felt, and how I hated having to go back to school at the end of each holiday. Long before that dreaded departure came I understood that I was cast out, banished to make room for the baby brothers who followed me. I remember my mother rolling and sculpting little balls of rice and dahl in her fingertips and popping them tenderly into Vijay's mouth with devoted concentration. I watched silently over my lonely untended plate, no longer existing for her.

I have tried so hard not to reject Pooja, to love her and cherish her. She is not rejected, or hurt, or jealous, she is simply not interested. We are boring to her, home is boring, her life is boring. I know she says such things deliberately to provoke me, but I cannot protect myself from the pain she intends. It distresses me deeply to have brought up a child so devoid of values and beliefs, so apparently shallow, so apathetic and self-centred. I blame myself for not having taken more time to teach them my values. I should have talked to them more about my childhood and my work in India, the union and political meetings I attended with such passion, and the vision that we all had then of how India could be. I tried a few times but their eyes glazed over after a couple of minutes.

"Okay Mum," they would say, "We've heard all this before and we saw the film about Gandhi, but it's not got India anywhere has it? There are still people starving and killing each other over religion so what's the point?"

"The point is that you should care about India!" I would cry in despair.

"But we do, Mummy." Anil would always try to placate me. "We just don't understand all the politics and it's not really our problem. We have to sort out our own lives first, don't we? We can't help what's going on in India."

"Anyway, that Hindu stuff's all about fulfilling your

destiny, isn't?" Pooja once intervened belligerently. "Well, this is our destiny here and we're just getting on with it like good little Hindus." I winced at her cutting tone.

"Don't mock, Pooja, it doesn't sound nice." My reprimand sounded lame even to my own ears. "You know I've never asked you to be religious, that's up to you. I'm not religious myself. But I do want you to grow up proud of your heritage."

It always felt like banging my head against a brick wall, and when I examine it in the cold light of day, what have I given them of India, my India? A little puja ceremony once or twice a year for Diwali and Navratri, a ceremonial thread for Pooja to tie around Anil's wrist once a year, an occasional visit to the samaj for a wedding or a festival, and the food I cook at home. It's through my cooking that I hoped I was passing on what is special and different about our history, about India. I tried to woo my children to India by filling the house with aromas and textures, the delicate smokiness of northern breads, clouds of steam rising from cooked rice, the cream of southern coconuts and the nutty spices of Gujerat. But Pooja rejected my food from the beginning, preferring a square of yellow cheese between two slices of limp white bread to any mouth-watering dish I could create, and Anil ate happily enough in the privacy of our home but insisted on pre-packaged pizza and oven chips when his friends came to tea. I lost the battle on the food front as on all others and now I see my children drifting in a limbo, needlessly reinventing themselves. Sometimes I think that's not so bad. I thought I was coming to this country for that very anonymity, an escape from the weight of tradition and the constraints of living with my husband's family. But leaving home seemed to leave me more dependent on him and more trapped by his decrees as to how my life, our lives, should be. Reinventing yourself is hard to do alone and I fear for my children trying to steer a course through the soulless materialism of this country.

"Hi, Mum," Anil appears suddenly at my shoulder, a rucksack dangling from his hand, his cotton shirt open at the neck and unfamiliar in its crispness.

"Hello, darling. Sit down." I move along the bench to make room for him, feeling a flutter of nerves at this unusual encounter with my almost grown-up son. "I'm just having my lunch. Have you had anything?"

"Ages ago, it's half past two," he reminds me. He sprawls on the seat, shoulders sagging, long legs angled like a spider's. "It's just nice to have a chance to talk." I say nothing, my mouth full of bland white roll and watery lettuce. He surveys the sloping swathe of grass before us, and the playground beyond, as if looking for inspiration. "It's a lovely day, isn't it?" I nod and smile. Should I help him along a bit? I wonder. But he takes a long inward breath and begins by himself. "Look, Mum, there's something I need to tell you… " I clutch my can a little tighter, long anticipated openings bouncing wildly around my head like, 'I've met this girl …', or, 'You know Shelley and me have been getting on quite well…' The words that come are not what I have been expecting and leave me blank and uncomprehending. "… The thing is I've got a job."

"That's okay, isn't it, dear?" I say at last. "Aren't you managing on your student loan, then?"

"No. Well, yes. It's not about the money actually." He pauses, as if he is going to say more, and then gets up

135

from the bench and crosses the path to lean against the smooth grey trunk of the beech tree. He seems to be thinking hard and I sense there is more that he is finding difficult to say. I'm his mother. Surely it can't be that difficult to tell me? "The thing is... " he continues. "It's a full-time job and I've decided to pack in uni. I've told my tutor. I was hoping I could count on your support." I stop chewing, the masticated lumps of bread sticking in my mouth as my hunger evaporates.

"But Anil, you can't do that! What about your education? Why didn't you talk to us first?" I can't keep the wail of dismay out of my voice and I can see his shoulders tense up as I speak.

"Because I knew what you'd say." The violence of his tone surprises me. "Dad would have laid down the law and said no, without even listening to me, and you - " He stops himself.

"What about me?" I have to ask, though I know the response will hurt.

"You just follow whatever he says."

"That's not true." I sigh, but there is no conviction in my words.

"Whatever." He shrugs his shoulders and a silence falls between us. I can feel his anger. And I know I have let him down somewhere, but I thought what I was doing was for the best, always. I supported my husband. I supported my children. When they clashed I mediated between them. What else could I do? I watch a woman help a little boy climb laboriously up the steps to the top of the slide. She should hold his hand at the top, I think, uneasily, a little wobble and he could fall onto the tarmac surface below. I was so sure Anil was going to tell me there was something going on between him and

Shelley. I have wrestled with the possibility since I saw them together in our front room the other night. I have worried about Shelley's idiosyncratic lifestyle, her unknown parentage and the history of abuse that may underlie her birth mother's silence. And the fact that she is older than Anil. I have mourned the loss of our friendship and I have been hurt that she has not confided in me. I thought I had read what was happening, but now I find I have got it all quite wrong. The little boy sails down the slide laughing, and lands in his mother's arms. If she is his mother, that is. I shouldn't assume, when so many children go to childminders these days. At least I still have Shelley, then. I wonder if she knows about Anil's plans.

"So, what's the job?" I try to sound interested. Anil lifts his head when I speak and shifts his position against the tree trunk.

"It's working in a hostel for homeless young people, mostly sixteen and seventeen-year-olds who've run away from home or been thrown out and need help getting back on their feet."

"But you're so young yourself." As soon as the words slip out, I regret them. "I'm sorry," I whisper, as he rolls his eyes to the sky and shakes his head despairingly. "Anil, I'm sorry if I don't understand, but your whole future depends on your degree. You can't throw it away for just one job, however interesting or worthwhile. No one does that."

"You see." He sounds triumphant. "You just take Dad's line every time."

"You don't even know what your father's line is," I remind him, but I feel trapped. I know Ramesh will hit the roof and I will be forced to take sides between them. There will be no middle ground, no other kind of space allowed. Already, I seem to have no voice in this. There are so many things I want to ask him. Who got him into this? Why does he need to do it full-time? Why is he throwing away all hope of having an easy path through life? What did his tutor say? But I can't afford to alienate him any further. I need to keep him close and protect him from his father, so I ask none of these burning questions. Instead I wrap up the remains of my sandwich and toss it into a wire bin beside the bench.

"I don't know what to say, darling," I sigh. "I think you're making a mistake. When are you supposed to start?"

"Not till the end of next month. My tutor said I should finish the year at uni and take a year out, rather than dropping out completely."

"That sounds like a good idea," I see a chink of light in this nightmare.

"I don't know, Mum. I don't think I'll ever go back to accountancy so I don't see the point really, but I said I'll talk to him again next week."

What about talking to me? I want to scream. Don't I count for anything, after twenty years of feeding you and clothing you and worrying about you? But I don't scream.

"How did you get the experience to go for that kind of a job?" I ask lightly, carefully.

"I've been volunteering there since I started at uni, on a kind of befriending scheme. I must have mentioned it?" He avoids my eyes and I sense there is more to this.

"No, I don't think you did, and I don't understand why not. This just isn't making sense to me, Anil. Did you think I wouldn't approve of you doing voluntary work?"

138

"It's complicated." He sighs and jabs his toe into the grass at his feet. Then he scans my face, as if looking for a signal that it's safe to go on. I wait.

"There was someone working there." He clears his throat. "Bev. We went out together for a while." His voice sinks to a whisper as he speaks and I can see that it hurts him to talk about it.

"For how long?" I can't believe he's telling me this now, for the first time.

"Fourteen months."

"More than a year," I say, unable to hide my shock.

"And seventeen days," he adds with a faint ironic smile.

"Oh Anu, darling, come here." I reach my arm out, filled with sorrow at what he has been carrying alone. He returns to the bench and allows me to put my arm around his shoulder and squeeze him gently. "Why didn't you tell me, poppet?"

"You wouldn't have approved, and Dad would have gone ballistic. She wasn't a Hindu, she wasn't even Asian," he mumbles sulkily.

"So all the times you said you were staying at friends' houses after parties and going out..."

"I was at Bev's." He finishes my sentence for me, confirming a complete other life he has been living. I have completely failed to keep up in any way with how old he is or how separate he is from us. I am hurt and angry, and I don't understand how, but I know I have not been available to him or he would have told me about all this before.

"So you're not together any more?" I try to keep going, needing to extract as much information as I can before I say the wrong thing and he clams up again.

"No. She's gone to London, but we split up before that.

Actually, it's because she left that the job came up. I suppose I should thank her." He laughs bitterly.

"But why do you want to work there now, when she's gone? Surely it will just hurt you more, all those reminders?" For a moment I see a way of persuading him out of this madness.

"It's not just about her. It's about doing something I believe in. We both believed in it, but her leaving doesn't stop me wanting to carry it on. I can't explain," he finishes, shrugging off my arm in exasperation.

"Like keeping faith with something you both cared about," I suggest, placing my hands back carefully in my lap and trying not to feel the roughness of his gesture. He looks sideways at me as if I have finally said something he can hear.

"Yes, that's right. It is kind of keeping faith." He stares at the ground, concentrating, and continues slowly, "It's only what you're doing, and Shelley, and even Dad. You're all doing stuff you believe in. I just have to do something real, too. I can't live in libraries and classrooms any more. Can you understand that?"

"I can, darling, but look at us. We all got our degrees first. That's all I want you to be able to do. And your degree can be something you believe in too. You could change your course."

He sighs and shakes his head.

"I can't, Mum. I've been down that one. Honestly. All I can think about is the guys in the hostel and wondering who's kicking off and whether so-and-so is going to keep it together this weekend, and I'm supposed to be doing all this abstract theoretical stuff, and I can't. I just have to get out."

I see that there is nothing more I can say.

"It's your life, Anil."

"It is," he agrees, and looks pleased. He will congratulate himself on how well he has handled this conversation, how well I took it, never knowing what it costs me to give such a blessing. "By the way," he adds, as if offering an afterthought. "I've found a flat near work I can move into from next month, but I've got to pay a wacking great bond on it. I wouldn't have asked, but now you're working full-time as well, Mum, I thought you might be able to help me out a bit."

A cold sick feeling sweeps over me, a feeling of dawning betrayal. He has shut me out so deliberately for so long, and now it seems as if he has let me in only to ask for money. He has already taken decisions, made promises and commitments he won't go back on, without any reference to me. I always intended that they should carve out their own paths, but I saw myself as being part of the process. Here there's no role for me. Once Anil moves into this flat and starts his job, he'll be lost to me. No more buying him clothes, or doing his washing, no more snatched moments over breakfast on a Saturday morning.

"I'll have to talk to your father about that," I say coolly, deferring any response about the money.

"But I'm not asking him, I'm asking you. I thought you had your own money now, Mum. Aren't you allowed to make your own decisions about it?"

"That's not the point, Anil," I respond sharply. "You know your father and I discuss everything together." I know I am maintaining a fiction, but it suddenly seems important to hang onto some kind of bottom line about this. "And when are you going to tell him?"

"I was sort of hoping you might be able to do that.

You're so good at putting things calmly... " He looks sheepish. I can see the sense in it, but it feels like the last straw and I now want this conversation over with. He is hurting me in ways I cannot name and I want to be somewhere else.

"I think you need to talk to him yourself. I might not have understood and I wouldn't want to misrepresent you," I suggest, surprised at the edge of coldness in my voice.

"Fine," he mutters. "Shall we go?" He stands up and loiters restlessly on the path waiting for me to gather up my belongings.

As we walk briskly down to the road I realise the unfamiliarity of his open-necked shirt is not its smart crispness, but the fact that I have never seen and certainly never washed this shirt. Maybe it was his job interview shirt. I should be pleased he doesn't need me any more, but I can't find that sense of relief I always expected to feel on discovering my children have grown up. It's no relief at all, only a yawning raw chasm inside that moans and wails its emptiness through my body as if I am giving birth a second time, unwillingly and too soon.

Ermyntrude has begun to peel off the wall above the front door in little powdery flakes of black and white paint. Every time someone bangs the door a little shower of white dust trickles sadly down. As I swept up the tiny plaster fragments and curls of old paint strewn under her cavorting form at closing time today, I lectured her severely, "Come on, old girl, you can't give up on us yet. Pull yourself together. Stiff upper lip and all that." I was going to tell Eleanor about it when I went into the kitchen. In the past we would have had a laugh about me talking to the cows. But now something always stops me. Since the day when she first told me about Matt leaving, the day of the hug, I never ask her what's going on. Trying to keep everything kind of low key and normal is doing my head in a bit, but it seems to be the only way to get through the day and keep the cafe going, which is what I care about most.

Eleanor was emptying the dishwasher with her back to me when I came through from the cafe. She didn't look round. Her crumpled white T-shirt hung on thin shoulder blades, etched sharply against the limp material, and I remembered the feel of her shivering in my arms that day. I concentrated hard on filling the kettle and rummaging among the tea caddies on the windowsill. I was staying on for an anti-vivisection meeting so I was in no hurry to get through the clearing up. I stood by the window waiting for the kettle to boil and looked out into the yard. I tried to imagine tables busy with chattering customers basking in the sun, and terracotta pots brimming over with summer flowers. I felt we had lost the warm companionship of that day clearing the yard and everything felt complicated now. I couldn't see how we would ever finish the garden.

"Have you got any cover sorted for the cafe yet?" I tried to make ordinary conversation as I poured boiling water onto our teabags. Eleanor usually had lemon and ginger tea and I decided to have camomile, to relax me before the meeting.

"Nearly - we're interviewing five people tomorrow, all students. We can't offer anything long term, so I thought a couple of part-time students for a while might suit us and them." While she was talking her eyes followed the stubby bitten thumbnail she was digging into a long groove in the wooden table.

"Is Matt interviewing with you?" I slid a mug across to her carefully and she looked up and caught my eye with a fleeting anxious flicker of her eyelids. Her face was grey and tired as if she hadn't slept. When she continued talking it was as if she was looking through me to some anonymous other person standing behind me, like she was talking through a veil.

"I told him he has to. We have to keep running to capacity otherwise word will get round and we'll start to lose customers. Then we'll be in an even worse position and there'll be even less money at the end of it all for his precious adventures." She paused, looking down at the table again. We sipped our drinks carefully in the loud silence that fell over the room. There seemed to be no way to retrieve the ease we had had before. It would always be there, the knowledge that Eleanor felt something and I couldn't respond with anything similar. I wasn't sure how much longer I could stay with all this awkwardness. But with the cafe in such crisis I couldn't

144

leave too. When Eleanor finally broke the silence her voice was tense and strained.

"Matt moved out at the weekend, you know."

"Oh God, I'm sorry, Eleanor. I didn't realise." No wonder she was looking so exhausted.

"He's staying with a friend in Hillsborough and he took most of his stuff to his brother's in Manchester on Sunday. It's much better really." She sounded as if she was trying to be positive. "We were just arguing all the time."

"So he definitely wants out," I concluded, thinking that Ermyntrude had got it about right then.

"I'm afraid so. We need to talk about what you want to do next," Eleanor looked at me squarely and for the first time for days I felt she was actually seeing me. I was back in the room again.

"I want to stay here," I said at once. She frowned.

"If you stay, we have to be a team," she began slowly. "I don't know where we are with that right now… "

I didn't know what to say.

There was a loud knock on the front door of the cafe and we both jumped.

"That'll be your meeting. Let's talk about this another time," Eleanor suggested, gripping the corners of the table and levering herself up slowly as if she was aching and stiff.

The group drifted in slowly in ones and twos, which meant I had to lift the heavy metal shutter outside the front door and drop it again each time a new person arrived. Eleanor retreated to her upstairs flat and left me to entertain them and I became increasingly grumpy as everyone hassled me for drinks and snacks. I wished we didn't have to be so paranoid about security and could meet in the pub instead.

Ritchie was in charge as usual and his gaunt melodramatic urgency soon began to irritate me.

"I told you I've sorted the access issue," I explained to him patiently. "This friend of mine is getting us a map of the whole site this weekend and a male student pass to the biology labs next Wednesday. He says whoever's going to have it needs to be using it for a few days beforehand so they don't stick out too much."

"So where is it?" Ritchie interrupted me fretfully.

"He hasn't got it yet. Obviously. I just said he'll get it to us next Wednesday."

"Can we trust him?" Ritchie looked dubious. Carmen raised her eyes to the ceiling in exasperation.

"If Shelley trusts him that's good enough for me," she snapped.

"I want to sus things out in the lab as soon as possible. Do you think I could meet up with your friend? I really need to talk to him." Ritchie continued. I was sure Anil could do without being hassled by Ritchie and I was starting to wish I'd never involved him in the action at all.

"Look, he's just getting us the pass. He can't do anything else." My response was sharp. "He's not even in the science faculty, he's an accountant."

"But he might know things. The more people we talk to who know the university the better," Ritchie persisted.

"Let Shelley sort out what her friend's doing, she knows what he can handle. We don't want to freak him out and lose the pass." Carmen met my eyes with a sympathetic glance. She was my rock in these meetings, when Ritchie drove us both up the wall. Sam always backed him up with unfailing devotion and Dave and Angela just retreated into rolling joints and smoking them moronically. "Look, there's not much more we can do about the labs till next week. Can we talk about something else?"

"What about the halal butchers in Attercliffe?" Sam volunteered suddenly, "You know, for our next project."

"It's not vivisection," Angela pointed out.

"But it's cruelty to animals and it needs stopping or there'll be more and more of it with all these asylum seekers being bussed up from London," Sam argued doggedly.

"Whoa! Hang on a minute!" I protested. "More and more of what exactly?"

"Slitting animals' throats while they're still conscious." He glared at me defiantly and Carmen shifted uncomfortably in her seat but remained uncharacteristically silent. It was down to me then.

"Did you know there was a racist attack on the Asian meat shop in London Road last Saturday?" I asked Sam coldly.

"I did hear something about it," he murmured, looking vague.

"So you want us to be lumped together with a bunch of fascists, do you?"

"How do you know it wasn't animal liberationists? That halal slaughtering malarky is barbaric," he countered.

"Because they painted racist slogans all over the windows and I don't think the Animal Liberation Front would do that. Or at least, I hope they wouldn't." The possibility that he was right about who had attacked the shop began to dawn on me and I felt as if the ground was sliding away beneath my feet.

"I don't think we should leave animals to suffer for fear

of being called fascists," Sam dug in stubbornly. I looked round at the others and no one would meet my eyes. A brick wall of silence seemed to have suddenly reared up in front of me and when Angela finally spoke it was as if the previous exchange hadn't happened.

"What about a petition in Fargate again? That went really well last year," she suggested brightly. There was a ripple of nods and a collective sigh of relief at what looked like a way out.

"Might be more popular than what you're suggesting, eh Sam?" Dave nudged him. "People are funny about religion and we've got a big enough job on convincing the public as it is." Sam shrugged his shoulders.

"Well, if your lot aren't going to sort it, somebody else will," he muttered, almost to himself.

"What do you mean your lot?" I said quietly. "Aren't you part of us any more?"

"Of course I am," he snorted. "But we're not the only people doing stuff. There are other animal rights groups out there. Maybe one of them will take on those - those butchers." I could hear the word on the tip of his tongue and a picture of broken glass and a brick in a chalk circle flashed through my mind.

"Go on, Sam. Why don't you say it?" I realised I was shaking. "Say what you mean - those Paki butchers!" The others looked shocked.

"Cool it, Shelley," Ritchie soothed. "He didn't mean that. You're getting stressed about nothing. Carmen'll make you a cup of tea." He gave Carmen a look that said, get on with it, then, and she jumped up and hurried out to the kitchen. I doubted she would be able to find anything but, not caring any more, I let her go. I sat quietly trying to calm my breathing and get my head round what had just happened. I was feeling quite scared about being in an action with Sam in a few days' time, but what felt more scary was that no one else seemed to have a problem with him. They moved on seamlessly to discuss a sticker campaign the national organisation was launching to target cosmetic products tested on animals, and Carmen brought me a cup of hot Barleycup, which was the only drink she had managed to locate. I nursed my drink gratefully through the rest of the meeting and locked up on my own after they had gone.

When I got home after the anti-vivisection meeting I felt totally shattered. I was too tired to cook and paced round the house for a while, trying to occupy myself so I wouldn't have to think. I put a load of dirty laundry in the washing machine, watered the plants, and screwed the dodgy hinge on the bedroom door back into the soft splitting wood of the door frame. When I think about it now, it was as if I was waiting for something, and when there was a knock on the outside door at about half-past nine I wasn't surprised. I knew Eleanor and I hadn't really sorted anything out and we needed to talk further, but I wasn't sure I had any energy left to face it that day and my heart sank.

I opened the door and the figure looming in the dark startled me with its height and the width of the shoulders seeming to bear down on me.

"Sorry about this."

I recognised Anil's deep voice with relief.

"I've just had a fucking awful row with my dad and told him I'll never set foot in his house again. You wouldn't like to go for a drink, would you?" My first stab of fear was replaced with irritation. I was too tired for this and I had problems of my own.

"No, I wouldn't. I'm shattered." I opened the door further. "But you can have a cup of tea if you like." He tripped over the doorstep into the room, screwing his eyes up in the sudden light. As he struggled out of his bulging blue ski jacket, his arms seemed to flail in all directions and he seemed too big for my little flat. I wasn't used to impromptu visits. No one just called round like this.

"How did you know where I lived?" I quizzed as he sat down heavily on the settee, his calves nudging the coffee table and threatening to tip it into the fire.

"I looked in Mum's address book." He scanned my face anxiously. "Sorry. Is this a problem? Because I can go if it is." He started to lift himself from the seat again and my resentment evaporated.

"No, don't be daft. Sit down," I insisted. I turned on the fire in front of him and moved into the kitchen to make a drink. "Actually, I could probably do with the company." When I said this, he relaxed and leaned back slowly in his seat. There was something languid in his heavy-lidded eyes and open sprawling limbs that gave me a little tug inside as I noticed it. I also noticed he didn't offer to help. Hugh would have offered to make the drink himself, I thought, I need to write back and tell him what I feel about his new-found enthusiasm for all things American. I can't just give up on the friendship because of one letter, he's worth more than that.

"Bad day at the cafe, then?" Anil called across the counter that separated the living and kitchen areas.

"Something like that." I hesitated. "It's too complicated to explain. So, what were you arguing about with your dad?"

"Dropping out of uni." There was a mischievous smile at the corners of his lips and I didn't know whether to take him seriously.

"You're kidding?" I suggested cautiously.

"'Fraid not. I finish uni at the end of the month and I'm starting a new job on the first of July."

"How? Where?" I breathed, incredulous.

"Rafters. It's a hostel for homeless young people over at

Woodford."

"It's quite rough out there, isn't it?" I seemed to remember that estate being mentioned in a S.A.F.E. meeting.

"So they say." He shrugged his shoulders as if this was irrelevant. I watched the back of his head as he stared into the fire. His black hair was combed out from the crown in dense black swirls and I could just see the tiny craters of old chicken pox scars on the side of his cheek. I heard myself saying to Eleanor, "He's a bit young," and realised maybe he wasn't just a spoilt little boy dossing around at home with Mummy.

"God, Anil, that's so brave, I mean, it's such a big step to take." I placed a mug of tea on the table in front of him.

"Yeah, right. But I'm a bit up shit creek now without a paddle, practically speaking." He picked up the mug and leaned forward, looking into it dubiously. "What's this?"

"Peppermint tea. I don't drink milk so I don't keep ordinary tea bags, I'm afraid. Anyway, it's good for you." I explained without expression.

"Really?" He glanced up at me sceptically, one eyebrow raised under a shock of black hair, and I started to laugh. The dark purplish skin around his eyes creased into a smile. "I'll take your word for it." He took a cautious sip and tipped his head approvingly in that very Indian way that Veena sometimes has. "Not bad," he conceded.

"So what's the problem, apart from ditching your entire education and future career, which I presume you've already considered?" I prompted, settling down in the armchair by the window.

"Yes, I have already considered it, actually. Thank you

for realising that. I wish my parents would."

"Oh, I see." I said, slowly. "You've had a row with Veena as well?"

"Not a row exactly," he qualified. "But I don't think she understands either and she won't back me against Dad. The problem is I've got a wacking great student loan to pay back, and nowhere to live, unless I can find a thousand-pound bond by Monday."

"Can't help you there. But I'm surprised Veena won't support you," I said lightly. "She did some pretty wild things herself when she was young."

"Yeah, and then she married my dad." His tone was final and damning.

" - Who was also a revolutionary at the time," I dared to remind him.

"I'm sorry, I just don't believe it." He put his head in his palms and pressed his temples as if trying to force in the indigestible information. The backs of his slender angular hands were silken brown and their arched knuckles poked through his hair like small mountain peaks. I wanted to run my fingers over the craggy joints, and then a memory of the corrugated ridge of Eleanor's spine suddenly crashed into my mind sending shock waves rippling in every direction. Anil didn't seem to notice. "If I wasn't in such a mess with not having enough money, it would have been easier not to tell them at all, especially Mum. With Dad I can have a blazing row and I don't really care, but you know what mothers are like. If Mum's disappointed in me she won't shout at me, I'll just feel all this pain I'm causing her burning a hole in me wherever I go."

"God, I so know what you mean." The feeling in my voice made us both laugh, our eyes sharing an understanding of guilt-tripping mothers. I felt a twinge of unease at my disloyalty towards Veena, but I brushed it aside. "Does Pooja know?"

"Of course." He seemed surprised that I even asked. "We always tell each other everything. I know it looks like we fight a lot, but really we're rock solid."

I braced myself against the tide of hurt that wells up inside me when I hear of that easy primal solidarity. I so wanted a sibling when I was growing up, a co-conspirator, a fellow traveller, who would carry through our lives a sense of me from before we could speak, before we had memory even. I feel so orphaned without it. Anil seemed to see the cloud in my eyes. He leant forward and slid his hand along the arm of the settee.

"You know," he pressed a random spot on the rough woollen surface with the blunt square end of his middle finger. "It's really good to talk to you, Shelley. It's such a relief to tell someone who understands." He held me with a level gaze for a few moments and I felt warm and noticed. Then he tilted his head to one side and raised his eyebrows hopefully. "So? Will you put in a good word for me with Mum when you see her? I know she listens to you."

"Creep," I laughed. "Of course I'll tell her what I think, if she wants to know. But we don't talk about everything, you know. We're friends, but there are things I haven't told her, because I'm not sure how she'd take them, and there's probably loads she hasn't told me." As I said this I wondered what our friendship was worth if there were so many things we didn't share.

"Thanks, Shelley, you've really helped." He leaned over and squeezed my arm affectionately. "By the way, have you eaten?" he added suddenly. "I could order us a takeaway, I know a really good place in Broomhill that delivers."

I abandoned any thought of going to bed early and realised I no longer felt tired. While he phoned the takeaway restaurant on his mobile, I went out to the off-licence for some beer. The air was still and cool, and above the rooftops a full moon ringed with orange was floating in a milky haze of thin high cloud. I felt quite buoyant, in fact, and full of warmth and gratitude to Anil for disturbing me at a point when I really needed distracting from my thoughts.

When the takeaway arrived we arranged the foil trays on the coffee table and poured ourselves two glasses of cold beer. As we spooned curries and dhal onto our plates and tore off soft chunks of naan bread to scoop up the dripping sauces and pulpy vegetables, Anil talked about the hostel and the voluntary work he had been doing there for the last two years.

"I don't know what I'll do if Mum and Dad won't give me the money for the flat. I can't carry on living at home after all this."

"Have some more food, there's plenty left," I urged him, pointing to the half-finished curries beginning to congeal.

"Oh no, I'm stuffed." He looked around, "It's really nice in here. You were lucky to find something so spacious. Do you like living on your own?"

"It's all right," I shrugged. "It suits me at the moment. I spend so much time at the cafe I wouldn't be much company for anyone else. But I don't suppose I'll miss it if I leave."

"You thinking of moving on then?" He took a swig of beer from his bottle and the muscles in his neck convulsed as the liquid slid down his throat.

"I'm thinking about it. This woman I met at Awaaz has asked me to move in with her."

"And?"

"And… I don't know. She's come here quite recently from Birmingham and she's got a child. I can't decide if it's a good idea or not." I saw Eleanor's white knuckles clenched on the steering wheel in dismay at the idea of me moving in with Tasleem. Thinking of her, I remembered our unfinished conversation earlier in the cafe, and the relief I felt when she looked straight at me at last and said we needed to talk. I realised how much I wanted things to be okay between us again. I wanted to see the curls around her head shaking as I made her laugh with my clumsiness, and her eyes crinkle and almost disappear in the spreading pool of her smile. I wanted everything to be back to how it was when I first started working there and felt I'd finally come home.

"Sounds a bit dodgy. A child's a bit of a drag, isn't it? What about your independence?" Anil cautioned.

"Oh God, I don't know!" I exploded suddenly, slapping my hands on the arms of my chair. I could feel the beer flooding into my head and I was aware I was being quite loud. I was starting to feel slightly distanced from the solid world of walls, and chairs, and plates that needed tidying up, and I tried to shake myself back into reality. "Actually, I think I could get a lot out of sharing with someone so different from me."

"And not so different," he reminded me.

"What do you mean?" I tipped my glass of beer right back to let the last drops trickle into my mouth.

"Well, you're both Asian women, aren't you?"

I felt as if I had run into a brick wall. His words took

my breath away. It was as plain as day, and as alien to me as if he had said I had two heads, I was just not that person he was describing. He saw something in my face and pulled back hastily.

"Not that it's anything to do with me, of course. I guess you'll be fine wherever you live." He wiped his hands on the paper bag the naans had been wrapped in and leaned back with a sigh of satisfaction.

"So," he breathed out with heavy emphasis. "What now?"

There was a coyness in his question and the winsome tilt of his dark head that made me wonder, with a small lurch in the pit of my stomach, if he was flirting with me. I looked back into his steady eyes and tried to unravel the moment, his question, the knot in my stomach, the reach of his long slender hand along the back of the settee. I shrugged and interpreted his question as literally as I could.

"There's no pudding, unless you want some fruit, but we could have coffee if you don't mind it black."

"And then I suppose I ought to go, though I don't know where." He sighed deeply and shook his head as if trying to rouse himself.

"You don't have to, I mean, I'm sure you're very well acquainted with settees. I don't know how this one measures up?" I stared absently into the fire to demonstrate my indifference to his response, but I wanted him to stay.

"Well, if you don't mind, that'd be great. It's a fine settee and I think I've missed all the last buses to anywhere useful."

"Don't you need to tell someone?" I thought of Veena. This could get complicated.

"They'll assume I've gone to stay at a friend's. I do have other friends if it's a problem."

"It's fine." I began gathering up the litter of curry trays and plates and plastic bags. "Do you want some coffee?"

"I'll make it," he sprang up suddenly. "I'm not a complete waste of space, you know." I smiled at his accurate reading of my thoughts. We carried the debris of our meal into the kitchen and I disposed of it while Anil made the coffee.

"Your coffee, Madam," he placed the mugs ceremoniously on the counter and drew out one of the barstools motioning me to sit down. As I lifted myself onto it, he held the back of the seat steady, his hands lightly touching my shoulders. He perched on the other barstool opposite me and leaned his elbows on the narrow counter, his hands encircling his mug of coffee. There was a long reflective silence in which we stared into our coffees. The kitchen was badly lit as I hadn't thought to turn on the spotlights over the work surfaces. When I did think of it something stopped me moving towards the light switch, I preferred the soft-edged cavernous gloom. When I lifted my eyes I met Anil's level gaze appraising me as he sipped his coffee. I thought I should have felt awkward, but I didn't, I met his gaze and felt kind of held again. His face was so close I could smell the hot bitter coffee on his breath. I felt if I moved I would break the spell of understanding between us. A voice somewhere in the back of my head was saying, "What the hell are you playing at, Shelley? Have you gone completely mad?" I couldn't be bothered listening, it was late and it had been a very long day. I felt stretched like elastic straining to hold together my reality as it expanded at the speed of light into some outer universe.

The warmth of the fire didn't quite reach as far as the kitchen and Anil noticed me shuddering a little in the cooler air. He reached for his jumper, which he had discarded on the settee earlier.

"It's a bit chilly now," he remarked. "Why don't you put my jumper on?"

"I could get my own from the bedroom," I responded truthfully, but I took the jumper he handed me and pulled it on. It was rough and warm, knitted in thick, tickly, grey-green wool that settled on me in misty folds smelling of varnished wood and sweat and smoky student bars. I shrank with the shock of such intimacy drawing me in and wrapping me in Anil. The jumper reminded me of Hugh and for the first time in ages I just wanted to run back to the dingy room in his student house where we spent so many nights together. I remembered diving into the saggy, yielding, feather-cushioned lair of his bed, rolling sweetly in the crimson fluid haziness of wine and candlelight and the saxophone harmonies he played on his CD player during our fumbling undergraduate lovemaking. I knew I didn't love him like Mum loved Dad, and I didn't expect to stay with him forever. But we took each other seriously, we cheered each other up when we were miserable and shared lots of good times, private jokes, funny, intimate moments that no one else would understand. If I had to get married for my parents, or community, or whatever, like some people have to, I often thought I'd have been quite happy to be married to Hugh. I missed talking to him most of all, that and the intimacy of waking up next to him.

"Penny for your thoughts," Anil broke the silence. I

laughed, a little embarrassed, and floundered desperately, trying to think of something to say.
"Nothing really."
"Come on, you were miles away," he protested, "Must have been something pretty serious."
"Just someone called Hugh that I used to go out with," I admitted.
"And what happened to him?"
"We split up when he left university and now he's in the States. It was fine with both of us, in the end."
"Do you miss him?"
"Sometimes." I hesitated, feeling a little cornered by his spotlight.

He seemed to sense this and sat back in the gloom. I peered at him curiously and saw the liquid gleam of his eyes, the shadow of stubble on his round jaw, his long fingers curled around his mug of coffee, the swirls of black hair along his forearms. I had to grip my own mug harder to restrain myself from reaching out and touching him, he was so real, so solid and three-dimensional.

"And what about your thoughts?" I challenged him, to distract myself from the strange unhinged feeling I had that I might float off somewhere at any moment.
"Me?" He shrugged his shoulders apologetically. "I was just wondering what you were thinking."
"That's such a cop out," I protested, indignant. "Come on. It's your turn."
"Okay," he looked at me solemnly, "I'll tell you what I was thinking, but you won't like it." My breath stopped for a moment in the briefest of silences that echoed like a bell across the room. "I was thinking how I want to kiss you." I sat quite still and there was his lovely gentle

brown face in front of me, and he didn't really belong to anybody and I certainly didn't belong to anybody, so why shouldn't we?

"Is that a good idea?" I clutched at some residual common sense.

"I've got something to be safe, if that's what you mean," he said carefully.

"Anil!" I laughed in astonishment, as much at my own misreading of him as at his presumption. "Do you make a habit of this?" He flushed and swore under his breath, looking down in to his mug.

"It's just responsible for us guys to be prepared, isn't it?" he muttered. "Look, I think I'd better go."

"No. Don't go," I reached my hands up to his shoulders and pulled him towards me until his lips touched mine. They were soft and full and I opened my own to meet them and drew in his hot coffee-clouded breath. He moved one broad hand to rest warmly around the back of my neck and pushed his fingers through the short frizz of my hair as he pulled me closer. I closed my eyes to blank out the cluttered kitchen, and it crossed my mind that I still knew almost nothing about him.

"Is this okay?" he said in a low voice into my ear.

"I've no idea, but who cares?" I whispered hoarsely and we giggled slightly hysterically. I wanted to feel his warm hand cradling the back of my neck again and feel the melting inside when his lips touched my skin. "Come on," I said. I took his hand and he followed me across the living room into the bedroom next door. We undressed quickly, shivering in the unheated air and snuggled under the covers warming each other's smooth, strange skin, exploring each other's unfamiliar curves and angles and sensitivities to make love in the

161

watery yellow street light that seeped through the gaps in my thin half-drawn curtains.

Later I woke to the bright moon I had seen earlier shining into my eyes and found Anil curled towards me, his head resting on my shoulder, a heavy arm flung across my belly. I wanted to stroke his tousled hair, but I didn't want to wake him and destroy the safety of the moment. Lying there in the empty colourless pre-dawn, absolved by the moon, if I could just stop time, maybe if I stayed perfectly still I could delay tomorrow for a hundred years, like in the fairy tale.

The next time I woke, the room was flooded with harsh daylight and Anil was lying on his back with one arm supporting his head, looking at me across the pillow.

"Hi," he smiled sheepishly.

"How long have you been awake?" I yawned pulling the covers up over my shoulders and feeling suddenly very naked.

"Not long," he replied vaguely. He slid down under the covers and turned onto his side facing me. We looked at each other gravely.

"Hello you," he whispered again. Here he was, the boy who had let me into Veena's house for dinner that first day, who I had thought of as gangly and adolescent, lying beside me in my bed after a night of delicious passion. That'll teach me to call someone young.

"Hello yourself," I smiled weakly. "Now what?"

"I don't know," he sighed and turned onto his back again closing his eyes. I felt suddenly angry. He'd better not be regretting it. He'd better not say it was my fault when it was him who came round here banging on my door. I thought of Veena, and Eleanor, and my heart sank. Bad timing or what? I closed my eyes too.

"Hug me," Anil's voice was suddenly by my ear and his arms around me. I buried my face in the hollow of his neck and we lay there for a while hugging each other against the cool grey dawn. "I'll have to get up," he said at length. "I've got to go home and get changed. I've got an appointment with the bank and I'm supposed to be collecting that pass off Elliott for the weekend."

He had a shower while I made some tea and toast for both of us and carried it back to my bed on a tray. I dropped my pink towelling dressing gown by the bed and crawled back in between the cold abandoned sheets. Anil re-appeared wrapped in my biggest bath towel, glowing and clean-shaven, rubbing his hair vigorously with a smaller towel he had retrieved from the depths of the airing cupboard.

"Are you all right?" he asked, as he sat down on the bed beside me, searching my expression for clues to my mood. I studied his smooth cheeks mottled with small brown moles and pockmarks and his warm laughing eyes and smiled in spite of myself.

"Not bad, considering I was kept up half the night, when I was already knackered. What about you?"

"Great," he breathed out loudly, stretching his arms and revealing tussocks of dark fur under his arms. I remembered their musky smell in the night. "It was fun. Right?" He screwed his eyes up anxiously as he said this, as if anticipating a problem.

"It was lovely and it was just one night," I assured him. "We weren't asking for anything more, were we?"

"Nope." His reply was firm, but there was a hesitation in his eyes. I pretended not to notice and he began rummaging in the heap of discarded clothes on the floor. I watched him pull his jeans over slim legs and taut, hairy thighs. I looked at his shoulder blades poking through the dark maroon T-shirt and two faint tapering points of black hair reaching down the back of his neck from the cropped line around his head. Is this what I did it for? I thought, so I can lie here looking proprietorially at the back of his neck? Is this how Veena feels when she looks at him? I shivered at the thought.

After demolishing the toast and gulping down his tea, he leaned over and kissed me almost shyly. Fully dressed, he seemed more definitely Veena's son again and I felt vulnerable in my nakedness under the bedclothes.

"I'll be off then," he announced. "I suppose I'll see you soon. Are you doing anything after work?" He bent down to retie his shoelaces. In the silence I tried to work out what was going on.

"I need to spend time with the anti-vivisection group at the moment, planning the action. But I'll give you a ring when it's all over and maybe we could go out for that drink you offered me last night."

"That'll be good." He stood up. "Bye then." He flashed me a brief smile as he turned, but avoided my eyes and I thought I saw something else on his face, but I couldn't be sure.

I lay still listening for the creak and slam of the outside door, and Anil's footsteps thudding down the concrete staircase. The house was deafeningly quiet after he had gone. I turned my head into the pillows and smelt him. I felt drained and slightly queasy, as though I had been awake for days, although I must have been asleep for quite a few hours. I dared not glance at the clock, it was too solid and real. I reached over and turned its face to the wall without looking at it. I needed time to think.

Last night seemed unconnected to anything else and yet everything was different now, my bed was different, my room was different, even my old scratched tea tray with its Parisian street scene and traces of rust in the corners looked different to me now. The room suddenly seemed to be smothering me. I dragged myself out of bed and across to the bathroom to run a bath.

I poured foaming bath oil into the searing steaming water and sank gratefully into clouds of jasmine-scented bubbles. This felt like my last refuge. I couldn't even trust my bedroom any more, it was filled with confusion and ambivalence just like everywhere else. Lying in the lapping, soothing heat, I resolved to be honest with myself. I splashed little waves of water up over my breasts. Ritual cleansing, I thought, ironically. But surely I hadn't done anything wrong? It didn't feel wrong. So why did this eerie stillness feel like the lull before the storm? My arms lying either side of my body were a darker sunburnt brown against the pale caramel skin of my belly. I was so used to seeing myself, I realised I didn't really see at all. I wondered what Anil saw, what Eleanor saw. I remembered a day once when hordes of sixth formers descended upon the geography department for a university taster day. Someone was giving them a tour of the faculty and had roped us in to demonstrate the lives of 'real' students. We got into groups with them in the main lecture hall and tried to answer their questions about what it was like being a student. There was this one Asian girl in a whole class of white kids. She asked something mundane about joining societies and stuff, but she looked at me when she asked the question. When I think back to school I remember feeling so cool and together and sure of myself, but when I saw her on her own looking vulnerable and alone, it was like seeing myself for the first time and I thought Christ, is this how everyone else sees me? I thought about her for weeks. I wanted to know what she did in the end, but I didn't even know her name or what school she was from. It was unnerving to be so haunted by a complete stranger. Remembering this, I felt like I couldn't trust my picture of myself, it wasn't telling me the truth any more. What had happened the night before didn't feel wrong, but I just knew it was going to cause so many problems.

I stretched my head right back to wet my hair, arching my back and splashing water over the top of my head. I poured a little pool of green shampoo from the bottle into my curved palm and smoothed it over my head, rubbing its coolness into my wet hair and warm scalp. Through the rubbing, scratching sounds on my head I heard my phone ringing somewhere in the next room. It soon stopped and I wondered if it was Anil or Eleanor. I tried to tell myself that it was no use worrying about last night. Anil and I were free agents, so why should anyone else care? But what about Eleanor? And what about Veena? I sank down into the water again and put my head back so that the milky white lather flooded into the clear water and floated down the bath in bobbing rafts. Out of the water my hair stuck close and flat to my head like beaver fur, under the water it fanned out like the hairy tentacles of a sea anemone. The short strands were soft and fine as silk running over my fingertips. Any way you looked at it I wasn't thinking about Veena's feelings - else why would I have invited Anil to stay? I would have sent him home in a taxi, or made sure he didn't miss the last bus. I realised I had known it was going to happen when we were eating dinner, even maybe when I was walking back from the off-licence. Had I known even before then, long before then? I thought of previous encounters with Anil, that first awkward skirting around each other in the hallway at Veena's, the instinctive conspiracies to outwit his father across the dinner table. Even then there had been something, the something that Eleanor had picked up on immediately. But these little flirtations happen all the time, they happen sometimes with customers in the cafe, who persist in coming back and waiting to be served by me. It doesn't have to lead to anything. Last night was just our separate upsets colliding, and the beer, and neither of us wanting to be alone, and, yes, we do click, we work well together. I like him.

I hauled myself out of the bath, wrapped a towel around myself and walked over to the cabinet on the wall. In the mirror I saw my eyes were startled, guilty, challenging. Approving my face, I found it stark and shadowy in the grey light, the dark-lashed eyes wide and liquidly attractive, the curve of my mouth strong and serious. It was the face of someone who might be fun to know, someone friendly and interesting, a brown face, exotic, some people might think. What did Eleanor think? Or Hugh? Had he known me? I certainly knew him. He was solid, I trusted that he had chosen me for myself and I still knew I could turn to his friendship if I needed to. A wild impulse flashed through my mind to get on the Internet that morning and search for a plane ticket to Philadelphia. But how could he help me know if I could trust Eleanor or Anil? I turned away from the mirror exhausted and disoriented, suspecting that maybe there was no one I really trusted at that moment, not my parents, not the woman who had given birth to me and let me go, and certainly not myself.

When I checked my mobile it was Anil's voice on the voicemail, hesitant and indistinct, as though he was not quite sure he had dialled the right number.

"Shelley? I was hoping to catch you before you go to work. Could you call me back on my mobile when you get this message?" As I listened, his parting glance at me, unsure, hurt maybe, swam before my eyes.

I called back, feeling a lurch of nerves in my stomach as I heard the ringing tone interrupted down the line.

"Hi, Shelley? How are you?" He answered in a voice different from before, a voice that seemed to say: I know you, I know all about you. I reeled at the breathy proximity of it in my ear.

"Is something the matter?" I ignored his question.

"I'm going round and round in circles about last night," he admitted. "I think we need to talk. Can you come out for a drink tonight?"

"I don't know," I hesitated. "Anyway, don't you need to meet your friend about the plans? We're counting on you for Monday." We weren't really supposed to talk about the action on the phone in case anyone's land line was tapped, but I tended to think that was more Ritchie's overinflated sense of his own importance than a genuine risk to the action.

"Don't worry about all that, I'm onto it. I can fit in everything I need to. This is more important."

"Is it?" I murmured. I found it hard to gauge what he was thinking. I could hardly even visualise his face, only the creases on his forehead and the serious, caressing gaze of his eyes as I remembered them watching me in the kitchen. Maybe he's right, I thought, we can't sort this out properly in a rushed telephone call where meanings become hidden and garbled. But to arrange another meeting felt like committing myself further, and made it harder to ignore. "You're not going to tell Veena, are you?"

"Of course not," he replied roughly. "Things are bad enough at home already." He paused and his voice softened. "Anyway, never mind about them. What about you?"

"I don't know," I felt trapped and wary of his concern. "I don't want to hurt Veena and I'm worried it's going to come out."

"I know," Anil sounded gloomy, "I'm not very good at keeping things from Mum, she always knows when I'm hiding something."

"You can't tell her," I protested in alarm.

"But it's going to be very difficult pretending nothing's happened. And I still want to see you, Shelley." His voice lowered to a hoarse whisper and a memory of his strong, confident fingertips in my hair flickered in my belly.

"We can't," I drew back from the telephone for a moment, appalled. "We absolutely can't. We need to forget it happened. I mean, we don't even really know each other."

"I think we know a little. I know it felt really great being with you last night," Anil urged in a low voice.

"This isn't helping at all," I sighed. "I think I need some time on my own to think. Can we just leave it till after the weekend?"

"After which time I will no longer be of any practical use to you." His voice was subdued and hurt.

"Now you're being silly." I countered defensively, feeling

the truth in his comment.

"Sorry," he muttered. "Ring me when you feel like talking, then. I hope Monday goes well."

"Thanks. Bye." I put the phone down. I was shivering. Probably not wearing enough warm clothes after my bath, I told myself sensibly, and wandered into the kitchen to make a drink. I felt sluggish and exhausted and a small needling pain had begun to press on my forehead just above my eyes. The uncleared tray I had brought in from the bedroom sat on the counter reminding me of our breakfast.

I really wanted to ring Hugh and tell him what an idiot I'd been. I wanted to set it all out before him and ask him to cast his wry gaze over the lot and pronounce on my fate. He was the only person I could think of who knew me well enough to believe this was something I could do. But I also remembered that we didn't work very well on the phone, apart from brief functional texts and rare stilted conversations from our parents' hallways in the holidays, it wasn't part of our student life together. Funny how I still needed to tell him significant things. I wasn't sure anyone else would understand the inevitability of what had happened. Or maybe it was that no one else would offer the kind of stoic acceptance that he always offered me. Hugh will always know me, I thought, with sudden clarity. He may swear allegiance to the Stars and Stripes every day of his life and become a raging fascist, but he will always understand me and will always see me as myself.

I decided to phone in sick. I couldn't work with this headache. I couldn't face the complicated atmosphere with Eleanor, and I needed to write a letter to Hugh.

13   Parcel

I feel a little foolish standing at the top of the iron stairs outside Shelley's door in a fine drizzle holding aloft my silver-lined pink umbrella: Connaught Place's most expensive, bought fifteen years ago on our last trip to Delhi. I can see that Shelley is surprised to see me and I immediately regret not ringing her first.

"Hey, Veena, hello? - what are you doing here?" she stumbles. "I mean - come in, you're getting wet." She looks tired and a little dishevelled. Even in the torn jeans and slogan-daubed T-shirts that are the unflattering style of her generation, she usually glows and sparkles. But today her dark-ringed eyes are blank and wary above pale sallow cheeks and she is wrapped in a large misshapen black cardigan as if she is feeling the cold. She is clearly coming down with something, I conclude, as I step into the room beyond the inner door.

"I only came to drop this parcel off for you from Anil," I struggle to extract the small padded brown envelope from my bag while my collapsed umbrella drips water on the carpet. "He didn't know when he was going to see you, so I said I'd drop it into the cafe for you. When I went there Eleanor told me you were ill and suggested I bring it round."

"Oh, thanks. Do you want a cup of tea? You can go through and sit down." She motions me past a small kitchen area and breakfast bar into a larger open space and relieves me of the parcel and my dripping umbrella. The flat is a little dark and the carpet and furnishings look well-worn, if not a little shabby, though I would never say so. The crowded shelves of herbs and spices, and the hanging clumps of garlic, give the kitchen area a rustic quality which reminds me of the cafe. I settle myself on the low sagging settee draped in a woven tapestry cover that I suspect has not been washed for some years, if ever.

"It's lovely in here, Shelley. So homely." Shelley flashes me a brief wan smile and I know she sees through my effort to be positive. She offers me camomile tea and I am reminded of our first encounter in the cafe.

"Why don't you let me make it?" I remonstrate, "You really don't look well." "Oh it's just a headache. I can't seem to shake it off. I'll be fine." She forces a smile and reaches for the kettle, ignoring my offer. I notice she has left the parcel unopened on the corner of the breakfast bar as though she already knows what is in it and is saving it for later.

"Eleanor asked me to tell you the cafe's fine." I raise my voice above the rising hiss of the kettle, watching her face carefully. "She's got a student helping her who started this morning. Seems a nice boy."

"She must be rushed off her feet." Shelley comments, concentrating hard on pouring water from the kettle.

"Actually, it was really quiet. I stayed for a bit and had a cup of tea with Eleanor." I picture the high-ceilinged room again, empty apart from two young women with a baby in a large complicated pram that seemed to need a table of its own. "We missed you, though."

It was strange being in there without her. Everything seemed to speak of her, the clatter of dishes from the kitchen, the jaunty tilt of the bold chalk script on the blackboard behind the counter, the strum and clap and breathy piping of Bolivian music playing gently from speakers mounted in the corners of the room, and the

172

cows most of all, kicking joyfully on the wall. Eleanor offered to join me when she had finished clearing tables. 'Please do," I replied, glad of the offer of company. She pushed a new disc into the music system and began to whip around the tables piling cups and plates on her tray and making quick energetic circles across the surfaces with her dishcloth, her lips pursed in a grim frown. I knew they were having problems keeping the place open and I felt sorry that what had started off for Eleanor with such vision and idealism had become so stressful and difficult. The joyfulness of the cows on the wall should be reflected in the faces of the staff, I thought. Maybe it isn't possible to create an oasis in the grey desert that surrounds us here? It struck me that this was the trouble with Awaaz. I felt so hemmed in by a jungle of bureaucratic demands and structures, funding bodies and agendas and committees, it wasn't the kind of centre I wanted for myself, never mind any other woman. I just couldn't see how to get past all that stuff. I felt the key lay here, with the cows, in the blue sky and green fields all over the walls, the warmth and good food. Even when it is cold and wet, there's a lightness and freshness in here like summer mornings, especially when Shelley's in. You can come and just sit and feel better. That's what we need in Awaaz, space to just sit and be. We need to be less of a conveyer-belt, meeting targets, solving problems, performing to other people's agendas. It should be more easy-going and homely; so you can just come and sit and chat or read or have a cup of tea without having to justify it with a form to fill in, a skill to learn, some information to find. I remember Shelley stopping to talk to me in the middle of her work the day we met, putting down her dishcloth, sitting on a chair. That's what I want in Awaaz. How can I explain this to Farah and Shahnaz? If I can only find the right language, give it an intellectual ring somehow with aims and objectives and an identifiable outcome…

"Hi." Eleanor appeared beside me, startling me out of my reverie. "Admiring our cows?"

"Yes, I was actually. I was thinking you've got something really special here. I hope you manage to keep it going." I explained as she sat down opposite me with a large mug of black coffee.

"Shelley's told you about the problems then? I don't see how we can keep it going when Matt pulls out. But something might turn up. You finished work for today?" She looked at me curiously. "Only you've been here a while."

"Yes, I just needed to drop this letter off to Shelley. Actually, I couldn't concentrate at work anyway," I admitted. "I've got a lot on my mind."

"Don't suppose I can help at all?"

"It's personal," I hesitated. "I'm a bit upset with my son and my husband. I'd really like to knock their heads together, the pair of them."

"Men are such selfish bastards," she said vehemently. "I'm sorry, I'm just a bit biased at the moment."

"You're so right." I felt a fierce pleasure at her anger and wanted to collect some of that anger for myself.

""You don't have to put up with it, you know," she eyed me mischievously. "Life's too short to waste on people who don't appreciate you."

I could see she was talking about herself but I found it comforting and strangely energising to suddenly be in company where there is no shame in admitting your relationship isn't working.

174

"It's not like that for me," I tried to explain. "You're right, I'm not appreciated, by any of them. But that's where my life is, I can't change that after twenty-four years."

"Personally, I think we can do anything we want at any stage of our lives if we want it enough." Her confidence had an edge of desperately trying to convince herself.

"So easy," I laughed. "But the real world is about commitments made for life."

"It's about habit, and you can always break a habit, even if it's hard to do." She looked across to the counter as more people streamed through the door and her new student glanced anxiously across the room at her. 'I'll have to go, but come round any time you need a chat, even if Shelley's not here. Or ring me. I mean it," she said, rising from her seat. "Any time." Then she hurried across the room to the young man's side. I hardly knew her, but I felt so cared for when I stepped out into the wet street.

"I was looking for you at the cafe because I wanted to talk to you about my own problems. But if you're not feeling up to it… "

"No, it's fine," Shelley's face relaxes into a smile as she comes to sit down beside me, placing two mugs of tea on the battered coffee table and drawing the armchair forward for herself. "So, what's the problem? Is Farah giving you more grief?"

"No, it's Anil." I see something like fear flash across her face. " - It's all right. He's told me all about the job, and Bev, so you don't have to keep any secrets. I did wonder how long you've known though?" I try not to show how much hangs for me on the answer to this question. "He only told me yesterday." She picks small burrs off her cardigan sleeve without looking at me and I find myself not believing her.

"I'm surprised. You've been seeing so much of each other lately." I can hardly believe he would not have told Shelley weeks ago.

"It's the truth," she shrugs her shoulders helplessly. "I was pretty surprised too, to be honest. He never said anything about working in this hostel before." She pauses. "Who's Bev?"

"He hasn't mentioned her?" I wonder again if I should have come. She shakes her head and waits for me to explain. I try to make it sound low key, innocuous, and wonder why I am playing it down. "She's someone who worked at the hostel. They went out together for a while. Didn't he tell you?"

"No. We talked about other stuff." She flushes and looks away quickly. There is something wrong, I felt it the moment she opened the door to me and that look of panic flashed across her face.

"What's the matter, Shelley?"

"Nothing. I just - look, I'm not such a great person to be around at the moment. I'm not feeling very proud of myself." She hesitates and I think she is going to say more, but instead she picks up her mug and begins sipping her drink slowly. "Did you hear there was another attack on Tasleem's house?" she throws in casually.

"Poor Tasleem," I am distracted for a moment from my focus on Anil. "She was so grateful that you and Eleanor came out to help her, she told me all about it. In fact she told me you might be moving in with her, which I was a bit surprised at because you seem so settled here."

"It's not that definite." She sounds irritated. "Everything's a bit up in the air at the moment with Eleanor and Matt splitting up, and the cafe not sorted. I don't know what I'm doing about anything." I am aware of her watching me, maybe trying to weigh up whether she can confide in me or not.

"I don't know what to do about Anil," I decide to offer her my confusion, in the hope that she will feel less defensive about her own difficulties. "If we were in India I suppose I would just put my foot down. It would just be totally out of the question for him to give up his studies. I'd have all the aunts and uncles and grandparents and even the servants telling me how he would be ruining his future. But then they said all that about me giving up my masters to come here with Ramesh and here I am with a good job and twenty-four years of married life behind me." I notice a flicker pass across Shelley's face as I say this and guess that she probably doesn't agree with marriage as an institution. "I've always told Anil and Pooja to do what's right for them. Be true to yourself, I said. But he's such a boy still, and he's had a difficult experience with this Bev. I'm worried he's not mature and experienced enough to know his own mind." "Were you when you married Ramesh?" I love the way she cuts through what Pooja so inelegantly calls, "the crap". "I was a very independent person when I chose to marry Ramesh. I'd lived away from home for years, at boarding school and then university. And Ramesh was different then, he was quite militant and daring," I smile affectionately, lost for a moment in the memory. "It was a long time ago."

"Well, I think Anil's more of a different person now than you realise - than I realised," she adds, thoughtfully.

I want to be as generous as her about my own dear son, but I am still smarting from his manipulation of my feelings and the cut of his financial agenda. I feel mean-spirited and churlish, but I cannot give him the credit she suggests. I will not be used, not even by my own child. But I must try to be cheerful with Shelley, who is clearly struggling with her own demons. "I am trying to support Anil. But it's a bit difficult when he chose not to tell us until he'd done it. You know how worried I've been these last few weeks, knowing something was going on and imagining all kinds of possibilities. I even thought at one point he might be gay." "Even?" she narrows her eyes suspiciously. "Like that would be the biggest disaster? Right?" "Well, no," I qualify carefully. "But it would be a lot to get used to, and it would affect all of us in so many different ways."

"Did you ever think I might be gay?" I cannot read her face at all as she says this and feel I am being tested without knowing the real question. I don't like this feeling of being played with, and I can only offer the truth, even if I am walking into a trap. "It did cross my mind when I first met you, your spiky hair, and your clothes, and there didn't seem to be any men around in your life. But then you told me about that boy in America, and you got friendly with Anil, and I decided I'd got it wrong - " "Lesbians can have male friends," she interrupts, and I am reminded of Pooja's barrister-style interjections.

"Yes, Shelley, I know," I snap. I had no idea I was so angry. "And if you give me enough rope I'll probably hang myself. What's your point?" She stares at me in shocked silence and colour slowly rises through her face. She covers her mouth with a hand as if she might cry and a choked whisper emerges from between her fingers.

"Sorry." "No, no," I cry in dismay, horrified at my outburst. "I'm sorry. I don't know what's the matter with me today. I'm so angry with Anil, I shouldn't be taking it out on you."

"Yes, you should." Her quiet insistent voice slices through my erupting apologies. "You should."

"What do you mean?"

"Anil was here last night," she continues in a strained monotone, and I feel my guts clenching as I realise what will follow. "We slept together."

"Oh. I see." I study the faded rag rug on the hearth, as my outwardly still body seems to reel backwards into the cushions behind me, struggling to find a purchase on this sliding sand. Neither of us says anything for a while. "I know it's really messy," she breaks the silence. "He came round because he'd had a row with his dad and he was in a state. It started off we were just talking about stuff. Then we got a takeaway and had some beer, and I suppose I was in a state too, about an anti-vivisection meeting. He was so nice and sort of... there." "Is that it? He was 'there'?" I can't help myself. I know nobody waits till they're married now. Not even Ramesh and I waited till we were married. But I am appalled that she can be so casual about it. Yet I can also hear how it happened and imagine the two of them slipping into it in quite a lazy why-ever-not? kind of a way late at night in the warm safe cocoon of this flat with the gas fire purring, dimmed lighting, soft music playing. I remember how it felt to 'surrender to the moment' and I am almost jealous. But then I remind myself that at least I knew I was going to marry the person I was surrendering to.

"I know it sounds totally irresponsible." She seems to read my thoughts. "I can't really explain - " "Please try," I encourage her. "I'm just struggling a bit to understand all this. First you seem to be wondering whether you're a lesbian, and then you tell me you've slept with my son. I don't know what to say, Shelley. Maybe I'm old-fashioned, but I think it's always dangerous for an attractive girl like yourself to be on your own in a house with a man you're not related to." She lets out a snort of irritation, but I persist with my point. "You must have known there was something between you and Anil before last night, I saw it the first time you came to dinner. But tell me if I'm wrong." I am trying to stay calm and centred in this unexpected maelstrom. That'll teach you, Veena Kumar, to go calling on people unannounced, a little voice in my head reproaches triumphantly. "No, you're not wrong," she admits, suddenly caving in, her shoulders sagging miserably. "It's a complete mess and you probably hate me." I suppress a smile at this. So like Pooja.

"You didn't do it by yourself," I point out. "I'd like to know what my son thinks he's playing at. And then sending me on errands to deliver parcels between you. What does he think I am?" I am aware of how hostile I sound, but I am suddenly tired of picking up Anil's pieces.

"The parcel's nothing to do with last night," Shelley insists quickly, "It's for my anti-vivisection campaign, honestly." She hesitates. "There is something else." Not more, I think, but say nothing, bracing myself for the next lurid confession. "You know that night Anil brought me to yours for dinner? And later on I went out to Tasleem's when her house was attacked? Well, I asked the police if they could contact Ramesh, because he wasn't at dinner, was he? And you'd said he was working. They radioed in to find out if he was on the duty solicitor list and he wasn't." I continue to wait, wondering how Ramesh could possibly be associated with this muddle. "He wasn't on the list," she repeats. "No one in the police station had ever heard of a duty solicitor called Ramesh Kumar." "But maybe it was the wrong police station?" I suggest, beginning to see what she is saying. "I don't think so. The list must be for the whole city, and they'd remember an Asian solicitor, wouldn't they? There can't be many." "So what are you saying? You think he's been lying?"

She nods and I find myself shaking my head and laughing. "No, no, Shelley, I think you're getting carried away with all your own complications. There'll be a perfectly simple explanation. I'll ask him about it if you like, but there's nothing sinister going on. We're old married people, you know, our lives aren't like yours, even if we might sometimes wish they were." "I'm sure you're right." She looks unconvinced. "Maybe I was confused. But it turned out we didn't need a solicitor anyway." There is a brief silence in which she studies her slippered feet and I sit very still allowing the ripples of everything she has said to wash outwards across my world rocking my moorings dangerously. Her revelations cling stickily to my skin like trailing cobwebs that won't brush away. I didn't ask for this, did I? I don't want to be part of this murky world I'm being sucked down into. And I feel I have come last in a race somewhere behind Anil and Tasleem and Eleanor, and even the boy in America. She looks up at me nervously, like a young child wanting to know if she is in trouble or not.

"I must be a real disappointment to you," she suggests.

"Shelley, I'm not disappointed, just confused." I refuse to be drawn into judging her. I can feel myself backing out of the door.

"Well that makes two of us," she says, "Because I haven't a clue."

"I just think you don't know who you are yet," I offer this seriously, hooked in for a moment in spite of myself.

"Oh, please. Not that roots stuff again," she flares contemptuously. I feel something snap inside me. I am so, so angry now. I stand up. "I don't know if I can help you with this, Shelley. I'm really not the right person to be talking to. I said to Pooja I wouldn't be too late today, she wants help with her revision, so I'd better go." "Oh, must you?," she sounds a little desperate as she rises to follow me to the door. "I feel like we haven't finished talking yet." "I'll ring you soon." I put my arms around her shoulders and give her a gentle hug. "It'll be all right." She clings to me for a moment and my body resonates with memories of cuddling Anil and Pooja, tucking them up in their beds with hot water bottles in knitted covers and reading them stories till their eyelids drooped and their heads fell heavily on their pillows. When I let go of her I notice tears in the corners of her eyes and I turn away firmly, surprised at the resolution within me.

"The train now standing at Platform 5 is the 16.05 to Bristol Temple Meads calling at Chesterfield, Derby, Birmingham New Street, Tamworth and Cheltenham, and arriving Bristol Temple Meads at 20.28."

My train. I sipped steaming black coffee from a cardboard cup, the bitterness burning my throat as it slipped down into my gut. My feet remained planted on the scuffed vinyl floor beneath the table. My mind quietly seized up, frozen, its needle stuck on the same circuit. I couldn't move. I really needed to get away, but now the moment had arrived, I couldn't quite understand how I had got there.

When Veena had closed the door behind her the day before, I hadn't been able to hold back my tears. I stood by the breakfast bar and put my hands to my face, pressing my fingertips against the bridge of my nose to stop the flood, but my face slowly screwed up with pain underneath my spread palms until great tearing sobs burst out of me and I had to grope on the counter for tissues to wipe my cheeks and blow my streaming nose. It was all such a horrible, unbearable mess and I had no one left to talk to. My hand, reaching for more tissues, brushed the brown packet Veena had brought from Anil. I tore it open and found the building plans and student pass I had been waiting for and a scribbled note from Anil: Dear Shelley, Here's the stuff you need. When it's all over, just bin the pass and my mate will report it lost. Thinking of you all the time. Love Anil xx. Something lurched inside me and I backed away from the counter in a panic.

"I've got to get out of this," I said, wincing at the loudness of my own voice. "I can't stay here." From that, everything else flowed. The sleepless night trying to work out an escape in my head, the garbled phone message left on Mum and Dad's answering machine this morning, the sagging rucksack stuffed with clothes snatched randomly out of gaping drawers, the struggle to lift Sky up fifteen steps to leave her safely inside the door of the flat, and my mouth going dry as I heard Ritchie's chirpy tone on the other end of the line. He was always brighter when we were about to do an action. He just loved the buzz of it all.

"Hi Shelley. What's cooking?"

"Nothing, I'm afraid. Look, I can't do the action, I'm going away."

"What?" His voice lifted in a slightly hysterical squeak. "What's happened?"

"It's a long story, but I just - I can't come, that's all."

"But can't it wait a few days? I mean, come on Shelley, we've been planning this for months. We need everyone on board."

"I know it's really bad timing, but I can't do anything else, I'm sorry. I'll leave the stuff you need from Anil behind the till in the cafe. You can pick it up from Eleanor in the morning."

"Is it because of what Sam said about the halal meat? Because you know we've dropped that. It was a pretty crap idea anyway. We're going with Angela's petitioning thing."

"I heard. It's not that. It doesn't make any difference." I suddenly realised it was too late. I wasn't going back to the group. Ever.

Eleanor looked at my rucksack in dismay when I stopped at the cafe on my way to the station. As she pushed the packet for Ritchie into the crowded shelf under the counter, I could see her struggling to find a way of asking what was going on.

"You don't have to leave, Shelley. I thought we were going to talk things over," she said, lowering her voice and glancing across the room at the pale angular young man clearing tables.

"It's not you, honestly," I tried to reassure her. "I just need to go home. I'll be back after the Bank Holiday, I promise." She looked at me searchingly, but didn't ask me about the action.

"Look after yourself, then," she said, quietly. I nodded, feeling tears welling up in me again and she leaned across the counter and squeezed my arm. "It'll be all right. Just tell Ermyntrude to stop moulting while you're gone because I haven't got time to keep clearing up after her!" I laughed with relief, seeing the wry smile on her lips and hearing the old grumpiness in her voice. There still seemed a thread of connection left there and I was glad I hadn't succumbed to my impulses to tell Anil or Veena about her. Maybe some things are better left unsaid to kind of subside quietly into the dust. I didn't look at the cows as I hurried towards the door, feeling their forlorn, reproachful eyes following me across the room. I could feel them now, sitting in my corner of this chrome and plastic travesty of a cafe.

Long minutes passed and my hands were still locked around the corrugated paper cup. The digital clock on the wall flicked through 16.03 and 16.04, until it finally flipped over into 16.05 and it was too late. I didn't even look out of the window, but something was moving in the far corner of my field of vision and, above the prattling canned music, I could hear the rising whine of the beast sliding away from the platform, on its way without me.

Shit.

I stirred the soapy froth on my cappuccino and tried to think. Everything was just going round in my head, the seventies' disco tracks, the explosive blasts and hisses of the coffee machine, sudden shouts of passing voices on the platform, harsh echoing station announcements, and through all that, the memory of Anil in the dimly lit kitchen, Veena's words, "Didn't he tell you?" How am I going to sort this out?

I stopped stirring the coffee and from my jacket pocket I fished out a biro I had picked up earlier from the breakfast bar as I whirled out of the flat. Maybe I should try and map it out. I unfolded the thick paper napkin they had given me with the coffee and spread it out on the table. I wrote 'Me' and circled it in the middle of the page. I looked at it for a while wondering where to go next. Then I drew a line out from the circle, like the spoke of a bicycle wheel, and wrote 'Mum & Dad' in a circle at the other end. I wrote Rehana nearby and drew a dotted line connecting me to her. I wondered about drawing a connection between her and 'Mum & Dad', but I couldn't feel one. I was not even sure about having a broken line connecting her to me when we had never met. She was hardly a presence in my life, hardly even an absence because there was no one real to miss. Yet my hand had drawn a connection that I couldn't rub out and, even if I could, it seemed to be no business of my brain's to interfere with what my hand wanted to do. Wondering about Rehana, I added up the years in my head; my age, twenty-three; her age when I was born, fifteen. I wrote the number thirty-eight slowly in brackets next to her name. I stared at it in disbelief. She had always been fifteen to me in my head, a slight fragile figure with an incongruous bulging stomach and long curtains of black hair hiding her frightened, haunted eyes. 'Thirty-eight' changed everything, the curling rounded matronly shapes of the numbers conjured up a whole new picture of a plump woman in a sari, a bit like Veena but without the grey in her hair, cooking rice in a tiny kitchen in Bangladesh, or Tower Hamlets, surrounded by a family of laughing noisy children. Children she had kept. God, this was so weird. I realised now that I hadn't really been ready to listen to anything about her when I was eighteen. I remembered being shown a sort of family tree thing with Rehana's parents and grandparents, brothers and sisters on it, but I barely glanced at it. The adoption social worker had tried to get me to talk about it, but I wasn't interested. I couldn't get my head round their strange names and I wanted to say, 'I've already got grandparents and aunts and uncles, so why do I need another set? They don't know about me, so why do I have to know about them?' It was clear I had just been a guilty secret between Rehana and her mother, an unfortunate accident, like a rotten tooth, pulled out, binned and forgotten. I came away from that meeting determined to have even less need of them than they clearly had of me.

I picked up my pencil again and extended the broken line joining me to Rehana beyond her name to the outer edge of the napkin. At the far end of it I wrote 'my Bangladeshi family'. I let out a deep breath. So, there they were, out on a long tenuous limb, a nameless, undifferentiated blob, but on the page nevertheless, human beings somewhere on the planet who had a connection to me, even if they never knew it. And for the moment it was enough simply that they were on the page. At least they were on the page. What about my birth father? I didn't even know if he was on the page or not, if he was in their space or not. I couldn't even decide if it would be better to know, or to remain forever floating in the bubble of not knowing, not saying, no one ever saying. I felt trapped in the silence and lightness of that bubble floating above the Bangladeshi family space and I started to circle the space round and round, with the tip of the pen, trying to hang anchor myself in the circle somehow, but I was slipping away into a void and there was nothing to hold onto. My bubble was being sucked into a down draught. I clutched the table with a sudden jolt and the pen clattered to the floor. A man at a neighbouring table bent down and picked the pen up for me.

"There you go. You all right, love?" he peered at my face anxiously.

"Yes, thanks. I'm fine" I assured him and placed the pen carefully on the napkin. I felt a bit dizzy and spaced out, and I couldn't quite understand what had just happened. It was like a dream, but I hadn't been asleep. I looked down at the rough marks on the napkin. I had taken the pen out to try to place where I was with Veena and Anil, and here I was, stuck with Rehana in Bangladesh, or wherever the hell she was, and the mystery of my birth father.

Dimly, I was aware of the loudspeaker announcing that the train now leaving platform 3A was the 16.15 to Plymouth via a string of stations that I didn't bother registering. Too bad, I had to finish this now.

On the opposite side of the page from the line to 'Mum & Dad' I put a line connecting me to Eleanor and the Dancing Cows to represent the different direction I felt them pulling me in. I drew a faint arching dotted line around the outside of the diagram connecting Rehana to the Dancing Cows in recognition of the cow incident in Scotland that both set me off on my path to veganism and gave me my baseless, but passionate, conviction that Rehana did not let me go willingly. I added the anti-vivisection group as an offshoot of the cafe, but didn't write any names beside them. I realised there wasn't anyone I could say I actually cared about. Or trusted. I shuddered at the memory of the silence that fell in our last meeting in the cafe after Sam started the halal meat conversation. A year ago I would have put Carmen down as important to me, but something had changed and we seemed to have drifted apart.

Next to the cafe I wrote Veena's name and from her there emerged a whole spider's web of connections, to me, to the cafe, our first and favourite meeting place, to Rehana because of Veena's knowledge of Bengal. From her name I drew a kind of diamond with her, Ramesh, Anil and Pooja at the corners all connected to each other by a web of criss-crossing lines. When I'd done it I realise I hadn't done such a web for Mum, Dad and me, I'd just shown them as a single unit connected to me by a single line. It looked flimsy beside the strong kite shape of Veena's family with all its supporting struts. Why, I wondered, haven't my separate relationships with each of my parents come through? Brushing this question aside, I found a space to squeeze in Tasleem and Huma and drew a triangle linking Tasleem, Veena and myself. I wondered if I should have put the cafe as a background circle, rather than as a distinct point on the web, but I decided the cows would not have appreciated being mere background wash, they see themselves as central players in my life and needed to be accorded due prominence (have I totally flipped now, I wondered?). Finally, I sketched in Tiger and Sky in a corner near me.

"Is that finished with, love?" a waitress demanded, balancing a tray on the edge of my table, and she nodded at my cold, half-finished cappuccino.

"Oh yes," I smiled distractedly, and she whisked it away and beckoned to a grey-suited man, who was hovering by the till with a full tray. "Room for you here, love," she invited him, pulling out the chair opposite me. Give us a chance, I thought. But she didn't know I was a fellow waitress, so I tucked the defaced napkin and pen into my jacket pocket and hoisted my backpack awkwardly onto one shoulder. I couldn't abandon my precious pencilled grid now, I had to complete it here in this crowded echoing anonymous space that was itself the hub of a host of radiating tracks. Here I was released from all the various corners I had dug myself into and I could take a step back far enough to maybe get all of my life into one camera angle, one wide-angled shot would do it. I walked along the high bridge flung across the platforms to its furthest end, remembering that there was a cafe and waiting room on the last platform where no one would mind how long I stayed.

There I found myself a quiet table in a corner by the window and took out my diagram again. The large room was once again awash with piped music, but softer and more middle-aged. A handful of people were sitting around drinking coffee alone or in small huddles, talking in subdued voices. Some of them looked like they expected to be there a long time. I considered the sprawling spokes on the napkin in front of me. Placing myself in the middle I would have expected it to look like the spokes of a wheel with the different people and interests in my life radiating out from the centre, but actually it looked more like a mountain range with two sister peaks flanked by various spurs and saddles. A single, bold, dark ridge linked the two main peaks and it was the shortest line on the page. I had no idea that Veena would turn out to be my sister peak at the summit of this straggling range. I sat looking at it for a while and then realised I still hadn't put in a line connecting me to Anil. That was my first impetus for this little game with myself and yet it seemed almost an afterthought in the final product. Reluctantly I drew a connecting line between us that had to cut across Veena's connections with Pooja and Ramesh. I sat back to contemplate my handiwork.

Looking again I spotted a strong central parallelogram with Veena, Tasleem, Eleanor-and-the-Dancing Cows and myself at the four sharply angled corners. I was surprised to see Tasleem located so centrally, I hadn't thought of her as a significant person in my life and the idea of being her lodger seemed more of a logistical solution for both of us than a measure of the closeness of our friendship. But it was that simple practical need that she had of me, and that we had of each other, that seemed like a refuge to me now. With everyone else there was 'stuff' to deal with, Mum and Dad, Veena, Eleanor, Anil, they all wanted me to talk to them about my feelings, work through my issues with them. The only person who wasn't hassling me was Tasleem. She just needed me for who I was right then in that moment, not who I might be when I'd worked it all out.

Glancing up at the overhead monitor as I emerged from the coffee bar, I noticed that there was another Birmingham train leaving in half an hour. Maybe it was possible after all to get a connection to Reading in time. But I wouldn't be going just yet. There was something else I needed to do first. A wall-mounted telephone booth stood opposite me. As I moved towards it my heart began to thump and a wave of nausea began to rise in my chest.

I dumped the backpack on the floor beneath the phone and emptied all the change from my purse onto the small ledge. In my diary I found the number I hadn't used for five years, but had religiously transferred from one diary to the next each year. As I pushed coins into the machine my hands were shaking and twice I dropped a coin onto the floor and had to scrabble in the dirt and dust to retrieve it. The ringing tone jarred through my body as the call connected and I had to force myself not to slam down the receiver when someone picked up at the end of the line.

"Ealing Family Placement. Can I help you?" A woman's voice, brisk, inattentive, I could see her examining her nails as she spoke, wondering if she has a file in her bag to smooth off that little nick before it started to catch on her clothes.

"Can I speak to Mary Savage?"

"I'm afraid she doesn't work here any more."

"Oh." I was crushed.

"What is it you want?" I could hear her thinking, I haven't got all day, you know.

"I don't know." I paused. I did know. "I want to trace my birth mother." The words I thought I would never say flew down the wire into the earth, spanned the two hundred miles to London in less than a second, whipped out of my mouth into a whirlpool of terrifying consequences.

"Okay," she said as if she'd heard it a thousand times before. "I'll put you through to Post Adoption. Hold the line." There was a click and a kind of humming silence. I could still put the phone down and no one would know. Five years ago when they asked me if I wanted to trace her I said I wasn't interested. I said I had two parents who loved me and that was enough for anyone; I didn't need to find a stranger who dumped me before giving me my first feed. I didn't need it then, and maybe I didn't need this right now. My hand twitched to replace the receiver just as a low voice buzzed in my ear.

"Hello?" When I said nothing, he continued. His voice was calm and measured and something about its gentle tone brought a great choking lump into my throat. "Hi. My name is Elton. I imagine maybe it's been hard for you to make this call. Would you like to start by telling me your name?"

"Shelley." I whispered, and the instruction board in front of me blurred in a sea of tears.

"Okay, Shelley. I know this is hard, but I'm here to help you work out what's best for you. You can take your time. I'm not going to make you do anything you don't want to, this is about your life." It was as if he'd been listening in to my mind for the last week, he was so spot on. I wanted to hug him.

When it was over, and Elton had all my details, I made a note of his direct line number, then put the receiver down. An avalanche of small coins clattered through the machine, most retained and some falling into the tray in the bottom corner. My change. I dug them out and looked at them for a while, puzzled. There was ten pence too much. Maybe the previous caller hadn't collected her change. I didn't know what to do. Someone coughed behind me wanting to use the phone. I closed my fist around the coins and walked slowly across the wide foyer, grazed by rushing bodies weaving frantic paths to platforms and taxis. I glanced up at the clock on the back wall of the bar to see that it was quarter to six. I didn't know what to do next. The threads of my life seemed to be slipping through my fingers with the passing hours. I wanted to tell someone about it all, but there wasn't anyone left to tell that I hadn't already upset. The information screen reminded me the train to Birmingham was still there.

"Come on, Shelley, get a grip," I muttered, glancing down at the defaced napkin I was still carrying around. My lines and scribbles looked suddenly pathetic. How could I have wasted two hours here doing that? I crushed the napkin hard in my hand and tossed it into the bin by the door as I headed towards Platform Five. As the bin lid swung shut a flash of regret sparked in my mind. I ignored it and hurried on.

I was standing in a crowd of bodies with heads all turned hopefully to the left, like a field of sunflowers, when my mobile phone rang. It was Tasleem and she sounded like she was crying. I stepped back from the platform edge to listen to her.

"Shelley, those boys are at the end of the road. I think they do something tonight - "

"Did you ring the police?" I interrupted.

"They came, but they say there is no crime, so now they gone. They can't help, but I think these boys will do something in the night. They are just standing and looking at my house. Can you come?"

"Actually, I'm just about to get on a train. I'm going to my parents' for the weekend."

"Oh dear. I'm sorry I disturb you." Her voice shrank.

"No worry. You coming to see us another time, then?"

"As soon as I get back on Wednesday. I'll give you a ring, I promise."

"Wednesday," she said, disheartened.

"I know, I'm sorry." I grimaced apologetically down the phone. "But Awaaz will be open on Tuesday; you could go and see Veena on Tuesday."

"When I go for English class today she's go home, Riffat says she is sick. Maybe she is still sick on Tuesday." I was shaken by this information. Veena had seemed fine when she called at my house the day before. I had never known her to be off sick.

"Maybe," I agreed. "I'm sorry, Tasleem, I've really got to go or I'll miss my train. I hope you'll be okay."

"I'm all right," she assured valiantly. "Have nice time with your parents. Goodbye."

"'Bye." I turned the phone off to preclude another interruption. Then the train from Newcastle was announced. Standing on the draughty platform watching the twin engine lights approaching, I could still hear Tasleem's mournful goodbye. She said the whole word, goodbye, slowly, with equal emphasis on each syllable, not swallowing the 'good'. There was something very resonant and final about the way she said it. I imagined her sitting on the long settee with the blue floral cover, Huma asleep beside her, her fat little

195

fingers curled into fists. I began to wish I hadn't been so rash with my little mountain range diagram. I would never be able to recreate it quite as it was on that crumpled scrap of paper lying no more than fifty yards from me in a tide of coffee dregs and sticky chocolate wrappers. As the train thundered towards us, something blew into my mind from earlier as I had sat staring at my drawing, something deep and irrational: guilt. Guilt at not having fought harder for Rehana. Guilt that I allowed myself to be given away as a baby. Yes, I was a helpless newborn, but, even so, I need not have become that sweet placid good-natured baby Mum and Dad told me about, I could have kept them up night after night, I could have screamed with colic. I should not have cooed and gurgled and given in so easily to the care of others. I resolved that this time I was going to hold on, even if I didn't know what I was holding on to. I was going to fight for Rehana, even if I never found her.

The train sighed to a halt and passengers poured out of each carriage door. I turned and joined the flood of arrivals streaming up the stairs towards the station exit. After spending all this time in the railway station I realised I needed to remain here, planted in this northern soil, to survive.

In the taxi to Tasleem's I rang Mum and Dad. They were disappointed, but offered to come and visit me on the Bank Holiday Monday instead.

"You're moving?" Mum repeated, uncomprehending.

"My friend, Tasleem, has invited me to move in with her." I explained patiently.

"Do you need any money?" she asked anxiously, "A deposit or anything?"

"Well actually, I wanted to ask you about the money

you've been saving for me -" This was not how I had intended it, but Eleanor and I needed to know what we were doing.

"Oh yes?" I could almost hear her brow furrowing suspiciously down the phone.

"Well, Eleanor and Matt are splitting up and Eleanor's looking for a new partner to buy Matt out and keep the cafe going. I was thinking maybe I could use some of my money to invest in the cafe and become a co-owner. Then at least I'd have a stake in the business."

"In going bankrupt, you mean." Disapproval oozed from each syllable.

"We're doing a business plan and we've got an accountant working with us now. I think you'll be impressed," I urged her, omitting to mention that Anil was unlikely ever to be qualified and that we hadn't actually started work on the business plan yet. There was a hiatus as she moved the phone away from her mouth and conferred with Dad. When she came back on the phone she said without expression,

"It's your money now, Shelley. You don't have to ask us." I felt floored. Were they angry? Disappointed? Was this her idea or his? It was so unlike them to just give up without a full-scale debate.

"Let's talk about it when you come over," I volunteered. "I'll ring you when I know what I'm doing."

We exchanged hasty goodbyes as the taxi drew up outside Tasleem's house. As I fished for my purse in my cluttered pockets, my unused rail tickets fell out onto the floor of the taxi. I didn't have the energy to retrieve them, too late to reclaim the fare anyway. I noticed on the taxi's digital clock that it was six forty-five. I must have been in the station for nearly three hours.

The staccato bleep of the phone rings impatiently through the house and Ramesh rushes to answer it. He leaves the door slightly ajar as he hurries out of the room and I can hear him talking in the hall. Normally I would return immediately to concentrate on the programme we're watching, but today I cannot erase the question mark Shelley has pencilled in my mind. I find myself listening to the low abbreviated responses he is murmuring into the mouthpiece.

"Hi. Okay.... mmm... Yes... Yes, I'm coming… about half an hour?... and me." He puts the receiver down and pops his head round the door. "I've got to go out. Might be a long one, so don't wait up for me."

"What is it?" I ask lightly, not moving my eyes from the television screen.

"The usual - duty solicitor stuff - you know. They haven't got anyone else. Is there a problem?" The surprise in his voice betrays how rarely I ask him anything about his work.

"No, no," I reassure, looking round. "Take care. Namaskar."

He disappears and I remain in my chair staring at the television without seeing or hearing it, the soft murmured tone of those last words, "... and me... " echoing in my ears. Why say, "and me," to a police officer or a clerk? What could it possibly be a reply to? My mind is racing and at the same time I despise such childish speculation, I feel invaded and demeaned by Shelley's insidious words.

When he has gone I get up and walk slowly out into the

hall. I stand for a few minutes looking at the phone and then pick up the receiver, pressing the redial button to ring back the previous caller. After three rings it is picked up and I can hear a woman's voice, slightly breathless as if she has run to the phone, saying, "Yes? Ramesh?" She speaks in a low throaty voice with a gentle musical lilt, Welsh, maybe, or Irish, I can never identify regional accents in this country.

" Sorry, I think I've got the wrong number," I say evenly. There is a pause and a silence in which I seem to have time to think of many things before her richly accented voice stumbles in confusion.

"Who is this?"

"I'm sorry to have troubled you," I put the phone down and dial the code to retrieve the number of the last caller. An electronic voice reads the number in a jerky monotone and as I scribble it on a notepad by the phone the numbers seem to swim before my eyes and I feel queasy. I return to the sitting room and collapse into a chair, shaking. I stare at the scribbled numbers. She must have known who I was, she'll realise from my accent, surely, and then Ramesh will know that I know. But what do I know? I look in the hall and the dining room for his briefcase but he has taken it with him. Which you would do if you were going to work. Or pretending to go to work. I feel confused and exhausted.

Pooja comes downstairs and surprises me rooting through the writing desk in the dining room.

"Want a drink, Mum? Have you lost something?"

"Just a friend's address. I thought your father might have it in an old address book, but I can't find anything." I straighten up and make an effort to smile. "Yes, I'd love a cup of tea. I'll come through in a minute."

I try to make idle chatter with Pooja in the kitchen, clearing up the saucepans from the draining board and wiping the surfaces, but I can hardly hear what she is saying there is such a clamour in my own head. After our drink I retire early to bed pleading a headache and ask her to leave the bolts off for Ramesh. There is not a flicker across her face as I tell her he is at work and I doubt my own silly suspicions, seeing only complete and unequivocal normality in her steady gaze. But upstairs in the darkness of the bedroom the shock of hearing that voice, so soft and richly intimate, returns to torment me for hour after hour as I wait to hear the key in the lock when he comes home.

When he arrives, finally, my nerve fails and I pretend to be asleep. I hear him moving around in the dark room, see his silhouette against the window folding his trousers and hanging up his jacket in that precise deliberate way he has, positioning the shoulder pads on the hanger with the pride of the newcomer making that extra effort to impress. I remembered how I used to watch him hang up his suit in the same way when he joined his first firm, my heart crying for his vulnerability, like a mother watching a child starting school. I knew how he struggled with those arrogant hard-edged English lawyers, how he learnt to dodge their jibes and match their sneering public school sarcasm. I watched him lose all his kindness in that place. But we were still a family then and he was still affectionate with his children, sometimes. I felt I understood why he was so distant and cold and preoccupied. I longed to find a way to bring him back to me. I remember with hot shame kissing the back of his neck one evening in the living room after the children had gone to bed. Just the touch of my lips would take his breath away in the passion of our first years, we were so aware of each other's bodies, linked invisibly across a room, breathing silently as one breath side by side, as we listened for his parents going to bed in the stifling Delhi nights, snuggling up together in the piercing cold of our first damp draughty flat in Loughborough. Now he was embarrassed by me, he moved away from my lips and turned to kiss my cheek politely saying that he was tired, and that he was going to bed because he had an important meeting the next day. I stood by his empty chair for a long time unable to move, waiting for the flood of shame and hurt to wash away. I wondered if this was just how it is after so many years of marriage, or whether the fault lay in me, or whether it lay in this cold passionless country that made a god of his work and forced us to wear nylon pyjamas and curl up in little foetal balls like squirrels to keep warm at night. Now I feel that hurt again with a new understanding. Watching him in the semi-darkness pulling his pyjama trousers over the bulging rise of his middle-aged belly, I realise I am looking at my own life slipping away: years of waiting, and trusting that my loyalty would be enough to take me to a place where I would one day be cherished again.

When he lies down quietly beside me, pulling the cover slowly so as not to wake me, I smell his stale smoke-filled hair and the musty earthiness of his body, I can stay there no longer. I wait until I hear his breathing slow into a familiar gentle snore and then I get up in one movement and snatch my dressing gown off the hook on the bedroom door.

When I switch the living room light on, I discover his briefcase in the middle of the floor, dropped by the chair he usually sits in. He must have rested for a moment when he came in, or checked the news headlines on the satellite channel before going to bed. I click it open carefully, holding my breath. I feel sordid and pathetic. I lift out his bulging, leather-bound diary and, perching on the chair arm I begin checking through the phone numbers in the back. Eventually I find the one I am looking for, sitting on its own in the 'K's between 'Keighley Magistrates Court' and "Iftiqar Khan', no name attached, just the number, looking as if it might be another number for Iftiqar. But how could it be? I heard the woman's liquid Celtic accent speaking his name with such familiarity. I put the diary back where I found it and turn the light off. Then I curl up on the settee in the darkness and watch the daylight gradually revealing the shapes and textures of a room which now seems alien and insubstantial to me.

He startles me, appearing suddenly at the door, rubbing sleepy eyes.

"You're awake?" he yawns, stretching elaborately.

"Too much to think about," I snap tersely. I am almost afraid now of opening the hornets' nest I have discovered. I hesitate on the edge of an abyss. If neither of us says anything it might be possible for life to continue exactly as it has done for the last twenty-five years and I will be safe in my routines and the ordinary, humdrum appearances that I relied on, even if they are fictions. But Ramesh has other intentions.

"Veena, we need to talk," he murmurs in a serious, almost deferential tone that I have rarely heard. He turns the dimmer switch to allow muted light to flood the room from the wall lights and walks over to the armchair by the fire.

"Can't it wait? I'm tired." I protest, feeling too drained for this encounter.

"You know it can't. Please. This is difficult for both of us, but it's better if we talk."

So there is no avoiding it now, no choice to remain in the old comforting illusions, no space for me to catch up in my own time. I am just dumped in this new reality because firstly Shelley, and now Ramesh, consider it best for me.

We sit across the lavishly patterned Kashmiri rug in a scene that could belong to any ordinary evening except for the late hour, the hush in the room and Ramesh's tense upright posture coiled with his intention to resolve this situation. I determine not to be resolved. I am not a situation. I am not another case to be mediated or compensated. I look intently at the intricate russet and navy borders of the handwoven rug and tell myself this is not really happening.

"You rang someone tonight after I went out, didn't you?" he begins.

"I got a wrong number," I respond evasively. "It happens all the time." I am not going to make this easy, but the habit of anticipating and meeting his need is very deep. I have to force myself not to comply.

"It wasn't a wrong number, that was Kath. Katherine Swain." I look at him, puzzled, waiting.

"Ed Swain is one of the partners in the firm. Come on, Veena. You know what I'm saying," he is beginning to sound impatient. "She said you realised who she was on the phone, and you know what was so amazing? I was glad! I've been wanting to tell you about her for such a long time," he leans forward, his eyes moistening earnestly. "I'm sorry, Veena, I didn't want to hurt you. But now that you know, we can both start to move forward."

"Know what? I don't know anything. I don't want to know," I mutter thickly and I am surprised to find myself fighting back tears. "I don't want to know about any of it."

"I know you're upset," he says gently. "But I've realised now, it's the hiding and the dishonesty that's come between us all this time. If we can be honest - sorry - if I can be honest with you, and we can talk about how we feel, maybe we can find a way to sort all this out." His voice is hoarse and choked with emotion and part of me wants to be convinced by him, wants him to make it all manageable for me. But I feel a dead steel coldness within, like the heavy closing of a door on a frozen vault inside me, immuring forever the long lying years of our marriage.

"I don't want the children upset," I manage to say. "Pooja's got her exams and Anil's got a lot to think about at the moment."

"Of course not," he agrees hurriedly. "There's no need to worry them, there's no need to change anything. In fact, I wouldn't want any of you to suffer." A small choking noise escapes from my throat and he looks appalled. "I didn't mean that. I know you are suffering - I just mean, whatever happens, you will have your home and everything you need. I will always provide for you."

"I can provide for myself," I assert in a dull voice, without feeling. "Give your money to the children. They deserve that at least."

He falls silent and I get up to leave the room.

"Wait. We have so much to discuss," he whispers in alarm. He reaches his hand out towards me, but when he meets my gaze it falls uselessly by the side of the chair.

"Another time," I sigh.

"Veena, sit down, please. I told Kath I won't see her while I sort things out here. I'll do whatever you need me to do to help you get through this," he explains, urgently, desperately. "Tell me what you need, Veena." I feel an impact like a cushion whacked against my chest as I hear this and the room recedes a little. I turn to him and say in a voice thick with tears,

"It's a bit late for that. I needed to say goodbye to my father. I needed to send his soul on its way. You knew I wanted to be there."

I remember the phone call from India about my father's death, my sister's weary voice pleading with me down the echoing telephone line to please come, now, our delayed voices colliding in the stratosphere, my mother sobbing and wailing in the background. I wanted to go but Ramesh said we didn't have the money, he was just starting his partnership, and what would be the point? It was the hot season and they couldn't delay the lighting of the pyre for me. By the time I got a flight, the funeral would be over, better to wait until we could all go for a proper visit. If I could have gone alone I would have, but I had no one to look after the children and Pooja wasn't even in nursery yet. We had only legal acquaintances or neighbours who were too old or too busy or too unfriendly. I had never felt so alone. I remembered my mother's warnings and knew she had been right about this country. I never forgave myself for not being there for her when she needed me.

"What?" He looks bewildered. "Why are you bringing that up now? For God's sake, Veena, you don't believe in all that religious mumbo jumbo, remember, 'opium of the people' and all that? You didn't even go to your mother's funeral when I offered to take you."

"For you, for our marriage, I stayed away from my own father's funeral," I hiss, emphasising each phrase separately. "It hurt so much I couldn't think. But I trusted you."

"And I took you. Remember?"

I remember. We did all go, eventually, when Ramesh could get the time off work and things were easier financially. It was two years late and by then my mother had retreated into a contemplative silence so remote it was hard to tell if she was even aware we were there. She was shrinking away into the dust before our eyes and spent her days at the ashram by the river cooking for the pilgrims and doing her pujas in an old white cotton sari, which she wore as she had never done in her life before, covering her head, pulled tightly over her thin strands of white hair and tucked under her chin. Despite her frailty, her presence gave me back an old strength and when the time came to return to Delhi, to my in-laws' house, I refused to go. I kept Pooja with me because she was too small to be without me and made Ramesh go on alone with Anil.

"How am I going to explain?" he protested angrily. "And how will you get to Delhi by yourself with a little baby?"

"She's nearly five and if I could travel on my own from Patna to Calcutta every school term when I was twelve, I think I can mange one train journey on my own now. Don't worry about me, darling," I soothed him, knowing it was not me but his parents' disapproval that he was worried about. Anil was bursting with excitement at the prospect of travelling alone with his father: just men together. He strutted around all day his thin chest swollen with importance. Only as the heavy, maroon carriages squealed and groaned and began to shunt slowly from the station did his little round face behind the iron window bars look suddenly forlorn as he waved frantically, and I stood helpless on the crowded platform with Pooja held securely and complacently in my arms.

"Another week isn't going to make up for not being here two years ago," my sister-in-law remarked acidly when I returned to the house. "She doesn't even know who you are. Her mind went when he died." I didn't reply. I wasn't trying to repair anything, I wasn't looking for forgiveness. It was more primal than that: I needed to be near her and I knew it would be the last time. I bought a tiny suit for Pooja and put on a plain cotton sari and each day we walked with her to the ashram. Pooja seemed to accept her silence as natural and was quite at ease chattering to us both as we walked the short distance to the ghats. When we got there she played in the dry dusty garden with the band of other small children who seemed to be loosely connected to the shrine. I sat in the inner compound by the open kitchen doors while the old people cooked, and followed the shade as the sun moved across the square of remorseless blue beating above. I had lost too many of the old ways to be able to cook the sacred food with the necessary ritual and purity, so I simply tried not to get in the way. I had a lot of time to think and sometimes forgot my mother entirely, thinking of Anil and Ramesh in Calcutta, and our life in England that seemed so unreal now I was back in the solid absolute reality of India. We only stayed on an extra week, but those days in the ashram seemed to expand to occupy months of my life. Time moved so slowly in the midday heat with the flies buzzing around puddles of water by the well, as I listened to the endless clanging of temple bells along the river bank. That waiting was the most profound meditation I ever engaged in and took me to understandings that I had to lock away deep inside me when we got back to England - where there was no space for knowing, only doing.

On the second day my mother brought me a small steel cup of cool water. I had been sitting on the steps that encircled the compound sunk in thought and felt only the faintest whisper of her sari against my shoulder. I looked up and she handed me the cup, her eyes fixed intently on her unsteady hand as little drops of water splashed out over the rim. I took it and thanked her, I dared not reach out to seize her hand or stop her walking away again. But I felt blessed and I knew that she had not lost her mind. Indeed, I began to understand that her silence was more a protection from the demands and clamour of my brother and his wife. She was not so silent at the ashram. I began to hear her discussing ingredients, asking after the health of the other elderly devotees, exchanging a small joke that would produce an explosion of cackles and splutterings around the echoing cavernous interior. I realised that she trusted me not to say anything on our return, when she would retire in silence to her wooden cot on the verandah with its rope mattress and thin dusty bedroll. On the third day she came and sat by me on the steps and took my hand. I tried to speak and started to cry. She patted my hand and shook her head sadly, giving a little sigh, "Aaiee…"

"Ammi - " I tried again. " When Abu died - " She stopped my mouth with her thin, bent finger.

"Nothing to say. You are here," she insisted firmly. "Come. Eat." And she levered herself slowly off the steps, leaning on my arm. After that she came often and sat with me, resting from her labours, and was sometimes missed in the kitchen. "Vasanti," they called when they needed her expertise. The name from her childhood that she had not been for so many years as a wife, mother and grandmother. We watched Pooja and the other children and I told her about England, about Ramesh's career, about my life as a housewife. She talked only of the ashram and her companions there, as if she had no interest any more in anything beyond its walls. If I had not brought Pooja and myself within the walls she might not have thought of me. The last day was unbearable and she began to withdraw again as if she too found it intolerable that time was about to split our cocoon. My train was at five in the afternoon so we left the ashram after lunch had been served. She gave Pooja a plastic bottle of Mysore sandalwood talcum powder, which Pooja hugged to her chest sending tiny clouds of talc up her nostrils. I tried to be strong but as she touched my head in blessing I noticed that her eyes were moist and I broke down. She turned away, stumbling slightly and murmuring to the others who had gathered around us. They led me to the auto rickshaw at the gate supporting me gently, a crowd of withered arms and crushed stained white saris.

"Don't grieve for her. She is at peace," one of the

women said to me kindly as she lifted Pooja into the auto beside me. I smiled and nodded through my sobs to show that I understood. My mother would die soon, among friends; there would be no need for me to return for her funeral.

I realise Ramesh is watching me as I stand lost in thought.

"Yes. You took me. But it was too late. It was too late for my father," I say sadly.

"So you stopped talking to me. You went away in your head," he laughs with sudden comprehension. "You did it, Veena, you started it."

"I asked you to sleep with your friend's wife, did I?" I sneer. "It started before that, when you pretended everything was all right at Firth Malleady's, with that awful racist man who gave you all the worst cases and humiliated you. Why wouldn't you talk about it?" He flushes and says nothing for a while. I have perched on the edge of the settee, drawn back into the room by my own need to be heard. I feel calm now. How many years have I not said that one thing, not wanting to cause a row, not wanting to be unreasonable? And for nothing. She probably wears those silk negligees they sell in John Lewis, racks of fine slippery gold and white, icing sugar pink, and shining, mysterious, temptress black. I despise him.

"It doesn't matter where it started," he sighs. "Let's not fight, there's no point. And we hardly ever sleep together. It's not like that. We mostly just sit and talk. We're friends."

Friends. I thought it couldn't hurt any more and that word hurts a hundred times more than all the rest. I breathe very deeply to steady myself and focus on getting out of the room in one piece.

"I'm going to get dressed. Pooja needs to get up at seven, she's got an exam."

"What do you want me to do?" he persists.

"Do what you want," I whisper as I leave the room.

As I stepped out of the taxi I noticed a charcoal sky looming in the west. The slate roofs of Tasleems's sloping street gleamed beneath a veil of livid orange-tinted grey. I looked around for signs of the lads she described on the phone, but the road was empty. I felt that same prickling on the back of my neck I had felt the night I went there with Eleanor, a feeling of invisible eyes trained on me. I knocked on Tasleem's door as the first heavy drops from the sky spattered on the pavement, advance guard for the storm sweeping down from the Pennines. Two teenage girls came round the corner, walking unsteadily down the other side of the road, their arms locked around each other's elbows, giggling and occasionally lunging sideways with squeals of alarm. Otherwise the street was silent and deserted. I took a deep breath, knocked and waited. There was no response. I knew she couldn't be out. I knocked again and stood back to look up at the windows. A curtain fell back into place. There was a muffled thumping of feet coming down the stairs inside and the sound of hurried footsteps in the hall. The raindrops were crowding the ground now with dark merging stains and cold rain lashed my head and neck.

"Just in time," I laughed as I ducked into her open doorway. "It's about to chuck it down." Tasleem let me in hurriedly and slammed the door behind me pushing to all the extra bolts and chains the housing association had installed for her after the last attack.

"You still here? You not going to your parents?" She quizzed, following me into the darkening living room.

"Come, come, get dry in here. I am so happy to see you." Her smile was warm, embracing me in folds of acceptance as she turned the light on and pulled thick green curtains across the windows over her tattered nets.

"I changed my mind about getting the train." I explained, sitting on the long bench settee. Huma was lying asleep on her back on the smaller settee, her arms and legs splayed out at awkward angles and her head on one side, tiny breaths coming in and out of her open mouth. The end of a scarf of soft blue material as thin as gauze was wrapped around her fingers. I noticed the material matched Tasleem's blue and beige shalwar kameez. One section of the gas fire was burning quietly and the television was on without any sound.

"Something happened?" Tasleem pursued, still bewildered by my appearance.

"Yes. Your phone call."

"You change your mind for me?" She looked at me doubtfully and I nodded.

"I felt sorry that you have to live like this, being frightened every night, I couldn't just leave you with it."

"This life is so hard for me," she agreed, shaking her head. "I don't ask for it to be like this, but I have no choice." She shrugged her shoulders in resignation. "Maybe I am unlucky person. First I have so much trouble from my husband. Now I have trouble from other people." Remembering what Veena had said in the S.A.F.E. meeting, I wondered whether to ask more about her husband. But I wasn't really supposed to know all that stuff about the domestic violence, it was an accident that when I met her in the centre I'd sussed that she was the person Veena had described in the

213

meeting. Tricky all this confidentiality stuff, I could see how Veena found it a struggle. I decided to leave it. We were both gazing at Huma.

"When I was little I used to fiddle with my pillowcase like that when I was falling asleep," I told Tasleem. I was not sure if I remembered this, or if the picture was one I had made in my head from hearing it told so many times.

"Always she holds my dupatta like this when she feels tired, and she moves it in her fingers like she is saying her namaz, over and over," Tasleem tugged the dupatta gently until it slipped out of Huma's loosened grip and then draped it around her own neck.

"Namaz?" I looked at her, puzzled.

"Her prayers," Tasleem explained as she sat down beside Huma. "You are not Muslim?" I shook my head. "Christian? Hindu?"

"I don't have a religion."

"No religion?" she breathed in amazement.

"Nope." My smile was unnecessarily triumphant.

"Your parents?"

Oh, hell.

"Not really," I answered evasively. "Can I ask why you've got the television on with no sound?" She laughed and leaned over to turn it off.

"It was Eastenders. I like. It is a good drama, but sometimes too much husband and wife arguing and the noise is upsetting me. If I have money I will get Zee TV on my television and watch beautiful films, with romantic songs and girls dancing in best fashions from Bombay and Karachi."

"But why didn't you just turn it off?"

"Then I feel too lonely. Huma is asleep and no one with

214

me, so if television is on, then at least I have some people with me," she explained simply. I had no answer to that. I lived alone too, but I didn't feel alone in the world like she seemed to. "Why you don't you come to see us, Shelley? Is two weeks now you don't come."

"I know, I'm sorry. I had a lot of stuff going off."

"Stuff? Going off?" Tasleem looked puzzled and I thought, this isn't easy, this language thing, it really makes you think before you open your mouth.

"Kind of, like, trouble," I explained.

"Trouble," she nodded, smiling. "I know trouble." She didn't ask any more, which surprised me. Instead, she wanted to know if I had eaten dinner.

"This time you will have dinner? Say yes." Her eyes were alight with excitement. "I have chicken pulao and lamb, it is so tasty."

"Actually I don't eat meat," I confessed, waiting for her horrified response. She looked at me doubtfully.

"You are joking with me?" she suggested.

"No, really. I'm sorry. You don't have to feed me, you know. I ate before I came out," I assured her. I was actually feeling quite weak with hunger, having hardly bothered with meals over the last two days, but I didn't want to create any more upset. However, she was undaunted.

"Then you have dhal and rice and I take out the chicken. And some salad, yes," she muttered to herself, and then, triumphantly, "So you are Hindu. I said this."

"No, no, no," I said, holding my head in my hands. "I'm a vegan."

"Okay, I understand," she soothed, plainly not understanding. "Your religion is Vee-Gan."

"It's not a religion, it's more like politics. Like being in a political party, only it's about food," I tried to explain. "I don't eat meat or any animal products like eggs or cheese or milk."

"Same as Hindu, then, but you are not Hindu," Tasleem affirmed carefully.

"That's right, except that some Hindus do eat meat," I qualified, thinking of Veena. I realised I didn't know whether Veena called herself a Hindu or not. I hadn't seen any shrines or religious imagery in her house when I visited.

Tasleem brought a small bowl of spiced toasted chickpeas and lentils from the kitchen, which she deposited in front of me, announcing proudly,

"Hot gram." She then disappeared to fetch more food.

I took a small handful of the mixture and nibbled as I gazed into the purring gas fire. The hot salty taste was familiar from visits we used to make when I was little to people Dad knew in the streets near his school, elders of the local Asian community whom we visited once a year on Eid or Diwali festivals. I remembered excruciating conversations about India, Dad waxing lyrical about his travels there when he was a young man and trotting out his showpiece Hindi phrases to general applause. A wave of helplessness would sweep over me as I waited for the inevitable story about myself and the accompanying barrage of sympathetic eyes. Mum would confine herself to telling me to sit still and eat properly and would take no part in the proceedings. There were usually other children but they were allowed to go somewhere else and play, their voices laughing and squealing through the thin walls of houses which smelt unfamiliarly of incense and spices.

It must have been on occasions like these that I first

heard Bengali spoken. I remember my father talking to a Bengali imam about staying in the YMCA in Calcutta and crossing the Hooghly on a river ferry to see the banyan tree in the Botanical Gardens. He said it was as big as a whole forest with its groves of trunk-like roots. His account of streets flooding in the monsoon was very popular, as was the story about his cycle rickshaw wallah getting into an argument with a taxi driver on Howrah Bridge and holding up the traffic in both directions. But as I got older, I had a feeling they were being polite. They listened because he was the primary school head teacher; really he was regarded as a bit of an oddity with his silent wife and his adopted Bengali daughter. I winced as I sat by Tasleem's fire remembering these occasions.

It was after such visits that they would try to talk to me about Rehana. They told me she had come from a place called Sylhet and gave me books about Bangladesh with photos of women working in bright green paddy fields, and fishing boats pulled up onto beaches lined with coconut palms. All they knew about my father was that the social worker who placed me with them thought he was probably Bengali as well because I was so dark. I had no way of judging for myself who I might or might not look like as I didn't even have a photo of Rehana. She had only looked after me for a day and only saw me once after she left the hospital, just before she was taken back to Bangladesh. No one had thought to take a photograph, or maybe she refused. I don't know. Whenever I am in a new situation it all seems to surface again. Maybe it's all the questions and always having to filter stuff and pace what I reveal or don't. I suddenly felt exhausted and not at all like eating.

When Tasleem came back into the room with a loaded tray she saw something on my face. She handed me my cup of tea, without milk but with a slice of lemon in it, saying kindly:

"You are tired. Here, drink this. I put a lemon for you." It was a novelty to be looked after, and such a long time since anyone had noticed that I was tired. Mooching around at home worrying about stuff had turned out to be more tiring than a whole day on my feet in the Dancing Cows. Tasleem looked at me with a smile of deep satisfaction. "Now you are here I feel much better. Those boys will see I have someone with me." A shadow passed across her face. "But what about your parents?"

"They don't mind. They're going to come and visit me another day instead," I reassured her.

"Is their place far?"

"A few hours. They live in Reading, it's the other side of Birmingham?" I raised my voice in a question, not sure how much she knew of other places in England. A frown pinched her face at the mention of Birmingham. "I know Birmingham. I lived there with my husband," she stated sadly. "It's good for you that your parents are here in this country." I realised she thought they were Asian.

"That's because they're English. They adopted me when I was a baby."

"Oh, I see." I wasn't sure she did, but she was lost in her own thoughts. "My parents are in Pakistan. They worry about me so much, but there's nothing I can do. We can't see each other. They had a lot of trouble from my husband's family. Maybe if I go there I bring more trouble on them. And I haven't got money for the ticket.

218

We are all suffering."

"I'm sorry."

"Maybe I try to save money to send a ticket for my mother to come over next year - " She jumped up suddenly, laughing at herself. "But what am I doing? You must eat now."

Tasleem spread bowls of dhal, rice, and spinach and potato curry in front of me. She nursed a cup of tea, watching me eat. I felt slightly unnerved. I knew the rice had originally been cooked with chicken and I probably shouldn't have been eating it. Even the dhal had probably been cooked with ghee from buffalo milk, but I was really touched by her efforts to accommodate my inconvenient beliefs and I ate with relish.

"So, how has it been here?" I asked a little guiltily, when my first waves of hunger had subsided. "I saw Veena last week and she said they sent someone from the council round to the parents of the boys you reported. I thought you hadn't had any trouble since then?"

"No, I didn't see them for two weeks till today. But I can't rest. Still, every time I hear a noise in the night I feel so scared." She looked at me carefully, waiting. I thought I had decided but suddenly I felt scared. All Eleanor's warnings crowded round my head.

"I'm completely stuffed. That was delicious," I sighed, leaning back in my seat with the dregs of my lemon tea. "If you stay here I can cook you dinner when you come from work. No meat, I promise. And you can walk to your cafe from here, it's very close." She looked at me wistfully, "It will be so nice. Huma likes you very much."

"Tasleem, I don't know. I don't think I can." I said, wondering how I had ever thought it possible. My night with Anil seemed to have proved that everything

Eleanor had warned me about was true. Our lives were just too different, and I had been naive and irresponsible to think they weren't. I saw tears in her eyes and mumbled, "I'm so sorry."

"I hate my husband for this," she sighed, looking down into her cup of tea. "He put me in this situation." This time I understood that she wanted to talk.

"Where is your husband?" I asked.

"In Birmingham, I think, or maybe he goes to Pakistan now. I don't know. We lived there in Birmingham. He is a very bad man. He hit me a lot. But my health visitor, she help me. She find a place for me here. She give me some money and take me to the train. She is so, so kind lady. I always remember her." I wasn't sure if she meant she would remember the health visitor throughout her life, or if she meant she was always thinking about her now. I quite liked the idea of the two meanings being rolled into one in those four simple words, like a haiku, or an epitaph: 'Remembered always'.

"And your husband hasn't found you?"

"Maybe he don't look, I don't know," she shrugged. "He has English girlfriend, he don't care about me."

"But how come you got a house in this area, when there have been so many racist attacks round here?" I felt angry that she had not been better advised.

"The house is so nice inside. When I see it, I want it. I didn't know about bad boys. And it is near the meat shop and Awaaz. I go to classes there, is really good for me. If I learn more English, I can get job, teach children maybe. I want to do something nice with my life."

"Did you know anyone in Sheffield when you came here?" I was curious.

"No. I come to refuge for women whose husbands hurt

them. I shouldn't talk about it..." she broke off anxiously.

"No, of course not, it's confidential. I don't need to know about it," I reassured her.

"Lots of people help me in the refuge. I am so happy I can make my own home now and look after my daughter." She paused, seeming to reflect on her own achievement, and then a sigh breathed from her lips. "But it is very hard living by my own." Her face fell and I was about to apologise again when she seemed to shake herself out of her sadness with a word I had heard her use before that seemed to mean, 'enough'. "Bas. Never mind. I am happy you are here now. You don't know Veena is sick?"

"No, but I haven't spoken to her since Wednesday." She saw my hesitation as I looked away.

"Something is wrong?"

To hell with it. I had to talk to someone.

"We had an argument." Tasleem's eyes widened in surprise.

"Why?" she breathed in amazement.

"I slept with her son."

She snorted into her tea and giggled.

"Tasleem." It was my turn to be shocked.

"Oh Shelley," she laughed, trying to straighten her face. "I am sorry. This is very serious thing, but you say it in a funny way..." She started chuckling again, and soon I was laughing too.

"Oh, dear. This is so bad. We shouldn't laugh," she said, wiping her eyes with the end of her dupatta. "Poor Veena. Poor you."

"I don't know about me, but, it is poor Veena," I said soberly, managing to control myself. "That was one problem, but I also told her something bad about her husband. He was lying to her, staying out late and not telling her where he was. I think that might be why she's off work now. What if they split up and it's all my fault?"

"Good," said Tasleem emphatically. "If he is bad man, he should go. Veena can find good man. It's not your fault. Men do these things all the time. I am not angry with my husband's girlfriend, I feel sorry for her."

"I think some of it is my fault," I demurred, grateful nevertheless for her impassioned support. "It was really messy me getting involved with Anil. I was supposed to be Veena's friend."

"Okay," Tasleem conceded. "I keep my boyfriends away from you." She delivered this in such a deadpan voice I had to look at her twice.

"Tasleem," I burst out when I caught the sparkle in her eye, "you are so wicked!"

"It's nice to have some fun again," she sighed happily. "In Pakistan we are four sisters, I miss them so much. Since I come to this country to be with my husband I didn't laugh at all, except with Huma, she is like my new little sister."

"Well now you've got me." Suddenly I knew it would be all right. The instinct that had led me there, that had placed Tasleem in the middle of my napkin picture, was a good one.

"You know about me staying here with you?" I continued. "Well, I'd like to try it. Maybe we should have a trial period, like, three months?"

"I don't understand," she looked puzzled. "You want to stay for three months?"

"No, I mean in three months' time we should check -

ask - if we're both happy. If you're not happy, or I'm not happy, then I'll go. We don't really know each other, do we? You might think I'm really untidy or I might keep Huma awake or - oh, I don't know." I finished helplessly.

" - Or Huma might get in your way. It's okay, I understand." Tasleem said seriously.

"I hope you do," I sighed. "And I need to pay you something each week, just like you pay the council." She looked worried.

"I think they don't allow that. I might get into trouble, they might stop my benefit."

"All right, then. Why don't I just pay half the bills and we can share buying food? That's not rent, it's just sharing and I won't be officially living here, I'll just be staying for a while as a friend. It'll be fine. You can save the extra money for your mother's ticket. But if you're worried, you can change your mind?"

"No, no," she protested. "You just tell me, when do you want to come? You move in tonight?" Her enthusiasm was infectious.

"I have to do something about my flat first, so it might be a week or two before I can sort everything out properly." I explained.

"Two weeks." She looked dismayed. "No. You come soon."

She insisted on giving me a tour of the house and as we walked round I tried to imagine it as my home. It was very empty and cold, despite being carpeted throughout in a thin dark blue cord. The back bedroom which I insisted was to be my room had no furniture or curtains or light bulb, it looked particularly uninviting in the anaemic yellow street light slanting down the alley that runs behind the houses. I told Tasleem I would sort out my own furniture and curtains. I wondered if Veena would help me, or if she would be concerned about me taking my immorality into Tasleem's home.

Tasleem left me to consider my room for a while by myself as Huma had woken up and was crying downstairs. I stood on my own in the dark room feeling the newness of it all. The stark uniform walls were somehow comforting, the emptiness of the room a relief, offering a new space in which I could start again, very simply, and try not to get it quite so wrong this time. Warm lingering smells floated up through the house of cooking spices and chapattis smoking on the open flame and I could hear Tasleem murmuring instructions and endearments to Huma downstairs. Mum and Dad would not understand, nor Veena, nor Eleanor, nor anyone else probably. They might try to dislodge me with their cautions and interpretations and reasons, but I felt my feet taking root in the floor, and a new kind of weight and solidity settling in my body, like being anchored at last. I knew I would be okay with all their doubts if I could just hang on to the feeling of rightness I had being in that space at that moment.

I took one last look around the room and as I did so, I thought I heard something crash outside. I moved to the window and looked out over the dark yard. At first I couldn't see anything, but then I noticed the gate to the yard swinging on its hinges and, with a lurch in the pit of my stomach, I noticed two figures right underneath my window their heads bent over something one of them was holding. I could hear their lowered voices muttering. Without thinking I banged hard on the window and they both jumped and looked around bewildered. Then one of them glanced up and saw me. Pulling his friend with him, he ran off down the ginnel. I could hear their heavy steps echoing down the tunnel and what sounded like laughter.

"What happened?" Tasleem appeared breathless at the top of the stairs.

"Just a cat," I lied. "I didn't want it to mess up your yard. The gate's not fastened properly, I'd better close it when I go out."

"Are you going now?" she asked sadly. "You can stay tonight. We can sleep on the settee and you can have the big bedroom."

"Don't be silly. You can't do that," I protested. "If anyone sleeps on the settee it'll be me,"

"So you will stay?" Tasleem was incredulous.

"Why not? I've got all my stuff with me." I could hide away here all weekend and no one would even know I was still in the city.

I returned to the living room to play with Huma while Tasleem found a pile of bedding for me. While digging in my bag for a pencil, I discovered there was a text message on my mobile phone from Anil: have u seen mum 2day? ring me on mob not at home. I responded straight away, perched on the arm of the small settee, while Tasleem arranged sheets and heavy patterned quilts on the long settee with 'help' from Huma.

"Hello?" His voice raised a flutter of nerves inside me, which I immediately felt annoyed about.

"Hi, it's Shelley here. What's going on? I heard Veena's off work."

"I was hoping you could tell me. Have you seen Mum today?"

"No. Isn't she at home?"

"No. Oh God, I really thought you might know." His voice shook slightly. "She's been gone since yesterday morning and she's resigned from her job. She left a note on the dining table saying she wanted some time on her own and she'll ring in a few days and not to worry. But no one knows where she's gone. Pooja's in such a state and Dad's useless, he's just gone to pieces and keeps saying it's all his fault." I felt a sinking inside.

"And he's okay about you being there?"

"He's on another planet, I don't know if he's even remembered about me dropping out of uni. Listen, you don't have to say where Mum is and we won't come to your flat bothering her or anything, but we really need to know she's okay."

"Anil, I'm sorry, but she really, really, isn't with me and I haven't seen her myself since Wednesday afternoon. We had a bit of a row, I'm afraid I told her about you and me."

"Oh. Right." He seemed stunned, or maybe just unsure how to respond. Oh God, I so don't know him, I thought. How did I end up sleeping with him? When he continued it was as if I hadn't spoken. "I think maybe the job has been too stressful for her and she's having some kind of breakdown. She's not used to such a high-powered role with all that kind of internal politics and stuff, and she's been working so hard. I don't know what to do."

"I think you should wait till she rings," I suggested. "And I don't think it's got anything to do with her work."

"Oh God, do you think it's our fault?" he groaned.

"No, I don't," He was starting to seriously irritate me. "We're not that important. And, by the way, why didn't you tell me about Bev?"

"Sorry," he volunteered with ease. "It didn't really come up. I was going to, eventually. Look, you must know something. Did Mum say anything to you on Wednesday?"

"No." I answered truthfully, thinking, it's more what I said to her. But I don't know it's that either, I told myself, I don't know anything. It could be about us, it could be about Ramesh, it might be nothing to do with any of us. If Veena had been depressed about work on Wednesday I was so wrapped up in myself that day I probably wouldn't have noticed anyway. I felt I had completely failed her. "I've got to go Anil, I'm at Tasleem's. Let me know if you hear from her. I'll ring you again tomorrow."

He let me go reluctantly and I tried to focus on Tasleem, who had brought more cups of tea and plates of sweets. But my mind was spinning with questions about Veena. What if I had started all this off by sewing a seed of doubt in her mind about Ramesh? I might end up destroying her life. How could I have done such a thing? How could someone so supposedly sensitive about cruelty to animals go crashing around in people's lives to such disastrous and painful effect? I listened to Huma's meandering chatter, my head throbbing with questions.

Sitting on the sagging sofa in the flat above the cafe, I leaf distractedly through yesterday's copy of The Guardian and drink lukewarm mint tea. My hair, unplaited, lies like a soft woollen shawl over my shoulders. Eleanor's shapeless jogging pants and sweatshirt hang lightly from my limbs with casual indifference, showing no interest in disciplining my spreading shape. I'm not used to feeling so unbound and I have a sense of floating as I move silently through the upstairs flat in my intangible emperor's new clothes. From below, the beat of strumming music rises, punctuated by the clatter of pans being put away as Eleanor and her part-time helpers close up. This is my retreat, my ashram, and Eleanor is my guru teaching me self-sufficiency and freedom from guilt. She is most caring in her silences and spaces, in the quiet undramatic way she smoothed my passage here, and the absence of sentiment in her manner. I am not to be pitied or sympathised with, I am simply here, and the space I slipped into seems always to have been here for me. Matt's departure is so recent the bathroom is still littered with half-finished bottles of aftershave. Discarded wrappers of disposable razors lie at the bottom of the plastic waste bin and his gaunt cycle with its drop handlebars lurks in the corridor downstairs awaiting collection. Yet I find it difficult to imagine a man living here, I have no sense of his presence in the flat, only the sense of him I get from listening to Eleanor. The tug of romance still lingers for her, the magical discovery of a soulmate who knows her like no other. I know she wants him back, one day, when he has grown up a bit more and learnt to appreciate her better. The thought of that day comforts her now and the likelihood of its arriving is not relevant to our discussions.

I don't know what she thinks of Ramesh for I never mention him. I prefer not to think of him, and it is surprisingly easy with nothing around to remind me. The absence I do feel is that of Anil and Pooja: Anil sprawled in front of the television with the morning paper, and Pooja popping me little quizzical asides as she passes through the kitchen to collect her cocoa or raid the fridge. I try to ring Anil on his mobile but it goes straight to voicemail and I can't think what to say. I know I am being unreasonable and melodramatic, and probably unfair to the children, disappearing like this. But I have been reasonable for so many years I feel I have reached a moment when I cannot bear to be reasonable for a second longer.

The morning Ramesh admitted the truth to me I stayed at home and buried myself in the kitchen cooking vast quantities of samosey and pakorey. I phoned Riffat to say I was feeling ill, which was true, and when she asked me, in a voice full of doubt, if everything was all right, I clenched my fingers tighter around the receiver and told her everything was fine, it was just a tummy bug, one of those twenty-four hour things. I put the radio on and tried to follow an arty discussion programme, but I couldn't process the brash convoluted sentences and arrogant abstractions assaulting me across the room, and eventually I turned the dial to a light music channel that soothed me with its gentle chatter and easy rhythms. I was aware of Ramesh at every moment. The unbearable weight of his betrayal lay like a blanket over my head and shoulders, smothering me, isolating me from the world.

When Pooja came home from school I thought for a while it was going to be all right, she was so ordinary and so herself, complaining to me about her history teacher's failings and the preparations for the school prom in May. If I willed it, for a moment, I could believe that I was back in that sensible ordinary world where things resisted my touch with their own unique solidity, instead of dissolving as I watched. If only the poisonous splinter of knowledge could be squeezed out of me again, I could pretend I had never known. But then Ramesh came home and I could hardly bear to speak to him. I don't know how I got through dinner that evening. Nobody spoke of Anil, who Pooja and I knew was staying with another worker from the hostel to keep out of Ramesh's way. But I could not think of him for the moment. I had little enough energy for my own battle and none for his. After dinner Pooja went out again to sleep over at Kate's house. Another time I would have complained about it being on a school night, but I was relieved to have some space in which I didn't have to pretend, so I let her go without a word.

Ramesh tried to talk to me when she had gone. He followed me into the kitchen and leaned against the fridge watching me. I had my back to him scrubbing the top of the cooker. When he spoke I felt a hand close around my heart like a great iron gate shutting.

"Veena, I don't know what you want me to do. I came home tonight for dinner because I wanted to keep things normal for Pooja. I thought that's what you wanted. But I don't expect you to cook for me or wash my clothes - or - Veena, are you listening to me?"

"Can't it wait? This cooker's filthy." I snapped tersely.

"You know we can get a cleaner to do that. I've told you that before."

"I thought we didn't believe in cleaners, I thought we left India to get away from having to have servants," I reminded him.

"It's not the same here, it's more equal, more dignified, they're not servants, they're just employees like anyone else - "

"How can it be dignified to clean somebody else's toilet? What would you know about it?" I was consumed with rage at his pompous generalisations, and, just under the surface, I could feel floods of grief rising at our lost ideals, our lost marriage, our lost intimacy. "Why don't you just go? I really don't want you here tonight."

A little while later I heard the front door close and the car start up in the drive. When I was sure he had gone, I fished Eleanor's number out of my bag and dialled it, holding my breath in suspense.

Half an hour later she was at the door, the engine of her yellow van still running in the street as if I had to make some desperate clandestine getaway. I would have made her a cup of tea, but she was too nervous, so I scribbled a quick note for Pooja and Anil and let her help me load my suitcase and bags into the car. She seemed slightly alarmed at the amount of stuff I had for a temporary visit but I don't know if I'll ever go back and I couldn't leave without my wedding saris, my jewellery, photo albums from when the children were little, and my old letters from India, shrivelled bits of paper holding memories more precious than a house full of things.

When I hear the crash of the security shutters coming

down on the front entrance, I know the other workers have left and I go through to the poky upstairs kitchen to warm up the dinner I have cooked for us. Soon Eleanor appears upstairs, throwing off her stained apron and hat. She is a small thin woman, with greying ginger hair and intense blue eyes, and a slightly desperate driven edge to her voice. But unwinding over a glass of wine in the evenings she reveals a gentler, more wistful and sentimental side that I feel is her real strength. She is a survivor and somehow she seems to hold the key to my survival as well. We are two shipwrecked sailors clinging to our upturned boat bobbing along together in a thick sea fog, trusting our fates to the elements and waiting to see where we land. "Cup of tea?" I offer and she throws me a grateful smile.

"Yes please, I could get used to this Veena, you mustn't spoil me, we're supposed to be getting you away from the kitchen sink."

"It's the least I can do. Besides, I've nothing else to do all day," I argue, warming her blue china teapot with steaming water. Already the furniture of this kitchen is familiar to my touch. I know the spurts and hisses of the temperamental whistling kettle, the slender handles of the Portmeirion mugs, the surprising weight of the cast iron frying pan, the gas ring that only lights when tapped, and the shelf over the washing machine that cracks your temple as you lift your head from the bin. This new kitchen fits me like a glove, and I could step away from it as easily as I have the last. I feel so light and airy at the moment, a nomad with my worldly goods in a sack just starting out on a trek into new territory.

"Have you been okay up here?" Eleanor asks, frowning

with concern.

"Of course," I laugh. "I'm having a wonderful time, watching lots of rubbish on the television and reading all your books. I haven't relaxed so much since I was pregnant with Anil." It strikes me suddenly how different my pregnancy was the second time around, with Anil an energetic toddler, not yet at school, keeping me on the go every hour of the day, Ramesh was at the lowest point of his difficulties at Firth Malleady's. We moved into a bigger house that I struggled to manage, suddenly finding myself isolated miles from the town centre, unable to drive, and about to have a baby. No wonder Pooja was such a difficult baby, she must have come out carrying all my stress from the womb, poor lamb.

Eleanor takes the cup of lemon and ginger tea I have made her straight into the other room and collapses in front of the television.

"Your son came in today." she calls to me from her seat in front of the television. "He was looking for Shelley, so I told him she's gone to her parents for a few days."

I serve the rice and vegetable dishes onto our plates and carry them through on a tray. I place it on the coffee table beside Eleanor. We balance our plates on our knees and eat our dinner in front of the television, something I would never have allowed in the sitting room at home, but I am in Eleanor's anarchic irreverent world now and I can be a student again, I can be a child, I can be whoever I want, I can even be me again, whoever 'me' is. There is a delicious unwinding happening here that I can only half sense. I think I have caught it and then it trickles away again, but I know I am tumbling, like a ball of wool unravelling, and I have no idea where I will end up. When all the wool has unwound, there may be nothing left but a frayed end and empty space, or maybe, at the end of the last strand, I will discover the real me that these layers of wool have been smothering all this time. An empty space feels quite attractive at the moment. I would quite like to float off into nothingness.

"Did he say anything else?" I ask lightly. Eleanor looks at me, weighing up what to say. Clearly there is more but she is not sure how much to tell me. I am not sure how much I want to know, I accept her protective filtering gratefully and leave it to her to judge what it is necessary to share.

"Maybe you ought to phone them soon. I think they're quite worried about you and getting themselves in a bit of a state. We don't want the police to start looking for you."

"But I left them a note saying I was all right - "

"Sorry, I'm just thinking of you."

"No, it's okay. I'll ring. I just wish people would believe me when I tell them not to worry." I feel a tinge of remorse for worrying my children and considerable annoyance that no one seems to have taken seriously the words of reassurance I left. Can I not have a few days to myself without causing a major incident? Apparently not.

"Speaking of escapees, or refugees, or whatever you are, it's a nightmare in the caff without Shelley. Do you think I should text her?" Eleanor looks up at me anxiously.

"No." I hesitate. "At least, I don't think so. She was quite - I don't know how to explain - troubled when I saw her. I think it might take her some time to work out what she really wants. One thing I know is it's not Anil, and that's not because I want to protect him."

"It's not me either," Eleanor murmurs, chewing a mouthful of rice thoughtfully. She sounds resigned and I tilt my head at her, remembering her account last night of an emotional moment between her and Shelley. I am not sure what to understand from this comment.

"How are you going to feel if - when - Shelley comes back?" I wonder, carefully.

"She'd better come back. I can survive her not fancying me, I just can't survive running the business without her." Eleanor scrapes impatiently at the last grains of rice on her well-polished plate. "To be honest, if we fold in a couple of months, what Shelley feels about me will be the least of my worries."

"Actually, Eleanor, I've been thinking about that. I've been thinking about a lot of things," I begin slowly, checking with myself that I am absolutely sure before I speak. "Ramesh and I have quite a bit of money now. Some of it was to get Anil and Pooja through university, but Anil has other ideas and there's plenty for Pooja. If we end up getting divorced and selling the house there'll be quite a bit more and I should have some cash to invest. Ramesh won't argue, I don't think, he has some sense of fairness about money, if not in other things."

"I didn't know you were getting divorced?" Eleanor looks at me in surprise and I realise I have covered continents in the long hours since this morning when she went downstairs to open up. "I have no illusions about a reconciliation in the future, Eleanor," I explain as gently as I can. "Ramesh and I can't go back from this. And the children are almost grown up, they don't need us to stay together any more. However we are in the future, I don't know if I can ever depend on him again."

"I'm sorry."

"Me too." I sigh, and wonder how this can be happening when he is also, still, my life companion, the soulmate with whom I crossed continents and brought babies into the world, the other half of the arch on which our family rests. There's a place inside me where it hurts so much that he let go of all that, but I have closed the door on that room for the moment. I can't face it. "If I come out of all this with anything, Eleanor, I'd like to do something to save the cafe. I feel like coming in here before my Awaaz interview that day really changed something for me. This is where my new life started. Maybe I could buy into the cafe, or become a partner - if you'll have me."

"Seriously?"

I nod, smiling at her disbelief.

"I know I drink milk in my tea and I used to cook meat at home, but I can be an excellent vegetarian, and a passable vegan if I have to."

"If you can save the cafe you can cook sausages up here every morning," Eleanor responds passionately, "Veggy ones, mind you!" She becomes wistful. "I can't bear to lose this place, it would break my heart to see somebody plaster emulsion all over my cows, I painted them myself you know. And all these in here." It is my turn to stare in wide-eyed amazement at the exploding dazzling abstract paintings I have been admiring scattered around the walls of the flat.

"They're beautiful, Eleanor. You should do more." She shrugs.

"No time."

"You must make time," I urge. "If we get the cafe on a secure footing, you are going to have a day off a week to paint, I promise. We could clear out the garage and make it into a studio and then you could exhibit your paintings for sale in the cafe!"

"Hey, I like that idea," Eleanor laughs. "You wait till you start working here, you'll find there aren't enough hours in the day to go to the toilet, never mind paint pictures." She piles our plates back on the tray and carries it out into the kitchen. I sink further into my chair. I feel tired so easily at the moment. Even though I do nothing all day I am often overwhelmed by exhaustion at unexpected moments. I know I should ring the house now, I said I would, but I don't feel ready. Eleanor was trying to help, but I have to trust my own instinct in this. I have to trust the sense I have of my mother's hand guiding me, my mother who always knew there was a fault line in our marriage. I feel I need just a little bit more time to complete the unknitting of my soul. I am lighter already, but there is still a bit snagging, holding me back. If I could wait just one more day I feel it would all be undone and I would be free of the tangle of all these years in this grey woollen country.

I still can't quite believe last night happened. It started so innocuously, the gas fire purring gently as I entered Tasleem's - our - living room, all three sections glowing orange and throwing a dry smothering heat into the room. I found the atmosphere a bit stifling for such a mild spring night, but I knew it suited Tasleem, and Huma was very happy running around in bare feet and unbuttoned sleepsuit. It was something we were going to have to work around, like the bags of chopped dead animal she lugged back from the halal butcher's this morning and stuffed into the freezer, and Sky's mud-splattered frame propped against the wall in the kitchen, spiky pedals and oily gears protruding into Huma's low-level range and waiting to snag bulging rubbish sacks on our way out to the bins.

"I think, maybe you are not coming back." Tasleem seemed even more jumpy than the previous night when I had arrived from the station. I collapsed onto the settee and unclipped my bike helmet from my sweaty chin. Huma pulled the fluorescent yellow bike clips off my ankles to release the baggy legs of my combat-style trousers. She put them on her arms like bangles and danced around the room showing them off to us. "Huma, give those back to Bhaji!" Tasleem's voice grated with tension and Huma's body slumped as if she had been hit. The bicycle clips slipped off her arms to the floor with a tinny clatter and she ran to her mother and hid her head in the folds of Tasleem's kameez.

"Has something happened?" I asked, leaning over to retrieve the clips.

"No. But the boys are here again. They see you go out and they are laughing at me. I stay behind the curtain, but they know I am here." There were tears in her voice and I stopped her, touching her arm very gently.

"I'm sorry. There was stuff I needed to sort out, and some food had gone off in the fridge, and I had to feed Tiger. Hey, come on, there are two of us here now. Come and sit down."

"No, first I make cup of tea and bring the dinner," she said brightly, seeming to recover herself. I was going to follow her into the kitchen, but she turned and instructed, "You stay with Huma. I don't like she be alone in here, so close to the street."

I held out my hand to Huma and she came to sit quietly beside me on the settee. The floor in front of us was strewn with the animal-shaped pieces of a wooden jigsaw and scraps of thread and material from Tasleem's sewing box. An empty baby's drinking bottle decorated with yellow suns and blue moons lay abandoned under the coffee table. It was impossible to take the idea of any danger seriously in this ordinary room, with the fire flickering innocuously and a soft pink light falling from the floral lampshade in the centre of the ceiling.

When Tasleem came back with a loaded tray, I asked if she minded me turning the fire off for a bit and she said,

"It's your fire as well, Shelley. You can turn on and off, you don't ask me."

The dhal was dark and grainy and rich with oily spices, and the chapattis were soft and floury. Huma nibbled a torn-off piece of chapatti as she watched me eat with intense fascination, but she declined my offer to help herself to curry.

"She's eaten while you are out," Tasleem explained. "She's hoping you will want a sweet next. It was our big Eid on Tuesday, and the workers from the refuge brought Huma lots of sweets and a big teddy bear."

I remembered wondering what was going on earlier in the week when I noticed a lot of young girls in glittering clothes milling about the shops on London Road. I felt bad that I hadn't known and something in me ached for Huma to hear that the only people she had in her life to buy her presents on the most important day in her year were refuge workers, who probably did it as part of their job. After we had eaten, Tasleem brought out a box of mixed Indian sweets and Huma dragged a teddy bear nearly as big as herself down from the bedroom to show me. I tried to imagine her face when they brought it and my heart warmed towards the anonymous women who were there for Tasleem and Huma in their most desperate moments and hadn't forgotten them now they had moved on from the refuge.

"After this, I take Huma upstairs and you can go to sleep here." Tasleem scanned my face anxiously. "I'm sorry there isn't a bed yet. We will get next week."

"Hey, I'm fine. I told you, this sleeping bag is really comfy and warm." I patted the nylon sack beside me, squeezed into a corner between the settee and the wall during the day. "In fact, it's probably more comfortable than the bed in my flat." And deliciously free of memories and complications, I thought.

"Did you see Anil when you went to your flat?" Tasleem seemed to read my mind.

"No. He's not moving in till his job starts and he can pay the rent. Anyway, he can't leave Pooja at the moment, until they find out where Veena's gone. It's four days now. I know the note said she was fine and not to worry and everything, but Anil wants to go to the police." I had become more comfortable talking to Anil on the phone, as we updated each other every day about Veena's absence and liaised about the flat. He had agreed to take it over from me as long as I carried on feeding Tiger, whom he claimed to be allergic to. I couldn't tell if he was trying to keep me hooked in somehow, but he seemed to be more relaxed about us being 'just friends' now.

"How is Veena's husband?"

"I think he's really upset too, but Anil's so angry now he's found out about that woman, he won't talk to his dad at all, so I don't really know what's going on with him." I tried not to let her see how worried I was about Veena.

By the time we had finished drinking our tea, Huma had fallen asleep on the carpet with her head and arms sprawled over the furry stomach of the giant bear. Tasleem lifted her briskly onto her shoulder and scooped up the bear with her free hand. I was amazed at how Huma slept on through being bundled around so roughly and unceremoniously. As Tasleem shifted her sleeping daughter to a more comfortable position on her shoulder, Huma stirred slightly and lifted an arm around her mother's neck before she dropped to sleep again instantly, her body moulded effortlessly around Tasleem's.

After they had gone, I settled myself on the settee and read for a bit until my eyelids started drooping. Then I turned out the light and snuggled down into my trusty sleeping bag. The room was hardly dark, even without the light, as the streetlight shone through gaps in the ill-fitting curtains. I drifted off to sleep quickly, exhausted by the roller coaster I seemed to have been riding over the last week.

I found myself floating down a street in a transparent plastic bubble past lots of other bubbles with a person in each one. We signalled with our arms to indicate when we were turning left or right, as though riding on a bike. Anil drifted past me in his bubble and we waved. Veena passed by in another bubble and seemed to be trying to tell me something. But we couldn't hear each other and I couldn't seem to stop my bubble. It drifted past the doorway of the Dancing Cows and I wanted to stop, but I couldn't find the brakes. As I drifted on towards town the bubble seemed to be getting faster and then I saw a kind of whirlpool ahead of me, like the mouth of a tornado, and the bubble was being sucked slowly, inexorably, into the airstream, spiralling downwards into the vortex in slow motion. I was shouting and beating on the plastic walls to get out as I was falling and I woke up suddenly, my heart pounding, breathing rapid rasping breaths. I lay still, trying to calm down, confused that there was no window in front of me at the bottom of the bed until I remembered I was not in my own room. I looked around and couldn't see anything in the darkness. Tasleem's front window did not seem to be anywhere either. My breathing was getting worse and I coughed violently. The understanding that I was breathing in smoke suddenly exploded into my awareness and I struggled clumsily out of my sleeping bag and fell onto the floor, where the coughing eased a little. Gripped with panic, I wanted to run in any direction, but I had no idea which way to go. I needed to stay calm. I could hear voices a long way off, maybe in the street. I tried to shout, but as soon as I opened my mouth it filled with smoke and I had to bury my head, choking and retching, in the pocketed air inside the sleeping bag. When I could breathe a little again I groped around in the darkness that was not night and found my jacket. I pulled my phone out of the pocket. The emergency services switchboard seemed agonisingly slow to me, although I knew there was no quicker way to get across my name and the address I was at.

"I'm in a fire and there's a woman and a two-year-old child in the room above me," I croaked, spluttering and coughing at each phrase. The woman interrupted me to say:

"The fire brigade is on its way already. Try to stay low down, on the floor if you can. Cover your nose and mouth."

I tunnelled my way back into the sleeping bag, but felt too trapped to stay in it for long. I prayed that Tasleem had shut her bedroom door, otherwise their room would have filled with smoke before this one. I could hear no noise above me. Surely they were not still sleeping through this? But that's what happens, I thought, the smoke gets you so you never even wake up before you choke to death. Oh God, why didn't I call the police when Tasleem said those boys were back tonight?

"Whereabouts are you in the house?" I was still clutching the phone to my ear with one hand, and holding my jacket over my face with the other.

"Front room downstairs," I gasped. My eyes streamed and I could see nothing, but felt a wall of heat in one direction, which I thought must be where the door was

243

into the hall. I can't die, I kept thinking. I have to get out, this isn't meant to happen.

"Can you reach the window?" The voice clamped to my ear continued to talk.

"I don't know," I breathed hoarsely, "It's very hot over there."

As I said this, there was a loud crash and glass seemed to splinter everywhere.

"Anyone in there?" a booming voice shouted.

"Here!" I tried to reply, but could hardly make a sound. I suddenly remembered from a women's self defence course in my first year that it was easier to make an 'O' sound than any other vowel and I bellowed,

"NO!" as loud as I could in my best self-defence voice, which came out as a cracked howl. Then there was a torch shining in my eyes and giant arms lifting me. A few moments later I was lying in the road in my pyjamas coughing my guts up into someone's tea towel. I looked up blearily into the eyes of the bottle-blonde woman from next door, who was leaning over me in a black negligee with a man's jacket slung around her shoulders.

"Are you all right, love?" In the dim street light I could see that she had tears in her eyes.

"Tasleem? Huma?" I croaked desperately.

"They're all right," a loud male voice behind her interrupted. "They got out first. It's you we was all worried about, you daft ha'porth!" Someone in a uniform covered me with a large blanket. I was so relieved I burst into uncontrollable tears and the bottle-blonde woman knelt beside me and lifted my head awkwardly onto her lap so she could hold me and stroke my hair consolingly. I could see she was caught up in the drama of the occasion and even in my pathetic watery state I wanted to say to her, if you'd been a half decent neighbour in the first place this might not have happened. I was glad to be removed from her arms and lifted onto a stretcher by the ambulance crew. Tasleem and Huma were already in the ambulance, sitting wrapped in blankets on a long sideways seat. Huma was resting back contentedly on her mother's lap absorbed in draining a large bottle of warm milk and looking sleepy. Tasleem began to cry as soon as she saw me.

"Oh Shelley, you could have died!" she sniffed.

"Thanks." I felt hysteria rising.

"I had to get Huma out first and then I couldn't get back into the house - "

"It's okay," I rasped. "There were lots of people, it was okay."

"You were lucky, love," a policeman, who was keeping people back from peering into the ambulance, interrupted. "The whole lot could have gone up any minute and no one would have been able to reach you." I lay back on my stretcher and closed my eyes, feeling suddenly dizzy and sick. The ride to the hospital and the next hour spent being checked over in casualty passed in something of a blur as we surrendered ourselves to the warm sleepy helplessness of recovery. Eventually I was confronted with reality.

"Is there anyone we can call, let them know you're okay, perhaps?" a crisp blue-uniformed nurse enquired as we lay in adjoining cubicles waiting to be seen by someone senior enough to discharge us. Not Veena, I thought. Not Anil, while their house was already in such crisis.

"Eleanor Charles, Dancing Cows Cafe, London Road," I replied, feeling a little forlorn that the closest friend I had to call on was my employer. "What about them?" I nodded at Tasleem and Huma.

"A worker from the hostel they lived in before is trying to find somewhere for them. Otherwise the council has a duty to house them in emergency bed and breakfast because of the child," she replied promptly. I glanced across at Tasleem and she made a face to show her opinion of bed and breakfast accommodation.

"They can come with me," I whispered, "Can I make the phone call myself?"

"Shelley?" Eleanor groaned on the other end of the phone line. "For God's sake, it's five o'clock in the morning. What's the matter with your voice?"

"Long story," I dismissed. Was it really five o'clock in the morning? I had no idea what time the fire had woken me in the night, or how long we had been in the hospital. I ploughed on trying to explain our situation in as few words as possible through rasping breaths. "I've been in a fire."

"Oh my God," she cried out. I felt my tears rising and knew I needed to get through to her before my voice gave out.

"I'm with Tasleem. We need someone to pick us up from the hospital." I tried to control the quiver in my voice. Her voice went muffled as if she had her hand over the mouthpiece and I thought I could hear her saying, "It's Shelley. What shall I do?" Was Matt back? I wondered, with a sinking feeling. He would not take kindly to me dragging Eleanor out in the middle of the night if he was. I didn't hear a reply, but Eleanor returned to full volume.

"Okay. You need to get a taxi, I can't fit you all in the van. I'll pay when you get here," she instructed firmly and I wanted to cry with gratitude for her bossiness.

"We could go back to my flat," I argued weakly, not sure I could face dealing with Matt.

"Don't be silly. You need looking after, you must all be in shock. That poor little baby - what's her name?" The voice behind her spoke Huma's name. It definitely wasn't Matt.

"Eleanor. Who's that with you?" I was very confused.

"Tell you when you get here. We'll see you in a bit. Okay?" and she put the phone down quickly before I could ask her any more questions.

The hospital lent us a couple of thin blankets to wrap over our nightclothes in the taxi. Huma had woken up with a vengeance and was full of chatter, wanting to bounce on our knees and climb all over the back of the taxi, which did not bode well for her introduction to Eleanor's flat.

When Eleanor flung open the front door of the cafe, a look of shock passed over her face. I realised we must have been quite a sight and we hadn't even noticed.

"God, you look awful and you stink." Eleanor muttered as she fished in her purse for the right change for the taxi driver.

"There was loads of smoke, it got me mostly - " I began to explain, and then I heard a movement and someone came in from the shadows by the kitchen door in Matt's green towelling dressing gown, curtains of black hair edged with grey lying loose and dishevelled on her shoulders, her eyes blinking in the sudden light. She looked different, younger and more vulnerable without her make-up and jewellery, and her immaculate clothes, but unmistakeable.

"Veena!" I spluttered, my charred voice cracking with the effort.

"Oh, you poor things!" she breathed in horror and swept towards us. She put her arms around me and pulled my head gently down onto her shoulder. I hung onto her sobbing and coughing and shaking with relief, while she patted my back gently.

"You're all right," I spluttered through my tears. "I was so worried!"

"Of course I'm all right, Shelley. Didn't anyone get my note?" her familiar mellow voice was puzzled and hurt.

"Yes, but Anil thought you were having a breakdown, and I thought it was all my fault telling you about Ramesh - " I sniffed, trying to control my sobs. "I thought if anything happened to you - sorry - "

"Everything that happens isn't your fault, Shelley," she said, very quietly, passing me a tissue from the pocket of her dressing gown. I didn't quite understand what she meant by this, but I was too exhausted to try and work it out.

"This is the problem with sudden disappearances. People panic." I was surprised to hear Eleanor speaking to her so sternly and saw a look of wry understanding pass between them.

"Okay, you win," Veena said to her, putting her hands up in surrender. "I'll ring as soon as they're awake."

"Hallelujah!" Eleanor exclaimed raising her hands to the sky with exaggerated relief. I suddenly felt like a stranger on my own patch and glanced around at the cows for help. What's the score, Winifred? I asked silently, someone please fill me in.

"Dhoodh, ammi, dhoodh," Huma pleaded, pulling at Tasleem's coat.

"She wants some milk," I told Eleanor, realising that I had begun to understand some of Huma's Punjabi already.

"Can we all go upstairs, please. It's not very comfortable down here," Eleanor put on her organising voice and ushered us briskly upstairs.

Hot sunshine washes over my bare arms and feet as Shelley, Pooja and I sit on the grass outside the Moorfield Community Centre, waiting for the other members of our Indian dance class to arrive. A tiny wind tugs at the pale yellowed grass stems trembling around me, but it hardly stirs the heat still pouring from the sky on this golden summer evening. Shelley is lying beside me in leotard-style leggings and a long white cotton kurta with delicately embroidered cuffs and collar that I gave her when I cleared out my stuff from the house. She is reading a travel book about India with her back to the sun so a shadow falls on her page. Pooja is facing slightly away from me touching up the immaculate paintwork on her splayed toes. Her feet are one of her best features, she always claims, and will continue to wear open-toed sandals long after I am snuggled up in woollen socks and stout winter shoes. She has come here straight from her summer waitressing job in jeans and a cotton top with a plunging neckline. How can I say anything when even her employer doesn't seem to mind what she wears? I doubt if Ramesh notices what she puts on in the morning now she's on his watch.

The silence between the three of us is comfortable. Cars rush noisily up and down the road beyond the wall of the these old gardens and the heavy beat of reggae music pounds from an upstairs window across the road. The community centre rises above us, a massive square edifice of red brick and coal-blackened yellow stone. It has been a family home to wealthy factory owners, an asylum for the mentally insane, a school, a hospital and now an adult education centre housing, among other things, weekly classes in bharatnatyam, dance form of the towering ornate temple complexes of southern India. Now I have left the stresses of Awaaz behind me I can finally enjoy some of their activities. I take a half day off from the cafe every Friday morning to go to women-only swimming sessions with Tasleem. Huma emerges from the crèche next door afterwards with a clutch of paintings and collages, which Shelley displays for her on the cork noticeboard in their kitchen, newly refurbished after the electrical fire in May that almost destroyed the whole house. On Wednesday evenings after we have closed the cafe, I change into a loose cotton shalwar kameez and walk up from the cafe to meet Shelley and Pooja, who usually arrive on different buses from town. We come here to learn bharatnatyam for a couple of hours. Or rather, Shelley and Pooja come to learn and I come to revisit the skills I learnt as a child. I come to let my body remember the rhythms and movements buried deep in my limbs and muscles and sinews that my mind had long forgotten were there. I try to calm my busy spinning head before we start, to prepare myself to approach the dance in a spirit of reverence and contemplative humility. Our teacher, Rekha, a delightful, diminutive woman from Gujerat with wide expressive eyes and long elegant fingers, reminds us that dance is an act of worship, it is a spiritual task. She drives all the way from Leicester each week to share her wisdom with us. Leaning back on my hands and looking up above the mossy slated roof of the centre I try to empty my mind, and my self, into the blue silences beyond.

Shelley puts her book down and sighs deeply beside me. "I can't wait to go. I almost wish I hadn't taken on the post-adoption project now."

"Don't be silly, it's only a three-month contract and you're so good with the children. Anyway, you don't want to go to India in August, it's still too hot," I advise, "A few more weeks and it will be much more comfortable. You'll be there by Diwali and that's what matters."

"But I'll miss Durga Puja in Calcutta," she says. "I've just read all about it, it sounds amazing."

"Shelley," I laugh. "India is a vast country and you have many years to live. Don't expect to do everything in one trip. You may just want to sit on one river bank and watch the world go by for six months. That's what I'd do if I could go."

"Come with me then." She turns over onto her stomach and makes a pillow with her arms, on which she rests her head and squints sideways at me, shading her eyes from the sun and waving cheerfully at two more of our classmates walking up the drive.

"No. Don't," Pooja counters with alarm. "She's not going anywhere until I'm at least twenty-one."

"The next time I go I'll take you with me, darling," I promise, patting Pooja's bare knee fondly.

"Hey, mind my nails!"

"How are my cows doing without me?" Shelley asks me, looking mournful.

"They tell me they miss you terribly and Ermyntrude is peeling more than ever in protest. But we think we've sussed out the cause now. There's something going on with the gutter over the entrance porch, which needs fixing, along with most of the rest of the building, but we can't afford to get anything done till my cheque comes through from the house sale." I wish immediately that I had not mentioned the house. I could bite my tongue.

Pooja snorts her disgust and, turning her back to me a little more, starts on her fingernails with the nail varnish brush. Her father has bought himself a stylish luxury apartment down by the canal with a stunning balconied bedroom for her, and has promised to buy her a car when she goes to university, but she remains angry, in waves, with both of us about everything, most of all about losing the house in which she grew up. I know it hurts her deeply, it's about growing up and not wanting to grow up and all the complicated currents that have coursed between us from when she was small. I worry that she will stop eating properly again and don't trust Ramesh to notice if she is eating or not. I will speak to him about it when we meet on Friday. I have agreed to let him cook me dinner in the flat and Pooja is going out so we can talk. I don't know if it's the right thing or not, but I know there's something there I can't carry on avoiding for ever. I have to sit across the table from him again, hear the mixture of self-importance and vulnerability in his loud unmistakably Indian voice, watch the knotted veins moving on his balding forehead, answer the need to communicate with me I see in his pleading eyes each time I encounter him now. I have to sit down with him and try and understand what happened to us.

"I must say I don't miss worrying about the building," Shelley's voice jolts me into the present again. "The Post-Adoption Project may only be a voluntary organisation, but it's a different world, whizzy swivel chairs in the office, loos to die for which I don't have to clean myself, and proper holidays. Compared to all that, the Dancing Cows was sackcloth and ashes. Not that I regret one minute of it. Anyway, you're in a different position from me, being a partner. Eleanor can't boss you around."

"She's all right, actually, I don't find her bossy," I comment lightly.

"Sorry," Shelley apologises and screws up her face, wincing, "I know she was there for you when I was pratting around."

"Doesn't matter, it's all water under the bridge now." I smile, signalling that I really don't want to hear about it. Our time together is too precious to waste on recriminations. Who knows where she will end up on this quest of hers to find Rehana, but I mean to enjoy her company before she sets off.

"Here she is, folks," Pooja shouts, stuffing her nail varnish pot into her handbag and giving her nails a final blow to dry them. A small red hatchback pulls into the car park and a dozen or so women pick themselves up from various parts of the lawn and straggle towards the pillared entrance at the front of the building.